PREJUDICE

Emmanuel Ikechukwu Azubuike

Edited by Mr. Titus Tion

Printed in the Federal Republic of Nigeria
By: Emmanuel Ikechukwu Azubuike,
2, Logone Close, Off Nile Street, Maitama, Abuja, Nigeria
Tel: 0811-497-7616, 0701-918-9751
E-mail:emmanuelazubs12@gmail.com

ENDORSEMENT

PREJUDICE is a suspense-filled storyline detailing multi-dimensional skirmishes caused by differing cultures, faiths and personalities. This novel tells our daily struggles to live in harmony with ourselves and the world around us, and yet often ending up stirring strife and unprecedented conflicts either intentionally or otherwise.

This work of art is painted in very colourful master-strokes by the skillful hands of a young artist who has demonstrated that he is indeed dexterous and diligent at what he does. The author being an astute craftsman; has proven to be an exciting budding literary persona who has a lavished diction.

PREJUDICE is a testament to the fact that in every generation, one can always find those talented and determined enough to add their voices to the record books of history for the benefit of humanity. For the elderly, PREJUDICE is refreshing and engaging, for the young, exciting and challenging to the intellect. I highly recommend it for all.

Emmanuel Ikechukwu Azubuike may be young and supposedly inexperienced but he has proven beyond doubt in this novel that he knows his roots, his faith and his generation well enough to provide insight and solutions to the complex challenges they face.

The effort of this young author is quite commendable, and I hereby append my endorsement.

Rev. Dr. William Okoye,
General Overseer, All Christians Fellowship Mission.

ONE

"WOW! LOOK at how gorgeous you are, my pretty little girl," Mr Adekunle Adefarasin said to his daughter, Funke.

"Daddy I'm not a little girl anymore," she said.

"You'll always be my beautiful little girl," Mr Adefarasin said as he cuddled her.

"Of course she's beautiful; she got that from me her mother, not from your ugly genes. Only God knows what charm you used on me, for me, the only granddaughter of one of the richest relative of the Oba of my kingdom to marry you," Mrs Bolanle, Mr Adefarasin's wife blurted from her closet.

They lived in a cosy house which was too big for just the three of them. The floor of their posh porch was tiled with marble. Besides, it was where their plush Porsche was packed; it was more of a decorative element because it was rarely used.

Their marble floor was black and glassy, coruscating like an obsidian stone, there were beautiful sculptures and majestic engravings on the cream coloured wall. A chandelier was right at the centre of the living room; they had guest rooms, dining rooms, a laundry room and kitchen at the ground floor.

Their ardent staircase led to the first storey, where the bedrooms, library, gym and a room filled with all manner of hodgepodge, with miscellaneous things hanging on the wall. The floor was aesthetically tiled and could look like a mirror when polished, and that it was at all times. Mrs Bolanle made sure of that.

The living room was beautifully wall-papered and where there was no wall paper, there was white paint. The house literally glowed in the night both in and out. Beautiful paintings, drawings and artistic work clad the walls of the house.

"But she's our daughter; you didn't conceive her all by yourself, did you? She's ours," Mr Ade accentuated the "ours" as he grimaced; he wasn't ready to duel with his wife again, she always won and he paid for losing. Mrs Bolanle his wife was a sore winner, she capitalized on her victories, and her perceived acrimony for her husband seemed abysmal.

"You said what?" Mrs Bolanle asked stepping out from her snug dressing room with her Gele half-tied and wrapper half-loosed, looking like she was ready to eat her husband raw. "Yes Funke is our daughter," she said suppressing the first outburst. "But she's nothing like you! You're scruffy, sluggish and skinny; our servants have more flesh than you do," she said tightening her wrapper as if getting ready to brawl.

"Your hands are like broomsticks and fingers like toothpicks, you have slumped-slouching shoulders, you can't even mistakenly be shortlisted to be a soldier, and they would prefer a stick to you because it can be used as a weapon, but you, nothing. You said she's our daughter, see your black-big-bulgy-ugly face, see her pretty cute adorable face, see how long and lanky you are, and see how balanced and buoyant she is."

"Mummy please stop! E-jor!" Funke protested. "Please stop I beg you, daddy meant no harm."

"Stop what? Stop telling the truth?" Mrs Bolanle said looking at Funke, raising her eyebrows. "Just take a look at him; he looks like a thirsty fish though in the middle of the ocean. He's wealthy but he's dried up like fish trapped in the Sahara desert, under its scorching sun."

Mr Ade who could no longer stand the lambaste, holding back tears, trotted away from the luxurious bedroom downstairs, like a dog with its tail tuck between its legs. Tears from his twitching eyes would have made matters worse; they would be like fuel for his wife to keep blazing her rage.

"Mummy let me help you tie your Gele," Funke said, trying to salve her mother's unabashed fury, knowing fully well the reason for her untamed outburst. A month earlier, her Uncle, Kayode, her mother's younger brother was preparing for his wedding.

Throughout that period her father who was a pastor in their church; Ambassadors for Christ, was fasting. The fast was called by the General Overseer of their Church for the leadership team to fast the first week of December to annul any nocuous plan of the Devil during the festive period.

Her father, after the first week continued to fast, and was extremely religious about it. He fasted from six to six without taking even water, and then prayed for an hour before he would break his fast by eating a trifle amount of fruits for that day. And there was a day he didn't even break his fast at all, he had to do that in the night of the following day. Her mother persuaded him to stop the fasting; she didn't want him to be looking like a dried up skeleton on her brother's wedding day.

She once said to him; "Why are you fasting? We are rich, we lack nothing, what are you fasting and praying for?" But her father doggedly continued till it was New Year and the wedding was just a week away. Her father was naturally skinny; now the fasting made his bones pop out. "You look like the malnourished Biafran children during the war," Her mother once lamented.

Before her brother's wedding day, Mrs Bolanle urged and coaxed him like fire melting candle to wear the very expensive agbada over the Ankara attire she paid their tailor to sew for him to hide his discomfiture structure. But on the wedding day he arrived without putting on the agbada, or the cloth she sewed for him. The attire he wore was too fitting to his structure. Her mother almost fainted when she saw him, her dear God-fearing Father.

Mr Ade in the sitting room downstairs; sat on their brown-leathered sofa, with tears streaming from his now red big eyes to his sunken cheeks, with his pale palms on his vein-interlocked forehead.

"God please give me the grace to go through this episode without retribution. Help me not to curse you, as Job refused to. Having a fiend for a wife is like having a wolf to take care of sheep during famine. My Father, I'm like a handicapped servant tortured for no just reason. Why did you let me get into this incongruous relationship, our marriage is a car with water in the place of petrol; we can't move at all talk less of making progress. My business consortium is soaring while my marriage consortium is suffering. I'm a rich wretched man, a riffraff in royalty. Help me oh lord," Mr Ade sobbed as he prayed.

"Forgive me oh my God for my inadequacies. Who am I to question your ordinances, what you long ago have ordained. Let your will be done in my life

and let your glory be manifested in and through my life, that all may know you are the sovereign God. I am but man."

TWO

"JOSEPH! Joseph!" Mrs Hannatu Yahaya kept calling her son.

"Will you stop that! Who are your referring to as Joseph? How many times will I tell you that his name is now Yusuf not Joseph?" Mr Habib Yahaya her husband warned.

"His name is not Yusuf anything," Mrs Hannatu refuted. "I and your late brother, my husband, his real father, named him Joseph and that's what his name will be, and you can't change that."

"I am your husband now, and you are my wife! I own you! You must do as I say, and that boy is now my son, do you hear me?" Mr Habib vociferated. Mrs Hannatu stared straight into the coffee-coloured eyes of the wolf in sheep's clothing. A hairy, handsome, slim, light skinned man, any woman could only dream of having for a husband. But he was haughty and very often spiteful towards her especially when it came to her new beliefs and he seemed bent on breaking them. She broke into tears as she grabbed his shirt with her sweaty palms as she shivered with her lips vibrating.

"Habib! Why are you treating me this way, why are you so harsh towards me? You said you love me and can't live without me. You persuaded me to marry you, saying you cared less about my beliefs and you won't interfere in it. But ever since we got married you've been interfering and trying to stop me. Why did you lie to me Habib?"

"That boy is my son now and his name is Yusuf," Mr Habib replied as he removed her sweaty hands from his shirt, nudging her away. He left their bedroom and banged the wooden door behind him. Mrs Hannatu fell on the edge of the bed, curled herself up as she cuddled their soft pillow while sobbing profusely. At this point she had forgotten that she was calling her son.

Joseph opened the door to the yellow painted room, lighted with the energy-saver bulb with sunlight also making its way to the room through the partially opened curtain; the room was tiled with regular white-like tiles. The fan was spinning slowly, jousting with the strong smell of Hausa perfume in the room. The small TV on the wooden shelf was displaying a channel that wasn't lucid, while the room was left disorganized.

Little Joseph saw his mother at the edge of the bed sobbing silently; he ran towards her and mistakenly kicked a small wooden stool which made him fall to his knees. His mother on hearing the sound from his fall, jerked from the bed to her feet because she didn't see him come in. As she saw him on the floor she scurried and carried him, walking to the bed while petting his tender legs.

"Are you hurt?" She asked with a weary face.

"No Momma," he replied.

"Thank God," She said as she gently dropped him on the bed.

"Momma, why are you crying?" Joseph asked.

"It's nothing my son, Momma loves you," she replied as she cuddled him. Tears were rolling down her swollen cheeks due to the agonizing pain she was feeling inside.

Just then lights went off, however, the sun got brighter. As the fan slowed down, the perfume pervaded the whole room resulting to upset of her stomach. What seemed pleasant before had now turned pungent, as such she started feeling woozy which made her stand abruptly and then tucked in sleepy Joseph into the bed.

She then scurried to the toilet sink in the bedroom close to the exit door trying to puke but she was retching. Frustrated, she locked the wooden door behind her and sat on the dry white tiles spotted with black motif, leaning and backing the door as she silently wept.

"What did I do to deserve all this?" She thought as she wept. *"God, have you forsaken me? Did I do something wrong that you are punishing me for? Where did I miss it?"*

"Do not be unequally yoked with unbelievers" started ringing repeatedly in her mind. "What does this mean?" She voiced to herself. "What does it mean?" She reiterated. "It sounds familiar; I've heard it somewhere," she kept mumbling as her weeping deterred. "Probably in church, during that marriage thanksgiving but I've heard it from somewhere else too. Oh yes! Yes! Mrs Adaeze told me this while I was preparing for my wedding, but I didn't take her seriously.

Oh God what does this mean? Nothing I do for my husband pleases him, he wasn't this malign the first year of our marriage. I prayed and fasted seeking your face concerning this marriage, but you gave me no reply, Jehovah. What do I do now, oh Lord?"

THREE

"JESUS CHRIST! Oh my God, what the hell is wrong with that woman?" Chigozie said vociferously.

"Will you shut up, don't call the name of the Lord in vain," Mr Nnamdi Okafor his father said from the driver's seat as he glanced back to look at his son who was still aghast by the pantomime he had just witnessed.

"I'm sorry sir, it was by mistake," Chigozie quickly responded.

It was a sunny Sunday afternoon, and they were on transit in their family car. Chigozie had just seen a woman, probably in her late thirties who was heavily pregnant, dressed in an Ankara gown with a big purple Gele which looked like a church's attire.

She had slapped a man by her side that looked like her husband, and then dragged a little girl most likely to be her daughter from the man, pulling the girl up her waist, and ran across the road holding her big black bag. She ran with great celerity and hauled the girl over the rail by the side of the road before herself jumped over with difficulty. She then trotted with the girl across the slower lane on the express way, ignoring people by the road staring at her in awe.

"Didn't you people see that woman?" Chigozie asked turning to his twin brother Chibuzor with a questioning expression.

"Nope, I didn't see any woman; can't you see I'm using my phone? Besides, what happened that you were shouting and gesticulating?" Chibuzor asked still looking at his phone.

Chigozie told his brother what happened. "Eziokwu?" Chibuzor exclaimed and guffawed. "You can lie eh, and you are becoming very adept at it sef."

"So you think I'm lying?" Chigozie hissed.

"Of course, it is not the first time, besides that's your expertise," Chibuzor replied.

"He's not lying oh, I saw her too," Osinachi the lastborn said from the backseat. She was sitting beside her elder sister Amaka — the firstborn, the "Ada" of Mr and Mrs Okafor.

Amaka's hollow idiosyncrasy made her oblivious to the charade going on in their auburn Sienna. She was busy doing nothing because her phone had shut down due to low battery; she killed it viewing people's status with her *GB* WhatsApp.

She thought about her wonderful life back at Abakaliki where everything seemed congruent with her lifestyle. She loved the place as much as she loved her hometown Afikpo, though she spent little time there. She and her family only went back to their village during the Christmas season when everything would be gleeful and bubbling.

She was brought back from stupor or her stimulated reverie when Chigozie wanted to confirm from her if she saw what transpired.

"Oh ho! Why can't you guys let me be? You're chasing away my cherished memory of what life is supposed to be like. I wonder why we have to relocate to Abuja, our life at Abakaliki was perfect, and we had our own house and business. Now we're going to go and rent an apartment, does that even make any sense?" Amaka blurted.

"Mechie onu there! Will you stop that your ranting, do you want to wake your mother?" Mr Okafor said with his face mussed. His beautiful wife at his side squinted and stretched her arms forward whilst yawning.

Mrs Nwaozioma his wife had been slumbering since they hit the road very early in the morning, journeying to the capital of the giant of Africa. Mr Okafor slid a slouching braid to the back of her tender ears. She had been working tirelessly throughout the past week preparing and packing for their relocation.

"Sleep on Ice cream, everything is okay. *Ihenine di naka* digi."

"Mrs Nwaozioma, uttered indecipherable words, wriggled and slept back. They had just left Lokoja, the capital city of Kogi State and were heading towards Gwagwalada usually called *'Gwags'* where the University of Abuja is situated.

FOUR

OH This overwhelming,
Never-ending reckless love of God,
Oh it chases me down,
Fights till I'm found,
Leaves the ninety nine

The song echoed from a church nearby.

"I *dey* yarn you the truth, you no wan believe, I tell you say I know that babe *wey* dey sing, I even know her brother *sef,* you dey here *dey* doubt. *Oga,* pick three, doubting Thomas," John said as he played a *five square* Whot card.

"I block," Tunde said as he dropped a *five-circle* card. "John I no fit believe you; ever since the day you lie say *na* Okocha train Ronaldinho."

"But *na* true na, I watch am for one *Teju Baby-face* Show for AIT. Okocha talk am by him sef." John said with a convincing expression.

"No be only that one, no be you talk say the new iPhone, if the phone mistakenly fall that ee get anti-gravity, so ee go slow down before ee go knack ground; and you talk say Jay-z and Beyoncé do their wedding on top plane. Guy you sabi lie abeg," Tunde said and sniggered sardonically. "Pick two Oga lion, you can lie for Africa."

Victor burst into laughter; he was sitting at the back of Tunde. Tunde was facing John who he was playing Whot with; they were all sitting on a wooden bench.

"But no reason am oh, John *na* veteran for woman affairs," Victor said laughing and Tunde laughed too holding his stomach as he rolled on the floor.

"Wetin be veteran?" John asked, wondering why they were laughing.

"Oga, go check your dictionary and go collect your school fees back, when people *dey* go class you go *dey* pursue skirt," Tunde said from the floor as his laughter reduced. "Later you go talk say *na* Frank Edward train

Don Moen," Tunde said wryly and continued laughing with Victor.
We go dey hail...
Hail God hail...Day by day...
All the way...All the way.

Another song echoed from the church.

"But don't these people get tired? How will they have service twice on a Sunday, in the morning and evening, nawa oo," Tunde said as he stood up from the ground while Victor was singing along.

"We all know you don't like church and it's because of your parents you still dey go Church, may God help you when you enter University where nobody will force you. Besides they're not having another service, don't you know that it's choir rehearsals? Or are you deaf or retarded?" John said and Tunde started clapping.

"You don go learn new English; now we no go hear word. Because of simple question I ask, you don *dey* use me shine. Abeg no *dey* use corner, corner way *dey* insult me, if you wan insult me tell me wela, no *dey* use style," Tunde said, gesticulating while he was talking. "But how they go *dey* do choir practice on Sunday?"

"Up NEPA!" People shouted from several houses in the Compound they were in. The compound was big, having about three different buildings which could house two residents in addition there was a smaller building that housed the caretaker.

At the centre of the compound was an open space where about five to six cars could be packed which turned into a mini soccer field for boys who usually played ball when the cars were fewer. Some of the houses were roofed with zinc and the others aluminium because there were old tenants whose houses could not be renovated because they were still living in the houses.

"Ah thank God," Tunde said. "Let me go and charge my phone."

"Forget that one, come and sit down let me finish you, you *wan* use style run, my guy wan escape. Come joor?" John said sardonically. Tunde hissed. Victor who wanted to go home too because of the light, hissed too.

"Chai NEPA have started again, they have taken the light," Victor said with disappointment all over his face.

"It's no longer NEPA again, it's now AEDC," John corrected.

"Oga *na* NEPA we know, no *dey* tell me that one," Tunde said.

"And you guys were doing *"I too* know" come and sit down let me humble you in this Whot game so that later when you see me, you would bend down and greet," John said as he chuckled, tapping the bench for Tunde to sit down.

"Oh it's because by chance you won me today that you're now feeling like one Whot boss abi," Tunde said putting one of his hands on his waist.

"I've won you nine times and you're calling it chance, come let me make it ten," John said.

"You eh, you can make mouth oo, that's how you will be lying for all those girls. Today no be my day, *na* why, if not, you for don *dey* collect. I wish say Abdulbasit *dey* here, he for change am for you," Tunde said wryly, facing John who noticed a Sienna approach their slightly opened faded black gate.

"Oboy see fine car oo," John said as he stood up. Victor, who was sitting at the other side of the bench, at the edge tried to maintain his balance but ended up felling off the bench and landing on the ground. The bench was like a seesaw, as John stood, the bench followed him and the opposite side where Victor sat, went down, sending the cards which were on the bench running down too.

"Dude, you wan wound me?" Victor griped loudly dragging John's attention to what happened.

"Sorry abeg, I *no* know nau. Look," John said as he pointed towards the gate of their compound for them to see what he was talking about. Victor turned his neck to look back because he was backing the gate. Tunde who was dusting off the sand which clung to his cloth after he rolled on the ground turned to see too.

"Is it the first time you're seeing the car?" Victor asked.

"Have you seen it before?" John asked.

"*Eben* na, it's for that man that has been living alone in that house," Victor said pointing to one of the houses.

"I know the man nau, but that's not the car he was using," John stated.

"Yes, even me too it's just once I saw it before he travelled," Tunde said.

"Ah no wonder, I never see this one before," John said.

"And it's like he came back with his whole family," Victor said pointing at the huge vehicle behind the car that was taller than the gate.

"Chigozie and Chibuzor come down and open the gate, welcome to your new home," Mr Okafor said to his sleepy sons while holding the brakes of the car.

"Daddy what's the name of this place?" Osinachi asked from the back seat.

"How many times will I tell you? It's Dutse, don't ask me again, besides you would even get tired of hearing it," her father replied.

Chigozie and Chibuzor opened the gate, and Mr Okafor drove in while the big lorry carrying their belongings packed outside the compound. Victor, John and Tunde helped Mr Okafor and his family to pack their belongings to their house after initial greetings. Other residents where busy peeping through their windows, looking at their new neighbours.

"What are your names?" Osinachi asked the three boys. John and Victor told her their names but Tunde was reluctant, Osinachi being sanguine, kept pestering him for his name. But he didn't capitulate, as he continued moving their belongings.

"His name is Tunde," John told her.

"Okay thank you," Osinachi said and ran inside their new house.

"Did she ask you Mr I.T.K, over *sabi* sabi. You'll be doing I too know every time," Tunde said indignantly.

"Sorry oo, small thing, see how you *dey* vex," John blurted. Tunde dropped the white plastic chair at the pavement of the house, and started walking towards his house which was two flats away from Mr Okafor's house.

"Where you *dey* go?" John asked.

"To the market to go buy you eyeglass, blind Bartimaeus!" Tunde replied as he approached his house which made Victor and Chibuzor who were carrying a wooden table together, burst into laughter on hearing his reply.

"You two are always cursing yourselves, you guys are opposite in almost everything, you're tall, his short, you're fair, his dark, you're slim, he get flesh pass you. But you guys are both daft," Victor said still laughing.

"It's you that is daft and retarded. See your empty big head," John said.

"But your head big pass my own," Victor said laughing.

"But yours is emptier than mine," John said derisively.

"Please can you guys stop insulting each other? I don't want our arrival to be the cause of rivalry in this compound. It's too early for a discord," Mrs Okafor said trying to salve the dispute.

"Yes ma," The both of them said in unison.

"We're just playing ma," John said.

"But ma, please what is... is discord?" Victor asked.

"Aunty don't mind him, he is too daft to understand. See how big your mouth is like goat own, instead of you to check your dictionary, you *dey* there *dey* ask stupid questions," John interjected.

"Oga know it all, what is the meaning?" Victor asked. Mrs Okafor ignored them and called Osinachi who just came out from the house to carry some of their property that she could carry, into the house.

"Osinachi, where is your sister Amaka? Don't tell me she's still in that car."

"She's not in that car," Osinachi replied.

"Okay, where is she?"

"Mummy, you say I should not tell you that she's still in that car," Osinachi said.

"See, Osinachi, I'm not ready for your gimmicks this evening, it's getting late. Since you learnt how to talk you've not stopped, go and call your sister for me, Osiso!"

FIVE

VEHEMENTLY, Amaka said, "If you people touch that plate again, I will slap the three of you!"

It was a dry Saturday evening during harmattan season. There was no light in their compound and the entire street. The incessant boisterous wind movement that took place early that morning scattered everything in its path that was unable to withstand it, leaving no one in doubt the season.

Every Saturday night, the Okafors ate together. This had been a tradition since Amaka could remember but it was not likely to continue because some things changed since they packed to Abuja. Mr Okafor usually came back home late while their mother who used to sew once in a while at her shop where Ankara materials and wrappers were sold, had to take tailoring seriously in order to assist and support her husband in providing for the family.

Mr Okafor had been staying in Abuja since the previous year when he was transferred because of some issues he had with his colleagues regarding his faith. Although, he had explained it to his wife, the children were yet to get the full story.

"But the plate is not in the middle," Chigozie protested with food in his mouth. He was sitting opposite Chibuzor and Osinachi on the rectangular wooden table. The table happened to be one of the things Mr Okafor insisted must be carried despite its size and age. He had bought the table before he even got married; he had told his children so many times the story behind the table.

The story was that, he had travelled all the way to Onitsha, straight to the best carpenter there known as Joseph Okereke. He was well known for how adeptly sophisticated he was with anything wood. As far as Mr Okafor was concerned he was the very best.

On getting to his workshop someone was already pricing the table, it was the last one available; and Mr Okafor wasn't ready to travel all the way to Onitsha again when another set would be made. He rushed to Capjoe, as fondly called; a derivative from carpenter and Joseph. As he approached him, he began pleading with him not to sell it to the dark complexioned, averagely tall man.

"Please how much is the table, I want to buy it, I've already come a long way," Mr Okafor said and the dark man who was casually pricing the table became more interested.

"Oga carpenter give me the table at the price you told me, I want to go," The dark man said.

"Alright let me tell my boys to bring it," Capjoe replied.

"Capjoe... Wait please, I'll add five hundred Naira to the price he offered." As Capjoe was thinking about it the dark man protested.

"Oga you know I came here first, I'm here with the money sell the table to me." He brought out the money and counted it to give Capjoe but Capjoe chuckled.

"You know I'm Igbo right? Action speaks louder than words, but money speaks louder than the both of them. So the person, who offers the biggest money, gets the table," He said and laughed sardonically.

"That's not fair at all, but I'll add extra One-thousand naira to the initial price. I know this man can't offer more than that five hundred naira," The dark man said, as he looked at Mr Okafor wryly.

"Going... Going..." Capjoe taunted Mr Okafor so he would offer more. Mr Okafor was deliberating in his mind. He wanted to buy additional furniture with the money, but the table was his priority and it was getting late, he had to drive back to Abakaliki before night fall. He had to buy it, if not he wouldn't gain anything; besides the dark man had just stepped on his ego.

"I'll add One-thousand naira to the money he offered," Mr Okafor said. Capjoe grinned so wide, he couldn't believe Mr Okafor would offer such amount of money; and was ecstatic by the fact that he was going to make so much money on the last table available which was considered to be the worst, because the best had already been purchased.

"Can you offer more than that?" Capjoe said daring the dark man, hoping for more. "Can you?"

The dark man grunted and shoved the money he was holding into his pocket and turned to leave. He was about five steps away when Capjoe said, "I know its only mouth he has, he has no money; penniless babbler," he said and hissed. The dark man overhearing what he said walked back.

"I rather be penniless than be a heartless opportunist like you," The man said and Capjoe guffawed and clapped with a canter beat.

"So you can be a heartless opportunist, but not like me?" He said laughing. "You're talking like you wouldn't do the same thing?"

"Stop taunting him, just give me the table, it's getting late and I have to travel back," Mr Okafor said pleadingly not wanting the man to offer something bigger because he had reached his limit.

"I have more money up to double the price for the table, but I can't stay here and watch you extort us even though you're one of the best here in Onitsha. Besides I know this man needs the table more than I do. If you don't believe I have the money, see." He brought out money from the black purse he was holding, which had a wallet inside, then counted the initial price for the table and gave the man. "I'm buying the table for him," the dark man said.

Capjoe was dumb founded. He collected the money, and he couldn't ask for the extra money added from the bargain because that would prove the veracity of his opportunistic idiosyncrasy stated earlier by the dark man. So he had to acquiesce.

"For me?" Mr Okafor asked in surprise. "Why would you do a thing like that?"

"Minus the fact that I want to prove I had the money, I just want to say Jesus loves you. I was into gambling and I was really good at it. But anytime I lost, I would become depressed, I had a mind-set of getting all or nothing, so I used to put in everything I had just to win, and if I still lost, I would become more depressed, if I won I wouldn't be satisfied, I always wanted more.

Sometimes in the middle of the night, I would go to the bar to carouse and while in the spree, I'll bet on anything just to make more money even though I had it. Sometimes I lost intentionally so that I could come back to my senses.

But the "all or nothing" mentality made me hustle the money back. My life was a malady, a total discomfiture. My quest for satisfaction only left me insatiable. It was really "chasing after the wind" as Solomon puts it."

The man continued talking since Mr Okafor was listening.

"My life had this insatiable void that couldn't be filled until I encountered Jesus. It will shock you that it was a mere gospel pamphlet which I saw on the floor after rain had drenched it that gave me salvation.

I couldn't read fully what was on it; the only thing I could read was "Jesus saves". I used to hear it from some "early morning gospel town-criers" as I used to call them because they usually disturb my sleep with their preaching. I never took them seriously; in fact I despised them and held them in contempt.

But after I saw that tract, "Jesus saves" kept ringing in my head morning, noon and night incessantly and I was compelled to go to a church to get answers to it. Fortunately for me I got answers.

As you can see me here, I'm free: no longer bound, no longer living in bondage like Andy Okeke," He said and chortled. "I have a choice now to do right or wrong. I'm no longer compelled to sin anymore like I was before. If I do, my conscience, sharpened by the Holy Spirit, convicts me and when I ask for forgiveness, I'm vindicated and the weight of guilt is lifted up.

Truly Jesus saves. And I'll like you to experience this joy and liberty I enjoy every day. Had it been you live here, I would have liked you to come for one of our services.

Again, I would like to state that we should be more afraid of sin than death. Because if we die without sin, we go to heaven to be with Jesus Christ, but if we die sinners we truly die, for we know the person who dies a sinner will be tormented in hell. That's why I fear sin than death. Please give your life to Christ."

That was how Mr Okafor became born again. What he knew about Christianity, was a mere shallow assumption. Mr Okafor and the dark man called Ejiofor became very close friends and he was Mr Okafor's best man at his wedding at *Christ* Ambassadors church, at one of their branches at

Abakaliki where he resided.

"So this table is older than me?" Osinachi asked with surprise.

"Of course yes; it is older than all of us including Amaka," Chibuzor said and chortled.

"Jesus! Amaka you've finished your food already?" Chigozie exclaimed.

"You're still calling Jesus name anyhow, upon Daddy warned you about it. Well it's not the person that has the biggest mouth that eats fastest but the person who's the hungriest, you know I didn't eat my afternoon food," Amaka retorted. The afternoon food was boiled yam and vegetable which she distastes.

Chibuzor, Chigozie and Osinachi ate the Eba and Egusi soup from the same plate, Amaka's food was separate. Amaka usually ate with Osinachi, but she didn't put their food together because she was hungry and Osinachi eats too fast.

"NEPA should bring light nau, for the past two days now, no light except in the middle of the night when everybody is sleeping," Chigozie lamented.

"That's a reason, to pray without ceasing," Chibuzor said as if singing.

"In season and out of season right?" Chigozie continued with the flow.

"Of course so that you can see the light."

"That's right, so we won't lose our sight."

"This is because, if we lose sight of the Light, we backbite and might think it's alright"

"And fall short of the glory of God like my battery that died because of no light."

"Who killed it?" Osinachi asked wondering how his phone, an inanimate object, could die.

"Help me ask him oo. I wonder how your battery died. Did it have an accident or it committed suicide?" Chibuzor said as he burst into laughter. Amaka and Osinachi laughed too.

"What I mean is my phone shutdown because of low battery. I know you all know what I mean but chose to behave as if you don't understand.

Osinachi, oya, clear the table," Chigozie said, vexed.

As she carried their plates to the kitchen the front door opened. "Daddy welcome!" Amaka, Chibuzor and Chigozie chorused. Osinachi who was in the kitchen ran to the sitting room to greet him. She hugged his legs and collected what he was carrying.

"Daddy what did you buy for me?" She asked as she went through what was in the polythene bag.

"I didn't buy anything for eating oo. I bought bulbs for the kitchen and backyard and some other things. Don't worry I'll buy you something next time."

"Okay," She replied sadly.

"Daddy there have been no light since yesterday night, they only flashed it twice," Chigozie said abruptly.

"Guess where there's light?... In Abakaliki" Amaka said farcically.

"Amaka are you still upset about our movement? Can't you bear with me? I did not come here on my own accord, I was transferred to work here and I decided to bring you guys along; I didn't want to be here alone besides Abuja is a good place to live in and I already thought about us moving here before the transfer."

"But Daddy why did they transfer you, I thought you were their permanent financial secretary there?" Amaka inquired.

"Amaka please allow me to rest first. I'm just coming back from work, and I don't think there's anything like permanent financial secretary, I'm just the financial secretary. Please where is your mother?"

"Mummy went out; I don't know where she went to," Chibuzor said.

"She went to the market to buy some things for the cloth she's sewing," Amaka answered.

"By this time of the night?" Mr Okafor questioned with a mussed face.

"She said that the woman that she's sewing for needs the cloth before Tuesday."

"Hmm, but it's really late," Mr Okafor said as he walked to his room.

"All of you wake up!" Mr Okafor shouted as he banged on the door to the room of his children. "It's Sunday morning and you're still sleeping by this time. Once its 7:45 and you are not dressed for church, I will drive out and leave you people. See your mother who slept very late is already awake. Prepare fast, I won't say it again."

For the harmattan breeze, sleep was very sweet; Chibuzor and Chigozie were sleeping on the same bed while Amaka and Osinachi were sleeping on another in the room. The room was demarcated with a wooden frame; one side for the boys, the other for the girls.

"I wish it was Saturday morning," Chigozie said as he stretched and yawned. "Chibuzor wake up, I hope you know that it's your turn to wash the car?"

"Which turn? Don't even call my name oo, I washed the car two times before you washed, so technically it's still your turn," Chibuzor said as he squeezed the pillow, hugging it tightly and turned to keep on sleeping.

"Literally it's your turn oo; it's turn by turn. *"Las, las,"* it's two of us that will wash it. So better wake up let's go and wash it before daddy comes back again."

"Gozie! Leave me alone, go and wash the car. Don't tap me again if not I'll beat you oo. You know I am your elder," Chibuzor said vehemently getting annoyed by his twin brother's disturbance.

"Because you are my elder by mere ten seconds you're shouting."

"Which ten seconds? It's twelve seconds," Chibuzor objected.

"What's the difference?" Chigozie asked sardonically.

"The difference is two seconds. Two!" Chibuzor muttered showing him his index and middle finger, like the peace sign, then pressing the pillow to his ears.

"Can you two stop making noise and go and wash the car. You remember the time mummy flogged two of you for this type of nonsense argument," Amaka shouted at them from the other side of the room.

"Osinachi wake up!" She said while tapping her. Osinachi jerked up from the bed and ran out of the room with great celerity whilst shouting. The three of them in the room were awestruck by what just happened. Osinachi the drama queen on reaching the sitting room stopped abruptly and slowly walked back to the room.

"Why did you run like that Osibaby? Do you want to give us

hypertension?" Chigozie asked as he stood up from the bed. They all loved their pretty, amiable, adorable and energetic sister; the last born of the family. Though she could be impudent, audacious and even impenitent at times, they loved her nonetheless. She had *Checkers custard* skin tone and black long soft hair.

"I had a dream," Osinachi said breathing heavily.

"Was Masquerade chasing you in the dream?" Chibuzor asked sardonically, exasperated that Osinachi's drama had chased his sweet sleep away.

"No oo, I was in a running competition. We were six that were running. I was the second and we were close to the finish-line, so I was using all my strength so I will overtake the boy in front of me before sister Amaka woke me.

"How come you were running with boys?" Amaka asked.

"I ran with the girls first. I dust all of them with big gap. So I went to run with the boys, because I've passed girl's level," Osinachi said as if she was debating.

"So you people started family meeting, this early Sunday morning? Amaka even you. At your age my mother, your grandmother was already married, taking care of her own house. You, you're here having a chit-chat when you're supposed to be directing your younger ones. Go and put rice on fire! Thank God I made the stew yesterday. And you two knuckle heads; go and wash that car fast, and you Osinachi go and take your bath right now before I open my eyes!" Their mother said, now looking at Osinachi after dishing instructions.

"But Mummy your eyes are still open," Osinachi said after waiting for a while.

"Osinachi I don't have time for this, because you are an egghead doesn't mean you should joke around with people, especially your elders. Do you hear me?"

"Mummy is my head like egg?" Osinachi asked with pursed lips, the lower lip more obtrusive, touching her head to figure out the shape.

"Osinachi! Bathroom, now" Mrs Nwaozioma ordered with her hands poignantly pointing in the direction of the bathroom.

"Yes ma," Osinachi said as she sprinted to the bathroom.

SIX

"FUNKE please go and tell your mother that, she should please hurry up, today is the last Sunday of the month and she knows its thanksgiving Sunday. We can't go late to Church today again. We've been going late since the beginning of this year," Mr Ade said to his daughter who was sitting at the backseat of their newly bought black G-wagon.

Mr Ade was literally forced by his wife to buy it. They had four vehicles, one being the G-wagon, then the Porsche which was rarely used, a Range rover and then a Hilux used mostly for menial jobs.

"But Daddy, can't mummy come with one of the other cars?" Funke asked.

"No, she can't. She made me buy this car, and I know she wants to flaunt it. But I wonder why she's lavishing time in the house. Please go and check on her my patience is on two percent; already dying fast."

Funke was reluctant to go, she had gone before and she knew she'll get the same answer from her mother to her father. If she went again she'll become their herald, more like a messenger sent back and forth.

"Yes sir," Funke said and muttered something that needed decryption to be understood before she opened the door of the exotic Mercedes. She walked upstairs from the garage which was at their basement. On reaching her mother's room, she saw her balanced on a seat, painting her lips circumspectly. She was so relaxed that Funke got enraged.

"Mummy!" She said in a somewhat low tone. "Daddy has been waiting for you for over fifteen minutes and we're running late but you're still doing make up," She offloaded those words breathing heavily.

Her mother's make-up was obviously copious; she still added make-up to make it more ostentatious. Her mother was already beautiful; Funke did not see the need of her packing make-up like someone hiding a tribal mark.

As an aristocrat nurtured and groomed by her mother who imbued class into her, she could not say more than she did, though she wanted to.

"So we've become mates, right?" Mrs Bolanle said as she started putting eye shadow on her eye lids so serenely which upset Funke the more. "Or has that thing you call your father poisoned your mind against me? Please calm down my sweet daughter I'm almost done here. Your father inflames small issues, screaming snake when it's just a thread."

She dropped the eye shadow on the desk carrying a mirror having a beautiful wooden frame, majestically stood up and walked towards her daughter like she was modelling her waist and her hands were stretched forward.

"Come here Keeki," a pet name she gave her. "Come and give your mother a hug." Funke was bewildered, she had expected her mother to erupt and spit out molten magma. She was already getting ready for word jousting. But her mother's words and composure overwhelmed the rising rage like rain on a flaming candle stick.

"But... But..." she tried to object but found no words.

"But nothing my dear," Her mother said. Funke became dicey yet docile; she gave her mother a hug. Then they walked towards the basement after her mother dropped the mirror and carried her ornamented hand bag.

"But don't ever raise your voice at me. Do you hear me?" Her mother said sternly.

"Yes ma," Funke replied.

"He has given me victory,
I will lift him higher, higher Jehovah,
I will lift him higher..."

Her mother sang, swaying and lifting her hands after handing over her lustrous bag to Funke as they walked downstairs.

"Hey, you... Ela or is it Tella."

"It's Stellar ma'am," the maid replied.

"I don't really care, make sure you clean and arrange the house before we come back; and tell that Okoro to add more pepper in that stew this time, I don't know whether they don't take pepper in their village, if not his salary would emaciate."

A boisterous sound was heard from the garage as Mrs Bolanle was dishing out orders. They were alarmed, Funke panicked, wondering what might have happened to her father. They all rushed to the basement.

SEVEN

"Yusuf is not following you to any church!" Mr Habib yelled.

"Of course Yusuf is not following me to church," Mrs Hannatu said as she kept combing her son's black soft curly hair. "Joseph is," she blurted and started singing.

I'm married to Jesus, Satan leave me alone,
I'm married to Jesus, Satan leave me alone,
My husband is coming to take me from here...
To everlasting home, everlasting home!

"You're indirectly calling me Satan right? If you carry my son to that noise making building you call a church, you'll know that Satan is still learning work," Mr Habib in his pyjamas said and snapped his fingers at her and stormed out of his room in rage.

"Momma, why is papa shouting?" Joseph asked as he twitched, his mother had mistakenly brushed his skin as she combed his hair.

"Sorry!" she exclaimed. "Your papa wants you to stay with him but I want you to follow me to Church, to meet and praise the One who created you and made you so cute and handsome. And there, you are going to have friends who are going to praise God with you," she said cheerfully as she tickled him.

Joseph who was serene and mild became animated and chuckled, then convulsed with laughter as she kept tickling him. "So once your shoes are put on and we eat we would be on our way, okay?"

"Yes Momma," Joseph squeezed a reply in the middle of laughing. After she finished tying his shoe lace, she rushed to take her bath, so they wouldn't be late. She had been going to church late, her husband always found ways to delay her with his incessant demands. Apart from that she had been going once in a while with Joseph to Church, so he wasn't so conversant with it, and she wanted all that to change.

A while later, after they had finished eating, Mrs Hannatu started looking for the key to the ash coloured Camry, bought for her by her late husband Ibrahim who had changed his name to Elkannah; the same name of Hannah's husband in the Bible instead of Abraham which was the Hebrew name of Ibrahim.

She ransacked the whole bedroom for the car key and then decided to ask Habib; her present callous husband. She knew it would stir up argument and rigmaroles that she was not ready for but she had no choice, she was already running late.

"Honey, please do you know where the car keys might be?" She asked in a serene manner in order not to provoke a fracas.

Mr Habib was a quick-witted-prodigal son, an awful foolhardy in academics. He didn't see any reason to study; his father was a rich politician. His father's political party happened to be the one in power at the time. They explored every bit of privilege they could get, even if it were through corrupt means; seeing it as connection and their turn to join the league of political power-play and eat their supposed share of the national cake.

Habib didn't like school, primarily because he was book-daft but he was cleverly cunny in school. He maneuverered through WAEC but was unsuccessful with JAMB which would have hindered him from getting admission into higher institution but his father's money and connections made it possible.

While in school he would syphon money from his father with different dubious schemes and lies. He used part of it to bribe his way through school and funded his business. But things changed when his father died suddenly while in his final year in school. The reason for his death was politically suspicious. His brother and mother sponsored him through, though.

"You said what?" Habib yelled.

EIGHT

"OLUCHI! Oluchi!" a woman shouted her daughter's name, urging her to be fast so they would go to church as Mr Okafor drove his family out of the compound heading to Christ Ambassadors Church in town. There was this kind of rush-hour frenzy on Sunday mornings as if something very important was at stake. The road in their area was very bad. Rain had eroded most of the road the past season. Its galloping nature and traffic jam used to cause some delay.

"Daddy, please what's the name of the Church?" Osinachi asked from the back seat of the car.

"It's the same church we've been attending back in Abakaliki; the one here in Abuja is the headquarters," Mr Okafor replied.

"Oh Okay sir," Osinachi replied.

Mrs Okafor was busy tying her Gele at the front seat with the aid of the rare-view mirror while humming a hymn.

"Awesome, astute Ada acknowledges, admonish and assist any aged apathetic adult.

You can't beat my alliteration composition, its way better than all the alliteration you've said," Chibuzor said as he chuckled and smirked at Chigozie. They have been playing a game named Alliteration, in which each of them would put together not less than seven consonants that could make a sentence.

"You can boast eh, because you managed to conjure something that looks like it makes sense," Chigozie said as he was trying to compose his own in his mind.

"You say what?" Between you and me, who use to boast most? If we can measure your pride and ego, it will be like the innumerable books John was talking about, of which the whole world would not be able to contain," Chibuzor said wryly.

"Which John are you talking about?" Chigozie asked inquisitively.

"You see yourself, and you'll be claiming to be a walking Bible. Simple thing you don't know. It's John in the Bible that wrote the gospel according to John, and he said if all the things about Jesus were written down, he suppose the whole world would not be able to contain such a book," Chibuzor narrated.

"Abeg, forget that one, I still beat you in Bible quiz and quoting scriptures," Chigozie blurted.

"You read to win, simply put. I read to know and I can use it later like now," Chibuzor said.

"You just want to defend yourself, you also read to win. But I won," Chigozie grinned.

"Now listen to my own alliteration; Pedagogue's perilous, precarious, pugilist, prodigious, prodigal pupils pari passu panoply pantheon pandemonium. I should be crowned the king of alliteration. That's probably the best you've ever heard," Chigozie said boastfully as he laughed.

"King ke? No be only king why not god of alliteration. You just went and *join-join* words that didn't even make ant sense and you're boasting about it. You sounded like you were listing things starting with letter P," Chibuzor said and hissed, turning his face.

"What's *ant* sense?" Osinachi who was keenly listening to their discourse or rather dispute asked.

"It means small sense, I said it figuratively. But technically Gozie has ant sense," Chibuzor said and laughed, Osinachi laughed too.

"But literally I'm more sensible, skilled, smarter sharper, so see shame on you." Chigozie sputtered and laughed. "I'm on fire! I just produced a different alliteration and I know you didn't understand some words in the previous one."

"Who told you I didn't understand? The jumbled and incongruence nature of those words makes the sentence to lack meaning" Chibuzor said with a mussed face.

"Well, maybe your brain can't comprehend the irony and the other figure of speech I used in the sentence," Chigozie said.

"It's more of a simile or metaphor than an irony; ego freak," Chibuzor said sardonically.

"See we're close to the church. I don't want you two to continue arguing in church, better behave yourselves. You know this is your first time. First impression matters, good reputation matters more. But behave yourself," Mr Okafor said.

"Yes sir," three of them chorused. Amaka didn't reply. She was busy with her phone.

"Amaka! I hope you heard what your father said, don't go and start using phone in the church," Mrs Okafor sputtered.

"Wow, is that our church? It's so big, sheen and radiant," Osinachi exclaimed.

NINE

MR Ade and his Family were already in church. The loud noise that was heard in the garage was caused by a chandelier that fell and landed behind the G-wagon. Mrs Bolanle had insisted that the chandelier be put in the garage. "Of all places?" her husband had asked, but in the end she had her way.

Mr Ade forced himself not to say, "I told you so" or anything near that. That would have brought about another quarrel. The Church was a two storey building; the second floor was walled with glass to some extent and roofed with aluminium sheets. The Children church was attached to the main one on the ground floor.

A Charity House in the same building was where items were kept such as clothes, food, and other gifts used to help the less privileged in the church. The culture was; most of those items were stored so they could also be used anytime the church went out for an outreach.

The Teenage Church was a stone throw away from the main Church. It was formerly used as Children Church before the teenage body was formed by some teenage-loving teachers who pioneered it.

A book shop was beside it, it had gospel books and also CDs of recorded messages from the general overseer and any other pastor that preached. It also had sermons of other preachers both Nigerian and Foreign.

A mini restaurant and shop was close to the main entrance into the Church's compound; this was where food and snacks were sold after church service. The restaurant was mostly used by some pastors with their families and other church staff that resided in the church compound. The residential houses were behind the teenage church, it was a two storey aesthetic building.

Amaka and the twins followed their parents to the big church; Osinachi was ushered to the Children Church. But later on, whilst when Chibuzor went to the restroom an usher from the teenage church was sent to call teenagers to the teen's department.

Most teenagers had the habit of leaving the teenage church to stay in the big church. Chigozie was one among other teenagers ushered downstairs to the Teenage Church. They arrived as praise and worship was on going.

Chigozie was captivated by the voice of the beautiful girl who was leading the praise and worship. She was wearing a black jacket on top of a yellow blouse with a snug black skirt and a black striped with yellow, hilly shoe that looked like a wasp.

Apart from her dressing which was almost uniform to the rest of the choir members on stage, her composure and elegance kept him looking until he took his seat.

Later on, Osinachi came running to the teenage department, holding twenty naira almost above her head all the way from the children's church. Her mother had given her offering for herself and Chigozie; she had already given Chibuzor who was still upstairs. Osinachi ran towards the teenage church bawling, "Chigozie! Chigozie!"

"It's a lie joor," Adebayo said vehemently. "How can you say that you don't spend money that is less than hundred-naira? What of if you buy something of fifty naira won't you collect the change if you gave the person hundred-naira?"

"Me...?" Chigozie asked, putting his hands on his chest. "I rather buy something else or tell the person to keep the change."

"Mogbe!" Adebayo exclaimed putting his hand on his head, forgetting he was in church.

"Walahi, you rich oo!" Cyril also exclaimed at the next statement made by Chigozie.

They heard everybody clapping and they joined them, someone had just finished giving a testimony. One of the teachers, Uncle Gabriel, as fondly called by the teenager prayed for the testifiers and announced offering time.

"Blessing time!" The teenagers chorused back.

"I will like to see what you will give for offering," Adebayo said.

"Ah... I forgot to collect offering from my parents," Chigozie said with celerity mussing his face.

"But I thought you said you have your own money," Cyril questioned.

"Abi oo," Bayo concurred.

"Yes I do," Gozie said. "But my parents still give me offering money."

Osinachi boisterously opened the last door towards the back of the teenage Church. Half the teenagers turned back, Chigozie and his friends inclusive. There was silence for about five seconds; Osinachi perused the hall looking for Chigozie, when she spotted him she shouted his name and trotted towards him with the twenty naira in her hand, she was wearing a low high hill shoe which was making an obtrusive cadence that sounded like *koi, koi* as she scurried towards Chigozie.

Most teenagers watched the juvenile, to see what she was up to. The teachers also watched patiently as they didn't know what to do.

"Mummy said I should give you, for offering," Osinachi said when she approached him. She said it audible enough for anyone listening to hear, protruding her hand to give him the twenty naira. Gozie was aghast.

Eyes from different directions of the church were looking at him, he wished he could disappear. Adebayo and his other new friends stared agape for a while and then burst into laughter. The choir started singing with the beautiful girl leading.

All I have... is given to me by the Lord,
All I have is given to me by the Lord.

Everybody stood up and started clapping and singing. Gozie had no option, he couldn't deny that she was his sister, or tell her to go away. She was impudent and would not be easily deterred.

Being in total discomfiture, he grimaced and collected the money meant for offering and joined others who were going to the front of the church, just before the altar to drop their offering inside a big blue basket.

"No one who is born of God will continue to sin, because God's seed remains in him; he cannot go on sinning, because he is born of God. Check your Bibles. I didn't just conceive it in my head — first John three verse nine said so. The title of this message is *"Finishing Strong,"* announced the preacher.

Not everybody on their way to heaven will end up in heaven and not everyone on their way to hell will end up in hell. He that thinks he stands should take heed, lest he falls. God will surely forgive you of your sins when you repent, but sin has consequences, if you doubt me ask King David."

Reverend Ifeanyi Onyekwere, the General Overseer of their church; *Christ Ambassadors* was the preacher. He was ready to set the church on fire, he had already removed his black suit, folded his impeccable and immaculate white ironed shirt.

He was a radical preacher; though a veteran in the gospel and well advanced in age, he was still very agile, and always preached with convicted unction. He was a lion on stage but a sheep off the stage. He could be described as an eponymous epitome of a humble fanatic. He always preached about holiness, it was like his mantra.

Chibuzor was captivated by the sermon, and became so vivacious after the first five minutes of the preaching. He was at the verge of slumber while sitting down before the preaching started; now he was at the verge of his seat to stand and shout and to give surplus applause for the sensational sermon.

"Strive to live holy, the safest haven is Heaven," The Reverend concluded.

"Heaven is the safest haven, the safest haven is Heaven" Mrs Hannatu kept repeating it in her mind as she walked down the stairs after the service to pick up her son. Her husband had sternly warned her and even forbidden her from carrying Joseph to Church if not she would be responsible for the consequences that would follow.

Mrs Hannatu however took Joseph to church despite the frontal confrontation. They used public transport to go to church because all her plea for her car key fell on heartless deaf ears.

As she was meandering through the crowd she bumped into a woman, a friend of hers and her late husband. The same woman had assisted her and her family sundry times when they were facing challenges.

"Hey how are you doing my Sister? I hope you are doing well?" Mrs Adaeze asked cheerfully after hugging her.

"I'm doing fine ma, look at how you're just shining."

"Hmmm, seriously?

"Yes oo."

"It's the Lord's doing oo. I thank God for his mercies on me and my family. But you look pale, what's going on?" Mrs Adaeze asked with concern. Mrs Hannatu unwilling to bug her with her family issues again, shrugged, feigning a smile as she wriggled her fingers inside her leather black bag.

"It's nothing ma, I'm okay. I just... just..." Mrs Hannatu fidgeted.

"Just what? Please tell me what's going on, you're not looking like yourself. Please tell me, I hope it's not what I'm thinking? Is it what I'm thinking? Is it your Husband?"

Mrs Hannatu was in her grey Buba and thoroughly tied black scarf. Her dressing depicted her dull and gloomy inward feelings and now outward countenance, which showed she was finding it hard to countenance her husband's bigotry.

Mrs Adaeze was like her personal Catechist, she had munificently groomed her in the way of the Lord. Mrs Hannatu found it arduous to hide something from her, especially something that was so ample.

"Ye... Yes," she replied as her shoulders slopped. She had been admonished concerning the matter by Mrs Adaeze. She had warned her of the predicaments and hurdles she will probably face, if she proceeded with her intention then. Being faced with the reality, she feared being told by Mrs Adaeze *I told you so* and perhaps the admonition she was certain would follow. That was why she had hesitated; now she expected her to say so.

"I'm so sorry," Mrs Adaeze said sadly, opened her arms embraced her and whispered to her ears. "We are going to meet later, to discuss this, I'll call you in due time. Right now I have to rush home I'm expecting some visitors," Mrs Adaeze said, patted her on the back and scurried through the moving crowd.

Mrs Hannatu never expected that and so she was overwhelmed and sighed of relief.

"I hope you children enjoyed the service?" Mrs Nwaozioma asked as they approached their house.

"I did oo, that sermon was fire-branded, just like the preaching in our village," Chibuzor said poignantly.

"I've never been so embarrassed, all through my life like I was today. It was so disheartening. I just remembered now," Chigozie was saying.

"What happened? Who embarrassed you?" Chibuzor cut in, with a questioning look.

"Mummy please why did you tell Osinachi to give me twenty naira for offering?" Chigozie asked ignoring his brother, facing his mother who was in front, reading a form given to her by the women's leader, because she was a first-timer in Church. Mrs Nwaozioma paused for a while then turned sharply.

"And so? What if I gave you twenty naira for offering? Is there anything wrong with that? You have your own money, if you wanted to give a bigger amount, you should have used your money. And I was not having five hundred naira change, I only had one hundred naira and twenty naira change, so I gave your sister to give you and take her own." She turned back and continued perusing the form, obviously photocopied not printed.

"OK ma," Chigozie said then turned to Osinachi with rage. She was sitting at the back of the car beside Amaka who was busy chatting on her phone as usual and also having Chibuzor's ear piece plugged in. Chibuzor was watching intently to see the drama unfurl. Today had been good for him, from a powerful sermon to a live TV drama.

"Osinachi! Why on earth did you badge into the Teenage Church holding twenty naira so every single person could see, and telling everyone that Mummy gave you twenty naira to give me for offering?"

Chibuzor burst into laughter. He laughed to stupor tears rolling down his eyes. He couldn't help it. Mr and Mrs Okafor turned back, awed at what Osinachi had done this time.

"Are you serious?" Mrs Nwaozioma said in disbelief. "Eziokwu!" She exclaimed. "Why did you give your brother twenty-naira? When there was hundred-naira?

"Mummy you did not tell me how much to give Chigozie; and the twenty naira was a new one that's why I gave him," Osinachi said, justifying her deed.

"Do you know how much older your brother is compared to you, how would you do such a thing?" Mrs Okafor said at the verge of laughing too. Chigozie wasn't finding it funny, he was still looking sternly at Osinachi.

"Don't you ever try that again, it's even better I didn't even give offering at all, I hope you're hearing me?" He vociferated.

"Yes sir!" Osinachi yelled whilst saluting him, making a jocose of the whole situation. Chibuzor kept laughing. Chigozie was annoyed, but couldn't do anything about it. What hurt him most was that the girl he admired so much, who led the chorus, witnessed the whole drama Osinachi put up.

TEN

"CHIDERA, the coward, ran to the village panting heavily. The king's officers came and apprehended him, dragging him to the palace. The king, angry and furious, asked Chidera why he ran away from the battleground, asking him why he wasn't brave like the other soldiers who fought to death.

Chidera, who was made to kneel down, spoke up. "O king live forever, we all know that those who run from a fight live to fight another day. My king all the brave warriors or soldiers as you call them are all dead. It is wisdom to run away from a fight you know you can't win. Even the Bible says a living dog, which can be termed as a coward, is better than a dead lion which is regarded as brave.

By-the-way, you king didn't follow us to battle, you sent us to die for a land that is not rightfully ours, while you stayed home enjoying yourself; to me that seems to be not only a cowardly act but also a hypocritical one."

"What insolence?" the king cut in. "What manner of impudence is this?" Can you imagine such audacious temerity? What gives you the guts, the mind, the impetus to display such effrontery in front of me? In my presence, are you crazy?

You must be stupidly mad! Guards! Take this idiotic coward and give him several lashes of the cane on his runaway behind."

Osinachi kept reading from a story book, aloud, as they drove back home from Church some weeks later. Chigozie's stomach began to rumble even more on the hearing of the flogging, imagining he was the coward soldier in his current situation.

As soon as church service closed, his stomach started to yarn him some very disturbing, notorious stories. Unfortunately he was experiencing running stomach that came suddenly and uninvited. He couldn't rush to toilet because his family was already waiting for him. Now he was full of regrets more so on hearing that they were going for a member's child dedication.

On the road Chigozie tried his best to stay calm all in a bid to avoid being laughed at especially by Osinachi. The worst part was that he had laughed at her when she was almost crying in a similar situation.

"Chigozie, this one that you're squeezing your face, are you the coward about to be flogged?" Chibuzor said jokingly. Osinachi who was still reading paused and laughed. Chigozie ignored them because responding would make matters worse. His purging notification came in phases, and each session with added tension.

He thought about the toilet at home, he couldn't wait to use. The restroom at home at that moment seemed to be the best place he could be. *"You can't know how useful and pleasant a place is, until you desperately need it,"* he thought, also wondering how a situation such as that would make someone desire such a place.

To top up his capricious situation, the car was slowing down. His father came down to buy some gifts and fruits to give the family dedicating a baby. Fortunately his Father did not send him or any of his siblings. Mr Okafor always had a sense of satisfaction when he did things by himself because he felt he did it better and he always wanted the best.

After buying the gift, Mr Okafor was on the hunt for fruits by the side of the road. At this point, Chigozie's mind was full of agitation wondering when he would be finally home. A phase just passed and he relaxed a little then he saw his father move from one fruit seller to another — sweat started rolling down his face, he began sighing heavily as he was bitter about the development. Chigozie was strangely immaculately silent while his stomach sang like it was performing at an orchestra. He felt like a bunch of mad rats were running helter-skelter in his stomach as if trying to escape. But he wouldn't let that happen, it would be beyond embarrassing.

Breeze from the car window dried his sweat as his father drove swiftly after buying all he needed. Chigozie had a bit of relief as they got closer to their destination, only to get stuck in traffic.

"How is it possible that there's traffic build-up at this place on Sunday of all days?" Chigozie blurted, and regretted his outburst almost immediately because it appeared he triggered a higher dimension of stomach upset and he started sweating again.

Twisting, wriggling, squirming, turning from one side to the other on his seat; Chigozie was becoming more and more uncomfortable. He wished he could come down from the car, and run home instead of going to the house of the family dedicating a child which was on the same route to their house but way further.

"Wait, what's wrong with you? Why are you behaving like someone that is possessed?" Chibuzor asked sardonically. Chigozie tried to compose himself, cleaning the sweat that clad his face.

"Nothing, I'm just feeling hot; and leave me alone, don't be asking me nonsense questions, me and you who looks like someone that is possessed?" Chigozie asked trying to ward off further interrogations.

"It's you oo," Osinachi replied from the back facing Chigozie.

"I agree, I'm possessed, you too you're possessed, everybody is possessed; it depends on what possesses you," Chigozie said facing Osinachi then turned to his mother.

"Mummy please I don't want to go for the dedication."

"What do you mean by that? Why don't you want to go?" She asked.

"I have plenty things to do at home, and I want to start preparing for our school resumption," Chigozie said in a low tune, trying not to anger the restless *rats* in his stomach.

"All of us can't go home because of only you. Is your brother not going to school too? Didn't you both get admission? Why do you all of a sudden want to go and prepare?"

"But Mummy it's not the same school na," Chigozie whined.

"You still have enough time to prepare before your resumption. You can't tell me it's because of school you want to go home, except there's something else."

Chigozie, determined not to let the cat out of the bag by saying why he really wanted to go home kept silent for a while. They were getting closer to the junction they could divert to their house, but where the ceremony was to be held was way ahead. Mr Okafor was driving passed the junction and Chigozie started calculating the time they would spend against how long he could hold back the purging palaver and it was not adding up.

"Mummy I have running stomach, I want to use the toilet. Please can you give me transport money, let me take bike to the house from here?" Chigozie said, like his life depended on those words. Osinachi, Chibuzor and Amaka who was no longer using the earpiece burst into laughter; even their parents laughed too but not as they did.

"So that's why you've been shaking like fish, with no water to swim in. See bush na, just help yourself," Chibuzor said still laughing, Chigozie ignored him.

"Yesterday night you were busy eating everything and anything. After eating that remaining rice and beans all by yourself, you still ate Eba and vegetable soup, and you bought bread and groundnut for yourself. But that's not even all, I've forgotten the remaining, and I warned you. He who eats alone dies alone," Chibuzor said and kept laughing.

Chigozie said nothing.

"You should have said it earlier. Wait small let your father pack, you can still get bike from here to the house," His mother said calmly.

As the car stopped, Chigozie slowly came out of the car with his native outfit that he so valued because he thought it quaint. He had picked the style and everything, and he wore it only on special occasions after ironing. But since the day he wore it out and saw a beggar wearing a cloth that had the same material and similar design with the cloth, the cloth lost value in his eyes. He wore it casually like every other church cloth.

Chigozie collected the bike fare, alighted from the Sienna and flagged a bike rider down. He climbed the bike carefully enough to control all the nerves in his body. With each gallop on the crooked road, his heart was in his mouth. He started praying in his mind. The sun's heat increased and drenched him in sweat.

Soon, he arrived at the compound and stopped the bike man right at the gate, and wasted no time with the rider. He rushed into the compound towards his house but half way he froze, and couldn't move any longer. He felt so heavy, that any movement made, would release what he had been holding for more than an hour. Luckily, the compound was partially empty, no one was outside.

He stood on that spot, looked this way and that, turned round on the same spot, did like he wanted to pick something from the floor in case someone was looking and wondering why he stopped in the first place. Then he walked slowly to their house, so slow that a snail would seem fast— almost as if he was tiptoeing.

As he reached the door to the house to open it he realized he wasn't with the house keys. It was still in the car and he had no idea when they'll reach the house. At that point, he gently sat down on the veranda and started sobbing.

ELEVEN

Mrs Hannatu was astounded on reaching the gate to Mrs Adaeze's house. The house was big and beautiful; she had no idea someone in the same church she has been attending lived in a house so magnificent.

Mrs Hannatu had followed Mrs Adaeze in her exotic sky blue Hyundai for the discourse Mrs Adaeze had told her about Sundays ago concerning her marriage to a heathen.

Mrs Hannatu had had several bitter confrontations with her husband, each one being worse than the one before it. She had always done her best to play down each clash but to no avail especially when she stood her ground.

Joseph most of the time was the subject of argument, but in recent times money and issues bordering on faith had emerged top of the dispute chart. Mrs Hannatu was a natural entrepreneur, she was excellent in business but her husband Habib was parasitic, and made unreasonable requests that were capable of plundering her thriving business.

Mr Habib had once tried to enrol Joseph into an Islamic school but Mrs Hannatu whisked Joseph to church and left him there in the care of one of the pastors until the issue subsided.

"I sympathise with you for the fact that your marriage is like a malady to your faith in God. I have seen how obsequious you are to the things of God, in spite of your husband's incessant squalor schemes. I heard he wanted to give your son to an Imam to make him one," Mrs Adaeze said.

"Not so, ma, he wanted to enrol him in an Islamic school, that is, from the principal to cleaners in the school, everyone is a Muslim, and I know that will influence Joseph as far as religion is concerned.

Like the Bible says train up a child in the way he should go, and when he is old he will not depart from it. If he grows up with Muslims he's most likely to end up a Muslim."

They were at the backyard of Mrs Adaeze's amiable abode. The ground was cladded with well-trimmed grasses where they sat under a big mango tree.

Mrs Hannatu had only seen the gateman and few house helps in the house but no family member. At the big backyard, where they were, there was a dried up swimming pool; albeit it was clean and sheen. They had started discussing about Mrs Hannatu's mismatched marriage and how incongruous their relationship was.

"Apologies for my misinterpretation, I must have heard it wrongly. I hope the issue has been resolved?"

"He has mellowed down on that issue, but he's still very arrogant and he would make me want to do things that are contrary to the Bible. The worst part is, my son is still a child and therefore docile and subjugated to his rules because I'm not always around and he is his father."

"I wish I could give my son to a priest like Samuel was given but I don't see the feasibility because I also want to tend and care for him. I love him so much," Mrs Hannatu said at the verge of tears, one hand in her black handbag the other clutched to the leg of the wooden table which was between them.

"God is our ever present help in time of trouble. Take heart, the Holy Spirit is always available to comfort and guide us. It would pain me more to say *"I told you so"* because I didn't admonish you on the matter just to feel good or predict what would happen. But experience, as people say, is the best teacher," Mrs Adaeze said as she removed a white handkerchief from her brown bag and gave her to clean the tears she tried so hard to hold back from gliding down her smooth cheeks.

"I know you'll find it hard to do what I'm going to tell you now, but God will help you. I hope you're listening?" Mrs Adaeze asked, seeing Hannatu was ostensibly distant like a person in deep thoughts. "Are you?" She asked with a bit louder tune.

"Yes ma, I'm listening," Mrs Hannatu replied as if she had just been woken from sleep.

Mrs Adaeze had known Hannatu to be a vibrant and strong-willed young woman, who did whatever she set her mind to do no matter what the situation was. She seemed broken now, weary and distraught, someone who was about to give up.

"I know from your tears it hasn't been easy with you, it would have been easier if you were not with a child, but God knows why, everything has a reason and we can't question God, he's all knowing."

"Okay, now this is the difficult part. Practice the word of God literally, and by his grace your husband, will change his ways. Listen and adhere strictly to it. When Jesus said; "Love your enemy and pray for those who persecute you," he wasn't joking. Even when he said; "If your neighbour slaps you on the right cheek, offer him the left," he meant every word of it. In so doing, you don't have to fight, the Lord will fight your battles and you shall hold your peace.

Let me narrate a scene of a movie of an ancient happening I watched though I've forgotten the title. It was during the persecution of the church by the Roman Empire. Soldiers were haughty and heartless; they were bloody, brutal-belligerent predators who found pleasure in inflicting pain on their prey.

One of these soldiers was mercilessly kicking and beating up a Christian in the presence of his brother, the soldier gave the brother who was made to watch the grotesque scene a sword to fight for his brother, to avenge him.

With every kick and punch, he persuaded the watching brother to fight back for his brother. But the brother who was on the floor with blood streaming out of his body through cuts, bruises and malicious wounds, pleaded with his brother not to fight, saying; "He who lives by the sword shall die by the sword." He reminded the brother that; "Jesus said we should love our enemies and pray for those who persecute us."

As he was still talking the soldier kicked him to shut up whilst taunting his brother to retaliate. The brother, with tears streaming from his eyes, and his hand holding the sword shaking uncontrollably, was about to strike the Roman soldier who was kicking his brother, when his wounded brother shouted; "Please forgive him, for he does not know what he's doing".

Of course I know in his mind he was probably shouting; *"He knows, he knows exactly what he is doing, he is causing you pain and having me watch."*

But he stood there trembling and shaking without doing anything.

"It's not easy though, Christianity is not bread and butter or akamu. It's like warfare, but our weapons of warfare are not canal but mighty in God for the pulling down of strongholds, casting down arguments and every high thing that exalts itself against the knowledge of God.

Your husband is not who you should wrestle against, but you should contend with what is pushing him against you. The reason is; we wrestle not against flesh and blood but against principalities and powers, demons making people do evil.

"How do we do this fighting and wrestling?" Mrs Adaeze asked while rolling her fisted hands as if ready to fight. Mrs Hannatu was busy gawking at her like she was watching a movie, totally perplexed by the question, unable to give an answer. Mrs Adaeze wasn't expecting one anyway, so she proceeded with her informal sermon.

"In the place of prayer," Mrs Adaeze answered her question as she got so animated and abruptly stood up with a stance similar to taekwondo fighters. Mrs Hannatu was left agape, totally amazed of how energetic Mrs Adaeze was and she was a bit corpulent.

She knew Mrs Adaeze was way advanced in age and way older than she was, therefore, she didn't expect the lion-like outbursts of energy she was manifesting.

"Wow... But I don't understand what you mean," Mrs Hannatu said, baffled.

"You *ka… kabash* in the place of prayer. You will have to *rababakashaka lewun si karebe lambade seenkaka radabakalesoone ayayaa!*

That means you have to pray in the Holy Ghost! Utter words that can't be understood, speak in tongues; in several countless languages. Like a deer running for its dear life, you will contend like your life depends on it.

Apart from that, you will also take charge in prayer by resisting the enemy like a mother Dog; attack like a lion; wrestle and combat like a warrior; dominate like a gorilla; take over in the place of prayer.

Prayer is sine qua non for true Christians – a genuine believer. Since the days of John the Baptist until now the kingdom of heaven suffers violence, and the violent, the fighters, the contenders take it by force, no negotiation nor pleading but force.

"Become a warrior in the spirit realm, for everything in the physical emanates from the spiritual. So you have to solve the squalor scandals from the source --- the spirit realm. May God see you through this dire season of your life? Know this, you are a Christian, you cannot hate, I repeat you cannot hate your husband.

Although it is not easy at all, nonetheless, love him from your heart, bearing in mind his wicked ways and sacrilegious schemes are sponsored from the pit of hell. For every bad thing he does to you, flog him back with good, be too good for him to do you bad, and be completely blameless for him to find blame or fault in you. Do your best to make peace, peace and love should be your paramount priority.

Try to adhere to what I've said, read and study your bible, find joy in searching scriptures, the Holy Sacred word of God, with the guidance of the Holy Spirit. I say unequivocally, your family's life would be auspicious," Mrs Adaeze said as she sat down.

She has been gesticulating whilst talking, not realising she was under the hot sun which made her to perspire profusely. Mrs Adaeze wiped her face with a snow-white handkerchief to dry up the sweat.

"Please let's go inside Sister Hannatu and have something chilled to drink, the heat from the sun is becoming unbearable," she said as she stood up again.

"Alright ma, but I'll be leaving soon, I have to pick Joseph from Sister Shade's house before I go home; I left my car at home," Mrs Hannatu said as she adjusted herself after she stood up to follow Mrs Adaeze.

After drinking the chilled orange juice stored in the dining room, they proceeded to a room that was probably her library or office. It was filled with books and electronic devices. The room which was heavily air conditioned, had a television suspended on the wall directly opposite where they sat.

"My advice concerning your son is this; saturate him with the things of

God. Read a Bible portion to him morning and night before he goes to bed," Mrs Adaeze said while Mrs Hannatu nodded as if she was gulping the words that came out of Mrs Adaeze's mouth.

"Teach him how to pray, and also pray for him constantly. Teach him scriptures he will be able to memorise. It will be good if he learns them at his tender age. Now let's pray," Mrs Adaeze said holding Mrs Hannatu's hand.

"Holy and righteous God, faithful and loving Father, You said You'll never leave us nor forsake us. Forgiving and merciful Judge, show us mercy and forgive us all our sins. For, if we say we have no sin, we lie and the truth is not in us. Cleanse and consecrate our desecrated bodies with your precious blood. For our self-righteousness is like a filthy rag in your presence.

You're the Man of war, no one can challenge you, yet you're the Prince of peace. Fight our battles; fight the battles of my sister Hannatu. For, it is written that You shall fight our battles and we shall hold our peace. Tear apart her enemies and let those who seek her downfall never rise and those who make trouble against her begin to make peace with her in Jesus' mighty name we have prayed."

The both of them chorused Amen.

"May God help you, I'll keep praying for you," Mrs Adaeze said.

"Thank you so much ma, I really do appreciate," Mrs Hannatu replied sincerely.

"And again you need wisdom. Wisdom is profitable to direct. Alright let's go, I'll take you to where you can easily get a taxi to Sister Shade's house," Mrs Adaeze said as she stood up.

"Ma you don't need to bother, you've done enough for me already," Mrs Hannatu protested.

After much drag, Mrs Hannatu acquiesced.

TWELVE

"Holy and righteous God, Vinedresser of the true Vine have mercy oh Lord and do not regard iniquity in our hearts nor wickedness in our actions. Like the children of Israel, let there be no sorcery against us or divination against our loved ones. Forgive our trespasses for if we say we have no sin we lie, and the truth is not in us.

Help us to be like Jesus who's every motive was to please you and to do your will. Make us to be zealous like Phinehas the son of Eleazer to annihilate sinful habits and not live with it and flee from every appearance of evil like Joseph evaded Potiphar's wife.

Let us not be like the Pharisees who gave a tithe of spices whilst neglecting justice, mercy and faith which is more important or hypocrites who claim to love God but can't love the people they see. Give us wisdom to administer justice like Solomon and make us wise like him to know that giving attracts blessing and our tithes provoke prosperity.

Give us an excellent spirit like Daniel to be above our contemporaries and the grace not to contaminate ourselves with the things of this world. Help us not to be blinded by our abilities like Asahel who neglected Abner's advice but let us be like Moses discerning enough to take Jethro's advice.

Help us love you like Ruth who followed and assisted Naomi expecting nothing in return, and faithful to you like Ittai the Gitttite who was ready to die with David. Help us forsake the things of this world and cling to you like Moses forsook the pleasures of pharaoh's house to identify with the people of Israel.

Help us to be tenacious in the place of prayer like Eleazer the Ahohite who fought against the philistines until his hand stuck to his sword, and like Jacob who wrestled unrelenting until he received his blessing.

Help us believe in you like Jonathan knowing that nothing restrains you from saving with many or a few. Help us return all glory to you like Joab did to David not letting the place he conquered be named after him. Help us to keep our vows like Jephter did, no matter what is on the line, and let us pick our words carefully like Jacob did when he vowed to serve you the rest of his life.

Make us to be obsequious like David who you carefully designed and cut part *of your heart and put in him. Oh God help us to be bold and audacious like Elijah to speak your word caring less of the type of audience.*

Let us not be money lovers like Judas who traded the breath of life for few pieces of silver or greedy like Gehazi who preferred present riches to future prosperity. Make us to intercede for our loved ones like Abraham interceded for Lot his nephew. In Jesus' mighty name."

"Amen." Mr Okafor's family members chorused.

It was a Saturday morning, Mr Okafor was leading his family in a prayer session he had titled; "The Be Like Prayer". They usually said the prayer together every day of the week back at Abakaliki but it had been altered since they came to Abuja.

Mr Okafor had told his Children to pray it together while he and their mother would pray it together during the week days then on Saturday the entire family would pray the prayer together. Only Sundays were exempted because they prepared early for church.

The Be Like Prayer was prayed after the morning devotion that morning. That fateful morning, Chigozie was woken up by his sister Osinachi. It was their mother who sent her to wake him up. Interestingly Osinachi woke up earlier than usual that morning claiming to be tired of sleeping.

Chigozie was feeling sleepy almost throughout the devotion. He wondered why the sequence of the morning devotion praises was always the same. That morning his elder sister had started with:

This is the day,
This is the day that
The lord has made.

Instead of the usual:
Good morning Jesus,
Good morning Lord,
I know you came from heaven above

But immediately she finished with *"This is the day,"* she then raised *"Good morning Jesus"* then continued with:

I will enter His gates
With thanksgiving in my heart,
I will enter his courts with praise.

Then she raised another:
Take glory Father, take glory Son,
Take glory Holy Ghost now and forevermore
And so on and so forth, the sequence was always the same. After the praise and worship their father led them in their Church's daily devotional used mostly on Saturdays.

Before the time for prayer, Chigozie was hoping and praying in his mind that his mother would not lead the prayers. It was because any time she led prayers, they always spent way longer time, and it was usually Saturdays when nobody was leaving early in the morning for any business outside home.

Before, when it was time to pray, all of them would kneel down facing the chair but their mother had stopped them from doing that because most of the time they did so, they would mumble prayers and sleep off only waking up at interjections to chorus amen.

There was a Saturday when Chigozie had slept off completely even until they had shared the grace. His mother had told his siblings not to wake him, she then came close to him and voiced "In Jesus name!" he then chorused "Amen," and started shaking and nodding his head like he was still praying.

Osinachi had burst into uncontrollable laughter; he then raised his head realizing they had since ended the devotion. That day, him and his mother continued the prayer for almost an hour.

After all the supplications in his mind for his mother not to lead the prayer, their mother still led making them stand up to pray and from time to time she would shout "I can't hear you, I can't hear you, pray, pray, pray!" This was to make them voice out their prayers; they would increase their voices but with time it would decline again.

Chigozie loathed Saturdays because of the herculean chores that came along with it. They had to wash curtains, bed sheets, wash and mop their floors, clean the always dusty windows and furniture surfaces and they had their own clothes to wash too and so many other things to attend to. Sometimes they were even sent to the market to make some purchases.

That particular Saturday, their mother had told them that her maternal uncle was coming to visit. It was the same uncle who her elder sister stayed with, after their father disowned her for an issue their mother had not yet told them about. The uncle had come for a friend's event in Abuja, so he had told their mother that he wanted to visit them before he travelled back to Lagos where he was residing.

"Chibuzor, can you remember Chizoba back in Abakaliki?" Chigozie asked his brother as they were trekking back from the market carrying the foodstuffs they bought. Chibuzor was carrying a sack containing tubers of yam while his brother was carrying a bag full with other foodstuffs.

It was still morning but the sun was already grinning like it was afternoon. They had just left the market after buying everything their mother sent them to buy. They bargained for every commodity they bought, even the ones that the prices were lower than what their mother wrote because there was every possibility that some commodities would be higher than what she jotted down because they were determined to save money.

They had trekked coming to the market with the plan of taking bike back home but the money was not sufficient, so if they took bike going back home, their trekking coming would be in vain because they would have no money remaining.

They had followed their mother to market and seen her beat prices lower than half the asking price. Sometimes it seemed even wrong to beat down the price but their mother had told them no matter the price the market people sell their goods, they were still gaining out of it, sometimes even prodigiously.

Their father while bargaining would sometimes act like he did not really need what he wanted to buy all in a bid to beat down the price. Back then at Abakaliki, they bargained just for bargaining sake but now it was expedient they did so if not it could be detrimental to their well-being.

THIRTEEN

"Some girls and guys fake it until they make it; that is why it's not everybody you see on Gucci that know what sushi is or has legit bank accounts that can be counted with the elite, which is not a bad idea though. The law can't punish who it can't catch, that's why yahoo boys are just flexing cash in a country like ours that does not care about cybercrime. We have to meet men, people that matter for us to matter too," Chinelu said as she gesticulated each point she gave.

"Chinelu! You have started again with all this your money talk, you're always talking about money. I hope it will not put you into trouble someday, you have a good voice notwithstanding?" Funke said whilst chatting on her iPhone.

"Thanks but no thanks for the compliment. I know you're just flattering me. You have the best voice in our choir, and you've even ministered in the big church more than once. *Sha*, you'll not understand hustling, you have all you need at your disposal and lack nothing. People would kill to be like you," Chinelu said while standing.

"It's okay my dear, you are over exaggerating," Funke cut in.

"Abi oo!" Some of the other girls with them voiced out. They had all come for choir rehearsals. It was a sunny Saturday afternoon and they were all in the teenage department waiting for Uncle Gabriel; their choir master who used to conduct their rehearsals.

Funke was brought to church by her father who also came to church for a meeting of the church leaders. Funke didn't want to come for the rehearsals, she had earlier in the day decided to go out shopping for new clothes though she had tons of assorted clothes, mostly unworn.

Only a few were used either once or twice, so she hardly had a worn-out cloth. She hardly repeated a dress to church because she used to buy more clothes than she needed, no thanks to her aristocratic mother who spoiled her.

Her mother bought her what she wanted, even things that weren't of any use to her. At a point she didn't like the lavish spending but she got accustomed to it, and often threw tantrums if she didn't get what she wanted.

Thanks to her father, she had not become a brat yet. Funke was a brain box; she excelled in her studies and always topped the class. She would sometimes intentionally fail her exams when she wanted attention from her parents or want her demands to be met.

Her father wanted her to study in a federal university— he had told her that that's where he studied and that it was a major part of what made him to be what he is today. But Funke did not want that, she wanted to go to a private university.

She had said federal schools are for poor people or the commoners who couldn't afford private schools. Her father wouldn't hear of it, he made her to still apply for University of Nigeria Nsukka; a federal school which she didn't like. So she flunked her post Unified Tertiary Matriculation Examination (UTME), and succeeded in failing. Her Father was really disappointed; unfortunately for him, his wife was in support of her.

"Hello teenagers! How are you all doing?" Uncle Gabriel said as he entered the teenage hall. He was a jovial teenage teacher, he was so passionate about teenagers, and had sacrificed a lot to keep the teenage department running. He was the youngest among all the teenage teachers.

"Good afternoon sir."

"Where are the twins? I hope they are not coming later than me again," Uncle Gabriel asked.

"They are yet to come sir," Chinelu replied.

"Chibuzor, could you please walk faster? You are way too slow for my liking. We're going late, thanks to you," Chigozie said as he walked fast at the verge of running.

Chigozie had joined the choir and was doing very well. He has been applauded for his carriage and confidence on stage, he was not completely a natural singer, but he loved the spotlight and the applause he would get when he finished ministering, so he trained himself very well in order to perform.

Chigozie always wanted to be involved in everything, always sought to be at the centre of talk and drama. He was outspoken, friendly and cheerful, but often had mood swings.

Chibuzor on the other hand was scholarly, more brilliant academically. He was shy, docile but friendly. He could be competitive and sporadic but most of the times withdrawn.

"Who reminded daddy that we have rehearsals? Who asked for money for transport? Who reminded you that it was time for rehearsals? I can now understand why people say the first complainant always seems right until the accused person lays his case. Just thank your God that last Sunday's traffic was too much hindering us from going for the dedication, if not, you would have stooled on yourself," Chibuzor said and laughed.

The both of them were trekking to church from the bus stop where they alighted because there were no bikes available and they could not afford a cab. This was a way of life for them every Saturday since they joined the choir.

"Let's run, we're very late. I'm the one leading praises tomorrow and you're the one playing the keyboard," Chigozie said trying to shade his eyes from the scorching sun, as he turned back to look at Chibuzor who was lagging behind with his sagging trouser that he had been trying to hold up.

"If you want to run, run. The Bible says the wicked runs when no one pursues. Besides if we're late, we would have passed the Limbo and I'll be on my way to heaven. I don't know which of the two places you'll be going. Because if you're running you'll be like the people Psalms 1:4 was talking about," Chibuzor said wryly as he grinned to himself whilst adjusting his sagging trouser.

"It's you that will be blown away by the wind with that your trouser. It would be a farcical spectacle to see you blown away. And I warned you not to wear that slacking slacks but you'll be there forming big head small brain," Chigozie said as he laughed.

"If I decide to tie wrapper and attend rehearsals, is it your business? I am me and you are you. Everybody has his own perspective and preferences. So leave me alone!" Chibuzor said vociferously.

"If you tie wrapper and go to church, to God who made me I will deny you. I can't wait for ASUU to call off their strike so that I can resume school, so you'll stop dragging me back."

Back in church Uncle Gabriel had set up the sound system with the help of other teenagers. "We can't wait any longer! Let's start practicing before they arrive," Uncle Gabriel said.

Just then Chigozie and Chibuzor entered the church. Most of the teenagers were happy to see them but Funke tried to hide her joy. She had anticipated their arrival. She felt like she had seen one of them when she went to sit for her post UTME at University of Nigeria. But she didn't know which of them she saw, because she just discovered of recent that they were twins.

Her amusement came from the fact they looked so identical and she could hardly spot the difference either facially or stature-wise. They were around six feet tall, fair or outright yellow in complexion. But they unequivocally deferred in character and dressing. Chigozie was an unapologetic show-off dresser while his brother was more reserved.

"Why are you two coming by this time? You guys are so late that Kate who used to come very late came before you guys," Uncle Gabriel said trying to rebuke them.

"Sir we trekked from the junction by the express way," Chibuzor said mildly while Chigozie nudged him because he didn't want them to know they trekked.

"All the way from the express?" Uncle Gabriel asked surprised. "Why didn't you guys just take a cab?"

"We just decided to trek, the distance is not too far," Chigozie said trying to float the gravity.

"Sir, actually, we just wanted to save the money, besides to enter drop is really expensive," Chibuzor said as if he was confessing.

"Igbo people, *una too like money* fa," One of the teenagers commented jokingly.

"Very true, but who here doesn't like money?" Chinelu asked.

"Everybody likes money, but you people's case is too much," Kate blurted.

"*Hmm, kinda true sha,* probably the effects of the Biafran war, which made the Igbos to start from scratch, like from nothing, that could be the reason why. I know you guys know nothing about it," Chinelu said.

The hall became silent. Chibuzor and Chigozie wondered why.

"I'm sorry sir, it's because of this tortoise that we came late," Chigozie voiced, breaking the silence.

"How will you call your brother, your twin brother for that matter a tortoise?" Uncle Gabriel said cautioning Chigozie.

"Sir don't mind him oo, he use to talk before he thinks because of his snail brain," Chibuzor said sardonically with a smirk on his face which was always there anytime he felt he dropped a punch line.

"Hey, the two of you should not start this afternoon, we are already behind schedule. Both of you are children of God, so stop insulting yourselves. Insulting anybody is insulting God's creation," Uncle Gabriel said but Chigozie who always wanted to have the last say, and who was vexed on understanding the gravity of the insult given to him by his brother said; "Okay sir, but Chibuzor is a grandchild, or should I say great, great, great grandchild."

"God doesn't have grandchildren; all of us are his children," Uncle Gabriel said. "So let's start the rehearsals, and I'm inviting you all to the wedding of one of our Auntie's sister next week, so we won't be having rehearsals then," Uncle Gabriel said.

"Party after party," one of the teenagers excitedly said. "Yes oo," some of them exclaimed. "Party after party, after party after party," Chinelu sang with the posture of one who wanted to dance. "After parteeee," Funke sang using a falsetto, pitching her melodious voice for about ten to twenty seconds.

Chibuzor who was now sitting at the drums side hit the cymbal so hard and adroitly that it shrieked melodiously which was followed by boisterous clapping and chanting around the teenage hall.

"These pastor's children will just be kidding with their Father's repute," Uncle Gabriel soliloquized shaking his head. "So it's because of party you guys got so animated? Settle down so we can start."

FOURTEEN

Mr Habib was pissed up because of how docile his wife had been for the past few days. She was too caring and doting, not only for their son but to him. Her love and affection was boundless like a basket under a running tap which could never be filled, cheerfully giving away what it had.

She always avoided arguments so adeptly. He saw her altruism as too redundant and superfluous, so it irritated him the more and vowed to deal with her, seeing her piety and her selflessness as a decoy to have her way. He was determined to make it a debacle. Her excessive politeness was rudeness to him, making him feel like he was nobody, for all his schemes and ruses seemed to mean nothing.

It was now night and she was not yet back home from work. He has been suspecting that she was cheating on him. He had even dedicated a whole day to spy on her but found nothing compromising.

Mrs Hannatu was managing a grocery store – a joint venture founded by her late husband and her. Her present husband used that as a means to exploit her, asking for his share every now and then.

The grocery store had a smaller shop by the side stocked with clothes and cloth materials where she had an employee managing it. Her husband had come to the shop late one evening drunk with beer, he had a carousal at one of his friends clandestine Bachelor Party.

Intoxicated with alcohol, he marched to the store to collect money from his wife. On reaching the store he met it closed but the cloth shop was still open. He entered the shop shouting and bawling boisterously; "Where's my wife? Where's my money?"

The sales girl in the shop who was about to lock it up was startled and astounded by the berserk manner. Fortunately no customer was in shop to experience the ill-manners of Mr Habib who was drunk to stupor. Alcohol had made his demeanour very condescending.

"Madam is not here sir." Emu the sales girl replied with fear in her voice. "Where is she?" Mr Habib shouted holding the door of the shop trying to balance his staggering body.

"She said she was going to church for prayer meeting Sir," Emu replied. He then forcefully collected money from the sales girl that night and failed to reimburse his wife when she asked him for it; not even bothering to answer her in that regard.

Now Mrs Hannatu was on her way back from Bible school – a two-year programme organized by their church but she was held up in traffic. The study was awesome, as such she was recollecting things the pastor had said; "Who the Son has set free is free indeed; be anxious for nothing; no weapon fashioned against you shall prosper; you are the head and not the tail; greater is he that is in you than he that is in the world; love your neighbours like I have loved you," the pastor had simplified some abstruse passages in the Bible.

"Oga driver give me my change, I *dey* drop for here," one of the passengers in the car said. Mrs Hannatu had taken public transport to church because her car needed repairs and she did not have money yet to fix it because of her parasitic husband.

The people in the car had been discussing about politics which was now turning into an argument. "The Presidential Election is coming up and some people are Atikulated while the others are Buharified. PDP and APC are the two major political parties in this country, other parties are just adding to the number. So it is PDP, APC and others. The election this year is very critical, many pastors have predicted the outcome, others are still prophesying.

People are scared that the outcome could erupt another civil war in the country. Most people are already traveling back to their villages, selling off their properties. There is nobody in the country that isn't aware of the upcoming election.

The election is no longer a power tussle between the political parties, but a power tussle of tribalism and religion. Everybody wants to vote as you could see long queues early in the morning at various voting centres of people trying to get their PVC. Would you vote? Would you be part of determining the fate of this great nation Nigeria? See you next time on your favourite radio station, same time tomorrow to get the latest on

Rising matters." The broadcast from the radio had started the jousting in the vehicle.

"You must be Buharified, because if you are Atikulated, you will know that we are in the centre of traffic and I can't stop in the middle of the road for you to come down." The driver shouted back. "Oga, I beg of you, don't bring me into such baseless argument, I'm not supporting anybody. You people keep fighting for people that don't care a bit about you, besides the car is not moving as such I can easily drop. And for your information whether APC or PDP wins you'll still be a taxi driver," the lady said sardonically which made the passengers burst into laughter.

"You're very stupid for making that statement, see how fat you are like two elephants put together. Take it that you no longer have change from me because the space you have occupied is for two people, if you want to go down, you are free to do so." The driver blurted and swore.

"Oga, don't try me, as you can see, I am not joking; forget this dressing, I'm a Warri girl oo, I must warn you." The lady said vociferously. The driver laughed as the road got more liberal, they were getting close to the junction where he would stop.

"So you have enough guts to shout at me anyhow! Do you think I am your mate? Do you know where I come from? Warri girl, Warri girl," he mimicked her. You people are too war-like. I am an Edo man, let me tell you; I have capacity to change your destiny." Everybody in the bus voiced 'ahh!' Even Mrs Hannatu, as she rushed to come down when the Sienna packed. The driver and the well-dressed lady continued stoning themselves with insults as Mrs Hannatu boarded a bike to her house. She started musing on the election, wondering what the outcome would be.

Back at home, Joseph was crying, asking his father where his mother was; he started crying when his father lightly spanked him. Mr Habib had asked him if he was a Christian or a Muslim and he replied that he was a Christian.

Days before that, he had come back home from school asking his mother the same question. Because a Muslim girl in his class had asked him what religion he was, and persuaded him to be a Muslim.

Joseph perplexed asked his mother what religion he was, and she had convinced him that he was a Christian. He had told her of his friend, the Muslim girl and that he wanted to be like her.

Mrs Hannatu astounded by his persistence wondered what the girl must have told him for him to want to be a Muslim. Searching for words determined to convince her son with words he would understand, she told him that Muslims bow down with their heads to the ground leaving a permanent mark on their head praying to God who cannot be reached or talked to except through his Son Jesus Christ whom He had sent from heaven down to earth to die for the sins of the world and also for him and her because He loved them. And it's only through Jesus Christ who is the father of Christianity that they could communicate with God the Father. Fortunately for her Joseph seemed to understand, he had said "I want to be a Christian."

Now Mr Habib was trying to convince and persuade him that he was a Muslim and that his name is Yusuf not Joseph. Joseph utterly confused and bewildered began to cry. Unable to placate or curb Joseph's wail because of the absence of his mother, he carried him to his room and put him on the bed and locked the door.

Joseph cried himself to sleep.

Mr Habib came back to the sitting room of their well-furnished two-bedroom flat, there was light and it was brighter inside as the day grew darker outside. The room was disorganized, pillows on the ground, scraps on the table, a jug of tea was still on the centre table since in the morning, and the floor was littered with some clothes here and there.

He did not go to work that day, yet waited for his wife to come back home from work to clean up and arrange the disorganized house. But worse than that, he sat on the brown cushion in the sitting room musing on how to deal with his innocuous wife.

Mr Habib wore dishabille outfits to work; he worked in his late brother's enterprise now managed by his late brother's close friend. He initially wanted to take over its management but his mother refused saying; "This ship would wreck and sink with no friction if you touch the rudder, talk less of wheeling it."

She had known him to be unstable, sporadic and incapable of managing anything. Nonetheless, he was proficient in the position he was given, and played a vital role in bringing cash to the company because of his craftiness. So he couldn't be removed even though he dressed and behaved irresponsibly most of the time.

Mrs Hannatu walked into the house and closed the door behind her. She was surprised by the gaily noise she heard from the room. She scampered to the room door, opened it and saw her husband and son eating happily then they stood up and started dancing. Then Joseph ran to greet her while her husband came and kissed her forehead it seemed too good to be true, God had finally answered her prayers, her heart cry; suddenly rain started falling. She heard it hit the roof top like sticks rapidly hitting a talking drum then she felt drops of water dropping on her head at an accelerating velocity, she looked up to see where in the roof the water was leaking from, but as she looked up the water covered her face, as she wiped her face to see clearly, she woke up from her sleep wiping her face just to see that her husband just finished urinating on her face.

"So you just came home to come and sleep, and left the house for who to arrange? Better go and arrange the house and cook food for me?!" Mr Habib shouted at the top of his voice on his wife, startling her, she wished she could turn to a statue, apathetic. Mrs Hannatu was perplexed, in total consternation. She couldn't believe her eyes, she cleaned them again and again, and she wasn't able to comprehend what her husband was saying anymore. He was watching TV when she came home and she was so tired that when she entered the room she slept off. Soaked in the Lacasera coloured liquid that had drenched her cloth and pillow, she hoped to wake up from reality, praying it was a dream, wishing her dream was reality. Dumbfounded with tears mingled with urine that rolled down her pale fair cheeks she stood up and slowly walked away uttering not a word.

FIFTEEN

"Good evening Daddy. Daddy, please, what really happened in what some people call the Biafran war? I've been hearing about it but I don't know the full story," Chigozie asked after clearing the table, carrying the plates with his father's remaining food for him and Chibuzor to eat.

Osinachi was already fast asleep while Amaka was busy putting on and off her data while chatting on WhatsApp. In her mind, she was trying to make the dying battery last longer, not realizing the music she was playing with her phone torch on will drain the battery in no time.

There had been no light since afternoon when Chigozie and Chibuzor went to church unlike in the morning. Saturdays were days electricity distributing company staff usually moved around disconnecting debtors. Most times than not, the light use to be full during those Saturday mornings.

That day, Mrs Okafor had gone out to buy some things she forgot to tell her sons to buy for her uncle's visit, and some materials she needed for her sewing and Mr Okafor had already gone to work, when staffs of the electricity distributing company came for disconnection.

Some youngster neighbours such as Victor, John and Tunde tried to persuade and beg one of the three electricity distributing officers who seemed to be their boss not to disconnect their house.

Among the Okafor family, it was Amaka that was home when they came. She called John who called the rest of neighbours present to beg them particularly because she was enjoying the fan and watching television at that time.

She had not had time to watch for more than half of the month because of poor power supply. Amaka who was not fully acquainted with how things were done in her new area was infuriated as well as frustrated. She was accustomed to the metering payment system.

How can they bring the bill for light they had not used and cut the light they have not seen? John was trying to placate her, explaining what she did not understand or refused to understand.

What incited most of her fury was the fact that she had paid the money given to her by her father already to their caretaker, Mr Fashola, Tunde's father who had not paid the bill yet because, according to him, other tenants had not paid their share of the bill.

Unfortunately the whole compound shared the same bill. However, some were advocating that the light distribution be divided into blocks which consisted of two tenants each, while some including the caretaker were not in agreement.

Amaka suspected the caretaker was not in agreement of the proposal because of the extra money he got from the contribution and she suspected that he had used part of the money paid to him that was why he couldn't pay since he couldn't pinpoint who had not paid when asked.

But even the bill was way more than expected, she knew they wouldn't have brought superfluous bill if they had paid earlier. She pushed John away, who was more of hugging her than restraining her from striding forward and shouting at the electricity officers.

She released herself and walked home abruptly and banged the door behind her, telling Osinachi who was at the window watching to go and wash the dishes.

"See, I'm tired right now. Maybe I'll tell you next time. Why do you all of a sudden want to know?" Mr Okafor asked.

"We're tired of hearing the story in bits and pieces. Daddy please just tell us," Chibuzor said trying to persuade his father along with Chigozie. Their curiosity was triggered by Chinelu's comment that day during the rehearsals.

"I just came back from work not too long ago, I'll tell you next time. Better still you can ask your mother to narrate the story for you," Mr Okafor said. He usually doesn't go to work on Saturdays except there was something important to do. He was called earlier that day in the morning for some work-related issues.

Mr Okafor was trying to avoid telling the story. He didn't want to talk on the subject because it brought bad memories. It was like a horror movie only that it was real. He didn't want to instigate hate or animosity in his children. There was no way he could tell the story, without he himself feeling that he was being biased. His father had died from the war he didn't want to fight but had to.

"I'm indisposed!" Mrs Okafor hollered whilst treading her sewing machine in the bedroom, using her phone torchlight to see. Amaka walked to the room to sleep after running down her phone battery, leaving her father and brothers in the totally dark sitting room, which was lit by a dim rechargeable lamp.

"Daddy we're waiting oo, we're not going to sleep this night, and tomorrow is Sunday," Chigozie said. Chibuzor sitting on the floor by his side was facing their father. Their Father twitched, but they were unable to see it due to how dark the parlour was.

"Well, if you insist. The story is that, a group of people, to be specific the Igbos decided to rebel against the government, by declaring Biafra as their country and confiscating the countries resources within their new republic. The Nigerian army fought back and won, quelling the Igbo's insurrection and rebellion so we are now one country, one Nigeria and we live in unity thanks to the able and gallant Nigerian army. End of story. I hope I can rest now?" Mr Okafor said. He quickly stood up, and walked briskly to his room, leaving his sons astounded.

On entering his room, his wife picked her phone and pointed the phone's torch at him as if she was taking a picture, Mr Okafor on the other end unable to see her upset yet pretty face, was busy posing with his thumbs up and winking as if he had conquered his biggest fear.

"My sugarcane," Mrs Okafor said. She was putting on a false smile behind the light which her husband couldn't see. "Oga smart! Oya about turn; go and give those children a better explanation. Don't you think it's better they hear the story from you with a better knowledge and maturity on the matter than from someone else? The explanation should better be good enough if you want to sleep on my bed this night."

She then turned the phone torch to her face with the look of *better do it now, or else.*

That was part of what Mr Okafor loved about his wife, she was feisty at times. He slowly walked back to the sitting room like he was walking into a den of hungry lions, meeting Chigozie and Chibuzor sitting erect as they waited for him.

"A person, who wants to swallow a knife, should be ready to drink a whole river to push it down. He that buys a cat to chase away rat from his house, should not complain when the cat wails for milk or fish and litter the ground with its faeces," Mr Okafor said in Igbo as he sat down.

Chibuzor understood the interpretation in English but Chigozie didn't fully understand talk less of seeing any relation if there was, with the Biafran story.

"Curiosity kills the cat albeit knowledge is for the curious," Mr Okafor said as he cleared his throat. Chibuzor was placid while Chigozie was uneasy but tried to hide it.

"Daddy, stop over sharpening the poignant pencil, just draw! Go straight to the point," Chigozie said in his mind.

"As engine oil is to a car engine, so are some sayings to incendiary stories, an internecine one for that matter," Mr Okafor said as if he read Chigozie's mind. He cleared his throat again and sank into his chair, and placed his legs on a small wooden stool near-by.

"He who gathers wood filled with ants, invites lizard for a holiday," Chibuzor said while trying to figure his father's face in the partial darkness.

"The bird that takes flight from the ground and lands on an anthill should know that it's still on the ground," Chigozie said almost immediately. He didn't want to be out-witted by his brother.

"What are you two saying? What does that have to do with anything?" Mr Okafor asked.

"I thought we were giving proverbs, turn by turn," Chigozie postulated.

"Me I thought the sayings are preliminaries for this type of story," Chibuzor said jokingly. Mr Okafor shook his head, and then looked at the bulb opposite him instinctively; they just flashed light. He mumbled something in Igbo, while the twins hissed, noticing it too.

"A woman, a very beautiful woman, elegant and endowed properly in the right places was made to be a co-wife to a man of a totally different culture, who's manner of living, beliefs, values and ethics were diametrically opposite to hers.

The husband liked his other wife more because she had things they could both agree on, and he could coerce her to do his biddings if he wanted but his other wife was rebellious, the first one I mentioned. The docile and rebellious wife could agree on some things as well. The husband favoured the docile wife more; he bought her gifts, made her promises if she continued to be submissive and so on."

Mr Okafor leaned forward to see if his sons were still paying attention to his analogy, he was in the mood now, so they had to be too. He asked them if they were listening and they promptly concurred, so he continued.

"The rebellious wife was ambitious, maybe too ambitious, the husband despised her for it, and he didn't want her to be in charge of anything. He began to abuse his powers and authority, making rules to spite her and laws in the house that was not favourable to her.

The rebellious wife was exuberant, ebullient, talented, very industrious and resourceful. In fact she was embedded with all manner of resources and her husband exploited her and used most of the wealth on himself and part of it for his docile wife and the remnants for the owner.

She confronted him and took the authority of the house saying; "this house is not yours only, stop trying to monopolize it, it's ours not yours, stop being corrupt." Not long after that he retaliated leaving her bruised and wounded and he began to oppress, assault, molest, harass her, putting her into servitude in the same house.

She decided to leave him and her co-wife who did nothing to ameliorate their discorded relationship or make it congenial. So she decided to secede, fragmentize, divorce him before she is badly mutilated.

He was happy, at least his impudent recalcitrant wife was gone, she was carbuncle to his skin, pox to his wounds, a hole in his pocket, now she was finally gone.

But in a short while his eyes opened like Pharaoh when he let the children of Israel go. She was his major source of income, there was no one to serve and pay him. Anxious, alarmed and aware of his complacency, he hunted her down with the help of the person who put him in power.

He confiscated all her property and fought against those who wanted to help her. Under the guise of pursuit for peace and unity, he afflicted her with violence and there was more discord.

Her sustenance became limited, her help cut short. She had little or no chance of surviving if she continued resisting, because the person that was helping and supporting her husband kept supplying him with all he needed to annihilate her.

They tagged her independence as mutiny, but refused to label their violent act as pogrom. He forcefully took her back to live in peace," Mr Okafor said and sighed as if he remembered a bitter scenario.

"I hope with these few points of mine you two can let me sleep; I'm tired and I have Sunday school class to take tomorrow," Mr Okafor said and received no reply. "Hello! So you guys are sleeping!" He said and still got no reply and was in total discomfiture.

"I must have been talking to myself; my analogy must have been terrible, for them to sleep off. In any case, I have tried," He thought and sighed as he walked into his room.

SIXTEEN

Mr Okafor met another situation in the bedroom that will delay his rest – he met his wife sobbing. He was startled and moved closer to her wondering what the problem was.

"Don't you know we're married?" Mrs Okafor said with tears in her eyes. "Why would you use that kind of analogy? Why didn't you just tell them the real story? I hope you don't see me as rebellious and a boil on your skin?" Mrs Okafor muttered. Tears were rolling down her sleek pale cheeks. She then started shivering, holding part of an Ankara dress.

Mr Okafor was astounded, realizing his wife had some of the qualities or features of the woman he described, but he meant no harm. He scurried towards her, kneeling down by her side.

"No! No! No! I wasn't talking about you. I didn't mean to hurt you, I'm sorry. You're the air I breathe," Mr Okafor said searching for words.

"Please forgive me," Mrs Okafor said finding it hard to talk as she sobbed.

"No, I'm the one who needs your forgiveness, I'm sorry, please forgive me," Mr Okafor said while holding her hands to fondle it. Then he cuddled her, urging her to stop crying. At that point light was restored to the house.

"Sugarcane I have something to tell you before you sleep," Mrs Okafor said moments later after being placated by her husband who was now about to sleep. She had just finished what she had been sewing

"What is it again Nwaozioma?" Mr Okafor asked as calmly as he could, he was really tired and wanted to sleep, knowing he had to wake up early the next day being Sunday. "Can't you tell me tomorrow? I'm really tired."

Mrs Okafor walked to his side of the bed, shifted his legs making him a bit slant on the bed and sat down folding her hands with her lips pursed, staring forward, saying nothing.

"Jesus!" Mr Okafor exclaimed. "Ice cream I'm not falling for this at all," Mr Okafor said and started rolling to her side of the bed. Mrs Okafor turned, grabbing his cloth.

"Biko be patient, it's about my uncle that visited us today. You didn't even ask me about him," Mrs Nwaozioma said holding him. Mr Okafor now wide awake, quickly sat upright realizing that he didn't get to meet her uncle because he had to leave for work in the morning and had forgotten to ask her about him.

"Its true dear, sorry I forgot, how is your uncle? I hope he was not too upset that I wasn't around?"

"He really was, he said he had not seen the lucky man who got married to his beautiful niece, though that's not the main issue."

"Yeah I'm really lucky. So Ice cream what is the main issue?" He asked, now worried.

"You know my father disowned my elder sister Adanna, because she had a relationship with one Yoruba boy in school?" Mrs Nwaozioma said.

"Yes, you've told me that before," Mr Okafor replied wondering where this was heading.

"My uncle just told me the part of the story I didn't know. I thought my sister dropped out of school only because her relationship with the boy led to failure in her academics but my uncle just told me that the boy actually got her pregnant.

My sister was a very brilliant student, she excelled marvellously in her secondary school and her performance got her a scholarship to study in the university. Because of my sister's activism in school activities and SUG, the boy who was an aspirant for SUG president got involved with her to boost his name and political clout which led to their eventual relationship.

My Uncle said my sister and the young man were both in love which led to him getting her pregnant. This made the school that gave her scholarship to withdraw it when they discovered, because her results dwindled. My Father hearing about her pregnancy, was angry and disowned her, he didn't want his image to be stained being a renowned Catholic Church leader.

I never knew my sister got pregnant in school, I thought the reason my father disowned her was because her relationship with the boy made her fail her exams; because my father sternly warned me not to have any relationship with a Yoruba boy or any other boy while in school."

"Except me," Mr Okafor said kissing her cheek.

"See I'm talking about a serious thing here don't make light of it," she said turning her face.

"But was your mother in alliance with your father's decision?" Mr Okafor asked and Mrs Okafor started touching his neck as if checking his temperature.

"Haven't I told you that my mother past away when we were still tender?" she asked.

"Oh sorry I didn't know it was before then. So what happened to your sister? Didn't the boy take responsibility for the pregnancy?" he asked sitting back.

"My sister continued staying with my uncle in Lagos where her school was. The boy wanted to take responsibility for the pregnancy to prove how much he loved my sister but his so-called godfather told him not to do that until after the SUG election.

My uncle said that this was part of the man's plan to push his daughter closer to him. Because later on, the man's daughter had come claiming to have his child but before that, the boy had come to my uncle telling him that he would take responsibility for my sister after the SUG election. By that time my sister had already given birth to a girl.

My uncle said the girl was so pretty, as beautiful as my sister, seeing me you can tell how beautiful my sister was though she was way fairer than I and her daughter took after her. But from my uncle's description, it seems she had amber eyes which is rare," Mrs Okafor said as if trying to imagine it.

"So when the daughter to his godfather came claiming to have the Yoruba boy's child, my sister couldn't believe it because she held on to his promise that he would come back for her. She then decided to go and get answers directly from him and she got killed," Mrs Nwaozioma said as she cleaned her teary eyes.

"Who killed her?" Mr Okafor asked, curiously.

"I don't know for sure but I think it was the father of the girl that claimed to have his child. His son, the younger brother to the girl and his gang had visited my uncle in one night telling him that he had been trailing them and every move they made.

My uncle said his father had also sent him to kill the little girl too so that the Yoruba boy would have no form of relation with my sister Adanna but he decided to pity my baby niece seeing how cute she was. He warned them to keep away and they should not let him regret his decision. He said if they tried reporting, or contacting her father, they will all end up like my sister did.

This made my uncle and his wife to pack from their house in fear of him coming back to kill them."

Mr Okafor rubbed her back trying to console her.

"I'm sorry. But what then happened to your niece? Did you know you had a niece?" Mr Okafor asked hoping nothing bad happened to her.

"No, I had no idea I had a niece," She replied.

"Why didn't your uncle tell you or your father about her, all this while?" Mr Okafor asked wondering.

"He said my father in anger forbade him from saying anything about Adanna, saying he didn't care about what she now did with her life or even if she lived."

"So even when she died, he said nothing?" Mr Okafor asked.

"He lost contact with us and did not bother trying to get it back because of how my father had forbidden him from saying anything about her even though now he feels he had made a mistake because of recent, my father had contacted him asking about my sister and he broke down when he heard she was dead."

"So you too just found out that your sister died. I'm so sorry," Mr Okafor said massaging her shoulders. "So what happened to your niece?"

"My Uncle said it was not long from when my sister was killed that his wife, my Aunty died of malaria according to doctors but my uncle thinks it was something more than malaria.

As such, being unable to take care of my niece all by himself, he gave her to his son who had been married for years without a child. They happily received her and trained her as their own daughter but later on because of serious money issues my cousin sent her to his onetime friend who became rich, to work as a maid in his house to make ends meet.

Incidentally the friend stays here in Abuja. But my uncle doesn't know him or where he stays. I thought of her coming to stay with us but we too are not doing well financially at the moment. I had no idea my sister had a daughter, she's my closest relation apart from my father," Mrs Okafor said wistfully.

"What about me and your children?" Mr Okafor asked jokingly.

"Oh yes, apart from you people," she said sympathetically. On realizing he was joking, vexed, she lamented some indecipherable words in Igbo and turned to stand up.

"Ice-cream calm down, I'm sorry," Mr Okafor said holding her back. "At least your beautiful niece is alive and doing well, don't cry please. Don't worry, when we get our footings here in this Abuja and we're doing better financially your niece will come and stay with us," Mr Okafor said cleaning her teary eyes as she nodded her head slowly. He then kissed her forehead and hugged her.

SEVENTEEN

"OH NO! see this gown. Are you sure she's a pastor's daughter?" Cyril exclaimed gaping at the bride.

"You're surprised right?" Chigozie said as he chuckled. They all sat round a table in the reception of the marriage of one of their pastor's daughter and a man from another church denomination.

"I hope you wear something more decent during our wedding Funke," Chibuzor said cheekily.

"Ah!" all the teens exclaimed and laughed.

"Funke don't mind him, you can wear what the bride is wearing or any other dress you feel like during our wedding," Chigozie said dramatically.

"Hmmm," the other teenagers muttered.

John from their compound followed them to the wedding on the invitation of Chigozie. John being an outgoing person agreed to go with them also due to the fact that there was also free transport to and fro.

Funke, Chinelu and Kate sat with them. Funke had come with her parents who were special guest at the wedding. Her mother made sure they attended the reception which her father didn't want to attend because he had planned to have a meeting with his workers around the same time.

"Do you want people to think we're not in good terms or think we're fighting? You know there's a rumour about it, therefore, I insist you attend to prove them wrong." Mrs Bolanle had said and that was why he decided to attend the reception.

At the high table, Mr Adefarasin was forcing himself to look happy as church members took turns to greet him and his wife. Later on, he observed that some came to confirm what they've been hearing while others came to see his health status because he wasn't looking too good during his brother-in-law's wedding.

His wife whispered to him that among those greeting him are those who want their sons to marry his daughter while Mr Ade perceived that some women came to greet him for self-advert in case he eventually divorces his nagging wife. Mr Ade refused to believe it even though they were too coquet, using endearing words.

Funke couldn't help but blush with goose bumps and invisible rouge on her immaculately fine dark skin. She was partially speechless at what the twins said because they were incredibly handsome and ebullient. Her only issue with them was that it seemed like they began to sink into penury.

"For me, I can't marry a woman that is lackadaisically dressed or dresses anyhow. You know, the way you dress is the way you'll be addressed. I can't let anyone talk to my wife anyhow," Chibuzor said emphatically.

"Nwokem, calm down you know some girls around us are shabbily dressed. Chinelu no offense please, my brother can be blunt at times.

"No offense taken," Chinelu said. She was wearing a snug sleeveless slit-silver coloured gown with a hilly shoe, probably six inches. The gown was a bit below her knees, while the gown's slit was way above her knees. "But it's not by wearing Mary Amaka skirt that will make people address you with respect, but the way you carry yourself and your deportment inside and outside.

Some village girls, even some "holy holy" sisters wear blankets for skirts yet it didn't bring any iota of respect to them. I can assure you some of them are eye service Christians nothing more."

Chinelu assumed that Chibuzor said what he said to spite her, because they had a bit of an issue during the choir rehearsal the Saturday before. She had indirectly made fun of his dressing when she said; "A new graduate wore pink slacks and yellow top for a job interview. The interviewer after diligently perusing his outfit told him that the position available in the company is not for girls and laughed. The graduate feeling insulted told the interviewer plainly that he was not a girl but the interviewer ignored him and kept on laughing. The guy getting infuriated tried convincing the interviewer that he was not a girl while holding his sagging slacks up with one hand. The teasing interviewer who was making fun of him and seeing that his trousers were sagging off said I'm sorry but we don't employ mad people. The pissed interviewee was infuriated and left his sagging trouser to fall. It scattered the papers on the interviewers table while he was shouting; I'm not mad!'

The entire teenagers burst into laughter, Chibuzor inclusive for less than five seconds before realizing the joke was indirectly targeted at him. She had asked him later on that she hope he was not offended? Although his reply was no, it appears that his latest comment was a retaliation.

"God knows I was not trying to offend anybody, and if I offended you, sorry," Chibuzor said as he just remembered what transpired the Saturday before. He hadn't said what he said to offend or spite her, but on remembering what happened during the rehearsal, he was happy that he said what he said.

"Before you people start hitting each other, who would like to hear how this handsome groom met his Igbo bride?" Funke asked.

"Tell us," John replied and the rest concurred.

John who had been stealthily staring at Funke was now gawping at her. Chigozie had pinched him once or twice to stop. Her dress marvelled him, it was simply amazing. She wore a black gown which was aesthetically designed with blue Ankara, embroidered with pearl beads strategically fitted on the dress. One of the hands was short sleeve and the other long sleeve.

A beautifully sewed Ankara material, shaped like a ribbon was attached to the shoulder of the short sleeve like a wing. She wore a sleek girly black wristwatch on one hand and an ornamented bracelet on the other. She also wore an embellished bead necklace.

John was trying to familiarize himself with her and the rest, he knew none of them except Chigozie and his twin, he was loquacious and liked to socialize but he observed that most of them were above his class, they spoke constructed English, even their pidgin was constructed, so he found it difficult to communicate fluently because he was used to broken English.

The MC cracked a joke and there was a reverberated laughter. The MC made fun of one of the so called big men on the high table, most people laughed because he said what they couldn't say, it was like he voiced out their mind.

"Their first encounter was a total jumble, Onwubiko sorry Onachi was walking out of the market towards where she would get a cab to her house with the groceries and foodstuffs in her hands."

"Wait first, why did you call her Onwubiko?" Chigozie cut in, trying to grasp the meaning.

"Emmm, her name was Onwubiko, before her Father became a Christian, her mother was a Christian before him and she had three miscarriages and one stillborn in the first five years of their marriage, So when she was born, her father called her *Onwubiko* meaning something like "death have pity." He named her that because of the previous deaths. He also vowed that if she lived up to five years he would give his life to Christ and serve his wife's God. His wife named her *Chimebere* meaning; "God have mercy."

So at the age of five they changed her name to *Onachi* meaning "God's priceless Jewel," on the day of her fifth birthday her father gave his life to Christ and later on became a pastor."

"Jesus is Lord!" John exclaimed for no real reason.

"How did you know?" Kate asked.

"Her younger sister told me, our teenage teacher, Aunty Nancy. My Father and hers are friends so sometimes I go to their house."

"Please continue the story of how they got married," Chigozie said as he took the penultimate buns from the middle of the table. John who was having an indifferent deportment about the small chops and chin-chin that was on their table carried the last one; neither Chigozie nor Chibuzor had carried anything while the others on the table were carrying so he refrained.

Chigozie carried the buns seeing that it was almost finished but Chibuzor had not taken. Funke liked being central, she enjoyed the attention she was getting so she was ready to tell the story and answer all the questions that accompanied it."

"Talk and stop smiling," Kate said.

"I don't know who you're blushing for," Chinelu inputted.

"Who's blushing?" Funke asked.

"Where did I stop again? oh I remember; as she was reaching where she would get a cab, one man a taxi driver, running past her mistakenly hit her and what she was holding fell down, agonizingly one of the leather bags was filled with eggs probably two or three crates.

Her parents had been pampering her most especially her mother, but her father wanted to stop it because she was already big and of the age to get married. He told his wife to send her to the market alone with no escort, to buy things for some Nigerian delicacies and a particular soup so she was to cook it alone.

Her mother specifically told her to buy eggs, teasing her, she said she hoped Onachi comes back with the eggs unscratched, her father said he doubted it. Onachi wanted to prove them wrong. Alas the godforsaken Hausa taxi driver bumped into her, not scratching but smashing over seventy per cent of the eggs."

"Oboye, the guy go collect," John cut in.

"Shut up na, let her finish," Chigozie said being captivated like the rest with the story.

"Please continue," Kate said.

"Yes oo," Chinelu said enjoying the story-telling.

Cyril who was a northerner was silent, wanting to hear the end of the story, wondering why the Hausa person had to be the antagonist in the story.

There was a general applause in the reception hall; a crew of dancers had just finished performing choreography. The MC made fun of some of the dancers. Some grasped the joke while others were indifferent and some were having a chit-chat.

Later on the couple cut their three-step cake, which had pink and white fondant frosting after the spelling of J-E-S-U-S, and then a woman was asked what she observed as they cut the cake. The observer said she saw love, diligence and unity.

The MC here and there found occasions to make money for the couple and himself. At this point, he told the groom to stand at one end of the hall and the bride at the other end and demanded they dance towards each other as the music played.

He asked them to move only when someone was spraying money on them, he used something to mark the midpoint, saying he wanted to see if it's the groom's family or bride's family that had more money.

Fortunately for the two sides that were now one, both reached the middle about the same time, after people from the congregation, friends and family sprayed money on them. The congregation cheered and clapped when they met.

"So Onwubiko, sorry Aunty Onachi got infuriated, she had been hearing different negative things about Hausa, Fulani bike men and taxi drivers and their violence. She once heard someone was stabbed with a dagger while arguing for ten naira with a bike man and so many other related stories.

But she was ready to fight, all her home training and girly demeanour vanished away, she shouted at him in disdain, bathing him with affronts. She, blinded by fury gave him a hot peppery slap. On hearing the boisterous sound from the slap, those trying to calm the situation withdrew for a while.

Onachi was expecting a retaliation of her uncontrolled outburst from the taxi driver realising she had just committed a blunder. The brotherhood of the Hausa's was so strong, she had once witnessed how bike people had caused serious traffic, gathering at one junction, and every bike man passing the road stopped, ready to fight to death whether their person was right or not as far as he was their brother.

She expected the taxi driver, who was still holding his cheeks from the slap to retaliate, but to her greatest shock he did not. Instead, he apologized sincerely and tried to pack and arrange the eggs that survived the crash. He even told her that he would carry her to her destination, free of charge no matter how far.

Although, now regretting her action, she was still obstinate; she did not want to disappoint her parents by proving them wrong."

"Hmmm... You've started adding salt and pepper to the story?" John cut in. Funke was speechless, she was actually telling the story the bride's sister told her, though she was spicing the story but she was enjoying the attention she was getting. Culpable, she was dumbfounded. Besides John's forwardness piqued her.

"Is it your business? If she put Maggi, salt and sugar inside, does it concern you? Is it your story?" Chinelu attacked him. John could not reply, he just wanted to interact but unfortunately his statement seemed to be anachronistic.

It was time for the marriage toast, they all stood up and Chigozie opened the wine on their table and shared for all of them in disposable cups. The MC cracked another joke and they laughed and shouted "cheers!" Clacking their disposable cups that couldn't clack, and then drinking the wine.

"Why would they name this wine *Pure Heaven* as if there is a heaven that is not pure?" Chigozie asked and they all laughed.

"That is for pure clout," Chinelu stated and chortled.

"Please Funke continue the story," Cyril said as they sat down, and the rest concurred.

"Hmmm, very well then, so, Onachi, still being obstinate asked him who would pay for the eggs, he was bewildered; he told her he had no money on him then. He said that he would carry her for free to wherever her house was no matter how far. He then offered to give her his number so that she would call him to carry her wherever she wanted to go to for the next one week, for free. However, she declined saying she can't have the contact of a low life like him.

The bystanders waiting to watch a fight; went on their business since the fight was not forthcoming. A little bit pacified by his humility, she told him to wait there caring less if he did, so she could go and buy more eggs to augment the eggs that withstood the crash even though they were fragile.

"She was surprised to see him standing there, where she left him though she spent a lot of time buying the eggs. When she entered his car, she began to doubt his tribe, maybe he was Igbo planning to use her for money ritual after the embarrassment she gave him or maybe he was actually Hausa and he was carrying her to his gang and they might mutilate her before killing her. Or still he might be a cultist, she saw how built up he was, not too muscular but very fit, and his gang might rape her or sell her for prostitution, she reasoned all this on the realization that she was very beautiful.

See the way you people are looking at me, that's what Aunty Nancy said her sister told her, and that's what I'm saying," Funke said trying to vindicate herself from their suspecting and questioning gestures.

"Hmmm, me I will not talk oo. I just want to hear the end," Chigozie said. He then put the back of his palm on his other palm making a sound, trying to drag attention as one fat girl pushed his seat trying to pass at the back of his chair which was very close to the back of another person's chair behind him. Chibuzor who was sitting beside him and others who understood his statement laughed.

"Funke, who said you should stop, please continue," Chinelu said, facing Funke.

"Ok oo. Out of fear, Onachi from the back of the car started asking questions: asking him if he was sure he knew the place she described for him and he said he knew the area like the road to his own house – that he used to pass there, almost every day.

"Jesus Christ!" she exclaimed in her mind. *"Has he been trailing me?* She thought. However, she was intrigued by his good English. He's probably a professional serial killer or kidnapper; he may have finished school and because of no government work, resorted to this.

Swallowing her phlegm she asked him what tribe he was, still confused. He seemed too literate and civil to be Hausa, her preconception of them did not tally with his disposition to her, and he had even carried her load to his cab. He told her he was Hausa and was delighted about it, peering through the front mirror probably wondering why she was asking.

She then asked for his name to see if he was lying. He told her his name was Shekinah Melchizedek. *Are you a Christian?* Onwubiko asked surprised."

"Onachi. Onachi!" Chinelu said correcting her.

"Can't you see it on the programme? Onachi weds Shekinah," Kate said showing her the programme that was on the round table.

"I know but I'm used to Onwubiko because that's what her sister used to call her, that's the name she used while telling me the story."

"You people should leave her," Cyril said, delighted by the twist in the story.

"Please continue, don't mind these girls," John said.

"What is there to continue? You people can already see the outcome," Funke said.

"Kate and Chinelu, see what you people have caused, can't you guys keep quiet?" Chigozie voiced.

"Of course, what kind of question is that?" Kate asked.

"It was a rhetorical question, if you must know. No offence please. Funke just continue from the car side where you stopped, or I should say where you were interrupted," Chibuzor said trying to persuade her to continue.

EIGHTEEN

Funke said jokingly; "I will continue before some people start crying." Delighted that they all wanted to know how it went. "Where did I stop again?"

"You stopped where Onachi was asking the driver if he was a Christian," Cyril replied.

"Yeah, the presumed driver affirmed that he was a Christian; he told her that he was named Shekinah because he was born in the church,"

His mother had adamantly gone for vigil though she had been notified by the doctor that she would soon give birth and she was persuaded by her husband not to follow him to Church.

During prayer in the vigil contraction started.

His father was busy cabashing, praying and sweating, when she told him about it. He started panicking and freaking out, luckily for them they were at the edge of the last row and it was close to an exit downstairs.

He carried her downstairs; being twice her weight during their wedding. On reaching the door to go outside, rain started falling. It was so heavy that he did not dare take another step. His father was bewildered on seeing the rain, wondering what would happen next.

"His mother who was feeling the pain started tapping him rapidly, as though she was saying "why did you allow me to come?" He became confused and perplexed. He could not start arguing with his labouring wife, he turned around and noticed a bed at the end of the passage, and on reaching there he saw a pile of them. They were beds used for the Church's yearly conventions.

He gently dropped Shekinah's mother there and rushed upstairs to call for help. As Shekinah was narrating his birth story, he reached her house; she had been directing him as he was talking. He packed but she waited in the car to hear the end of the story.

He said that his father met one of the pastors who was still sweating as he was praying and explained everything to him, the pastor called the health workers he knew that were present at the vigil and they all rushed downstairs. His mother was boisterously shouting his father's name while he dashed upstairs for help.

The doctor did the needful with the help of a nurse who was also on hand. So she gave birth to him there and she named him Shekinah because he was born in God's presence.

"Well it was later on when he was bigger that his mother told him she actually wanted to give birth to him in the house of prayer like Leonard Ravenhill the author of *"Why Revival Tarries"* who was born in a prayer *meeting.* Her intention was that he becomes a preacher and writer like him.

Okay now that's the end of the story.

But wait, there is more to it, she became infatuated with him, she fantasized meeting him again, she was glad she collected his number, he had promised to take her anywhere she wanted for the next one week as a way of paying for the eggs. Therefore, she called him to drive her to places she didn't need to go to, she still acted impudent towards him, but she kept asking him questions about himself.

He was carefree, holding no grudge and answering almost all her questions. He told her the reason why his surname was Melchizedek; his grandfather was a humble noble Muslim; a religious and peace loving man, but his son, Shekinah's father, was recalcitrant and rebellious, he did anything to spite his father that's how he became a Christian – a very zealous one at that.

As soon as he became a Christian he changed his name to Melchizedek, knowing that Melchizedek in the Bible was a priest who had no record of a father or mother or tribe, as such, he practically and literally disowned his father.

His father condoned his conversion because he loved his son dearly but he abdicated him when he changed his name and cut all ties with him. In response, my grandfather vowed never to be a Christian, and so he died a Muslim.

Shekinah told Onachi that he didn't like the way his father behaved; he had zeal without knowledge. He said had it been his father preached to his own father, or at least try to still maintain a relationship with him, the story might have been different. He said his father married his mother; a person as stubborn as him. Although, he loved his parents so much, he could not hide the fact that they could be too extreme in their views.

"His parents had worried about his joblessness after his NYSC, thinking he was lazing about with his laptop all day long, unknown to them that he was making graphic designs and selling. It was their constant disturbance that made him get the taxi he was driving, even though he wasn't good at the job.

He said the day before he ran into her, he had not gotten any passenger because he could not hustle them, and so was determined to get his first customer that morning. It was in the process to call a passenger; he accidentally hit her.

After hearing this Onachi apologized with tears in her eyes. And that's how she fell in love with him and she was too beautiful for him to resist, though she was rash at times.

That's how their love journey started. But it met a brick wall because both parents despised the tribe of the other. Shekinah's parents gave him several reasons why he couldn't marry the love of his life so did Onachi's parents.

"Hmmm, and they are Christians, why should they be behaving like that? The story is long oh, Funke, please wait for me let me go and get something, I'll be back soon," Chigozie said as he stood up. But he was actually pressed and wanted to use the restroom, so he scurried out of the reception, meandering through some ushers who were already carrying food and drinks to the high table for dignitaries.

At this point the bride and the groom were dancing with their mothers, the two who were vehemently behind their husband's decision to oppose their children's choice of marriage. Now they were happily dancing together to the renowned *Sweet Mother* song by Prince Nico Mbarga.

Many sprayed tons of one hundred naira, some two hundred naira, few five hundred naira, while a handful sprayed one thousand naira as the two mothers danced with the couple.

Funke's mother, Mrs Bolanle was not left out; she sprayed one thousand naira prodigiously on them. Two women by the side whispered to each other. "See how this woman sprays money, she just wants to show off." The other one said. "True, she's seriously showing-off as far as I am concerned."

"Mrs Bolanle has started, she will use any opportunity to show people that she's rich, I know she must have cajoled her poor husband to give her tons of money, just to show-off, I pity the man," another woman said.

"Funke please continue the story, I'll give my brother the upshot later," Chibuzor said.

"Yes continue the story; it's getting more and more intense," Chinelu said.

"How is it intense when you already know the end?" Funke said sardonically.

"But wait, how come you remember everything her sister told you?" Kate asked.

"Well... I actually wrote it down, I like stories like it, and it's not everything she told me I'm saying. You know I wanted to study mass communication but my mother said that I'm too intelligent for that, I told her that's where people like Oprah Winfrey started from but she wouldn't take it."

"I hope you guys did not continue without me?" Chigozie said as he sat down with sparse drops of some liquid on his shoes.

"Obviously, we have not, some people have been using style to wait for you," Chinelu said looking away from Funke.

"Let me just round up the story, they would soon close," Funke said.

"They cannot close just yet, the main reason some people came here has not taken place yet," Chigozie said jokingly directing his joke at John. He had seen how John squirmed when Funke said the reception would soon be over; he knew it was because of food which had not gotten to them yet. Chigozie was also expecting food but it was not as lucid as it was on John's face.

"It's only you that know what you're saying," John said and shrugged. Which made them burst into laughter, they all knew that food was the main objective that brought so many people for wedding receptions, and it would be painful to come all the way and not eat, no matter how small it was. A few of course came just to celebrate with the couple but even that celebration seemed empty without food.

"Somebody told me a story of a man who went for a wedding reception, and when it was time, they all lined up to get food. The man was at the back of the line so before the food reached him, it finished. He was so distraught because he didn't get food so when it was time to share drinks he was the first on the line. But the people sharing said that those at the back did not get food so they decided to share from the back to the front. On reaching him the drinks finished, but when they shared toothpicks the unfortunate man got one," Cyril said laughing and the rest of them laughed except Kate.

"Wait first, why will the man line up to get toothpicks, when he did not get food?" She asked.

"I don't know, it's someone that told me the story, and when some jokes are repeated more than once they lose credibility – they're no longer funny again," Cyril said and the rest concurred.

"True talk, if it's explained it's no longer funny like this one I heard; a father was teaching his son table manners, he told him not to talk while eating, so when they were eating the boy saw a fly on his father's plate of food, he was about to talk but he didn't, abiding by his father's table manners of not talking while eating. So, the father not seeing it mixed the fly with his food and ate it. So if you start asking me whether the boy later told his father or not, the joke will no longer make sense," Chigozie said.

"Why did you have to say something like that about food? Now I feel like vomiting," Kate said wrinkling her face.

"Another table manner is; don't say anything disgusting about food before eating or while eating," Chinelu said.

"Before we start learning table manners now, can we please allow Opera Winfrey finish her story," Chibuzor said referring to Funke.

"It's Oprah not Opera, she used to be Orpah though, but because people could not pronounce it, they pronounced it as Oprah," Funke said smiling as if she had just learnt about it recently.

"Very well then," Chibuzor said.

"Please continue," Cyril said impatiently.

"I will but I'm trying to remember where I stopped."

"Shekinah kept on carrying Onachi in his car to wherever she wanted, collecting no money, and Onachi kept calling him. Her sister told me that sometimes Onachi would be having reveries while she ate, she would be smiling eating one spoon of food for more than five minutes, and other times Onachi would laugh when her sister was talking to her about something that was not even funny. It was obvious she was laughing at something that Shekinah must have said because she had a look in her eyes anytime she was thinking of him. She seemed to always daydream, even at night.

Nobody knows exactly how Shekinah was behaving in his house, but it was lucidly obvious how he was behaving from the speech he gave her parents when he came to her house. I wrote it down for future use in case my parents have an issue with the person I want to marry," Funke said as she searched for the page in her pretty and stylish jotter.

The rest of them looked at her intently wondering why she had written it down.

"It's not exactly how she told me but she was there when he came in to talk to her parents and she recorded part of it, she said he said: "Sir, Ma, thank you for letting me into your house and for giving me your audience. I believe you are Christians, I am also a Christian and the Bible says in Galatians 3:27-28; *"For as many of you as were baptized into Christ have put on Christ. There is neither Jew nor Greek, there is neither slave nor free, there is neither male nor female; for you are all one in Christ Jesus.*

Sir there is no rich or poor, no king or subject, no black or white, no Nigerian or American, no Tiv or Hausa or Fulani, for all are one in Christ; we are all one in Christ Jesus. As Christians I don't see why we should engage in tribalism, ethnicity or nepotism. It makes us no different from the unbelievers, how can we say that we are Christians then we have the same values like the world. Of course I know we are in the world but definitely not of the world.

Sir and Ma, I also know the contrast and differences in culture and values and even religion of the Hausas and Igbos is much, it was great before the civil war and still poignant even presently. However, it is not just the Igbos and Hausas, other tribes too have sharp differences in their way of life.

But being Christians we are now one in Christ, as such we should not allow tribalism to tamper with our faith. Sir, I really love your daughter, Ma I'm in love with her, I rarely breathe well when I'm not with her. If I don't marry her, I'll be dysfunctional, and I don't know if I'll be able to bear it.

Sir I know your daughter loves me too, I don't know whether it's destiny or fate that brought us together but I know God is aware and I perceive it is part of his plan and the devil can't do anything about it, stopping us is stopping God and as we all know that's impossible"

Onachi's parents said nothing but dismissed him.

"They didn't want to let go of their first daughter that took them years and painful death's to have to a person of a totally different background, they had heard stories of how Muslim men in Pakistan or some of the Asian countries would kidnap girls of other religions at a young age and force them to get married to Muslim men and convert them to Islam.

They dreaded that such a thing should happen to their pretty daughter. Shekinah later on took Onachi to his parents and told them something similar to what he told her parents, they were moved but they stood their ground. They told him there were other beautiful Christian girls from their people or other tribes. They feared of what would happen if war was to break out, they had heard of the genocide in Rwanda where the Hutus killed the Tutsis even those that inter-married.

The beautiful couple you see over there turned to God," Funke said gesturing towards Shekinah and Onachi who were now dancing a slow dance like a waltz, her head was on his chest, one of his hands was wrapped round her waist and one of her hands was wrapped round his, whilst holding their other hands together. They danced slowly to *Victory Belongs to Jesus* by Todd Dulaney which was playing in the background.

"They started praying to God and preaching to their Christian parents.

Their persistent prayer was like water that gradually erodes the ground upon consistent running over; God did His thing, their parents eventually melted down like butter in a hot frying pan. Their consistent prayer paid off, their unwavering love brought the two families together. End of story now I can rest," Funke said as she sighed out of relief.

"Wow, see how their parents are dancing like they have been friends for ages," Kate said.

"Such is life," John said as he saw an usher pass with food to a table close to the high table.

"But I wonder why there's so much enmity and animosity between the Igbos and other tribes?" Chigozie asked inquisitively.

"My grandfather's beloved twin brother was a soldier and he died in the war," Chinelu said mildly.

"My mother's uncle, who advocated for peace was shot in crossfire and was left paralyzed and he suffered from excruciating pain till the day he kicked the bucket few weeks later," Kate said palpably.

"Which tribe are you?" John asked.

"My father is Tiv but my mother is Yoruba from Edo," Kate replied.

"I Hope you don't fly at night?" John asked jokingly and the rest of them laughed grabbing the meaning. Even Kate laughed; a suppressed one.

"My father said his people told him that he had been bewitched when he told them he wanted to marry her," Kate said.

"It's okay! Let's stop talking about tribes, I know the war left wounds and scars but we can forget about it and move on, we should forget the past and look to the future with hope," Cyril said.

"Yeah, but we can move forward only if some people stop reopening the wounds by trying to monopolize what is for everyone and treating the original owners like second class," Chinelu said wittingly.

"They say a hungry man is an angry man, thank God food has come, you guys should please calm down," Chigozie said gaily.

"Yes oo." John concurred as the ushers shared the plates of food on their table. It was the usual, Jollof rice and fried rice, some had Fish while others had Chicken, and some had salad and others had Moi-moi with egg in it.

But some few people, who requested, were given pounded yam meal.

"In some weddings I have attended, people are told to queue up to get their food and are given the chance to pick what they want, some people even selected from pounded yam, Amala, Eba, Semo, then take soup like Egusi, vegetable, Afang, Ofe Nsala, Oha, Okra, Ogbono, but me I can't eat swallow in public," Kate was saying as Chinelu cut in.

"I know it will be Yoruba people's wedding, they too like party, *Owambe is in* their blood."

"That's true; I won't deny it. I know you people were waiting to hear what I will say," Funke said.

"Seriously, this food is very sweet like they used sugar in preparing it," John said as he gulped down heavy spoons of rice.

"Guy, every food is sweet for you. Funke are you not eating?" Chigozie asked.

"I don't feel like eating much, I'm full," she replied. She had only eaten the salad and half of the fish on her plate.

"Ah, John you have almost finished your food," Cyril said in surprise and they all laughed.

"Just like my sister use to say, it's not the person with the biggest mouth that finishes his food first, but the person that is the most famished," Chibuzor said and chuckled.

"Hmmm, some of you are pretending, even you Chigozie. I know that if you were in your houses now, the way you people will consume this food, it would take only a matter of seconds to finish it. Me I don't like to pretend, the way you see me now, is the way you will see me tomorrow. Some people in this wedding now will be acting like they have money but if you follow them to their houses, story will change," John said as he drank water after finishing his food.

"You are right John. However, calm down, nobody is accusing you of anything. By the way what you said is correct, we Africans know how to fake status. However, there's a difference between faking and composure or your carriage. The way you carry yourself will determine how people will address you. It is important we realise people will treat you the way you treat yourself," Chigozie said.

"Chigozie and Chibuzor you guys should please come early to church tomorrow, you know we have to rehearse before service starts, Kate and Chinelu you guys have to come early too. Goodbye I'm leaving; my parents are leaving," Funke said as she stood up to leave.

"Funke, so you did not see me, no problem bye-bye," John said wryly.

"Sorry, bye," Funke said and dashed away.

"John! John! Must you be noticed? If I'm Funke, I won't even answer you. You're just full of yourself; did she call Cyril as she was going?" Chigozie asked.

"It's okay you guys used me to catch fun today, next time I'll not follow you attend this kind of wedding. Please let's start going home, people are leaving, the wedding is over," John said.

NINETEEN

"DADDY YOU'VE not yet told us the story of Biafra or as some call it, the Nigerian civil war. We're tired of hearing incomplete stories especially now that the election is coming up. There's tension everywhere, I've even heard that some people are traveling back home to their villages for fear of the unknown," Chigozie said trying to persuade his father while sitting on their couch beside him.

The twins had been talking about it since they left the wedding reception. It was night now; their charged rechargeable lamp illuminated the parlour. Their mother had told them that the food they ate at the wedding was their lunch, and their next meal would be dinner.

They had just taken their dinner made up of Eba and Okra soup which Chigozie loathed while his brother ate. He could eat any food without discriminating; as such he had more flesh than his brother. Lights went out immediately they finished eating.

Mr Okafor unaware that the twins pretended to sleep the last time when he tried to explain what happened was compelled to tell them the story all over again. He dreaded to use another analogy so he wouldn't hurt his wife because her sadness was misery to him. He would do anything to avoid hurting her.

But things were getting hard for him and his family. He had come to Abuja expecting the worst so he would not be disappointed, but what he got was worse than the worst he expected. His salary was not able to feed him and his family as such things were indeed hard.

He had been transferred to Abuja because he was too righteous to be the accountant. He kept no secrets of sharp practices in a corrupt system like the one he was working for. So the transfer was their way of punishing him since they had no powers or grounds to sack him.

Now in Abuja, he was shackles to the freedom of his colleagues who seemed to be above the law. He was supposed to be promoted before he was transferred, but he was told he would be promoted when he got to the Abuja office. But the people in charge in Abuja refused to promote him;

they also refused to send him on any field work, so he would not get any allowances since he was unwilling to change figures by adding zeros.

He was practically stranded, depending solely on his salary which was hardly enough because Abuja was more expensive and he had rising needs, his two sons had gotten admissions; he couldn't leave one and train the other since they were twins.

There was even a time he was tempted to succumb to the pressure but he resisted the idea knowing that God would not be happy with him. He remembered a passage in the Bible that says if you faint in the day of adversity your strength is small. God had been so good to him and his blessings outweighed his present predicaments.

"I hope you two would not sleep off like last time?" Mr Okafor asked. The twins looked at themselves and turned and looked at their father.

"No we won't," they replied.

"The reason I'm telling you the story is for knowledge sake, and so you two will stop disturbing me. I don't know why they stopped teaching history in schools, and I wonder why you guys did not go and read about it. During our time we searched for answers, our parents hardly had time because they spent their time working to send us to school.

We had no one to help us with assignments; because our parents didn't go to school, so they couldn't answer the questions that were school related. But things have changed now, if you are not watching TV you'll be playing game or chatting on your phone. If you are not using your phone, you'd be outside playing ball or playing card, no time for your books except during exams, and you read to pass exams not to know. Nigeria's school system has been besmirched, they don't teach for you to know but just to pass exams.

Most of the things you learn in secondary school, we were taught in elementary school which is what you people call primary school nowadays. I hope you two are listening?"

"Yes sir," they replied.

"Okay, go and check if your mother is still awake, ask her when the first putsch took place," their father said.

"Daddy what is porch?" Chigozie asked.

"Putsch not porch, I mean the first coup d'état in Nigeria," Mr Okafor replied.

"Oh Okay," the twins said on realizing what it meant. They scurried to their mother to ask her. They met her reading her Bible with her phone torchlight; she had finished praying at the time.

"Mummy, daddy said we should ask you when the first coup d'état in Nigeria happened," Chibuzor asked on reaching the room first.

"Can't you see I'm reading my Bible? Besides why does he want to ask me?" she asked them.

"Hmmm, Mummy, I think he wants to see if you know, to prove something to us," Chigozie said.

"Your father wants to test my memory this night, tell him; I think it was towards the second week around 14th or 15th January, 1966. The putsch was led by Chukwuma Nzeogwu.

See, you people should not come here to ask me any question again. Tell your father that tomorrow is Sunday and he has Sunday school class to take, he should narrate what he wants to narrate fast and allow you two to go to bed," their mother said.

The two of them were still surprised that their mother could still pinpoint the date, and leader of the coup d'état so they excitedly replied "okay" and walked back to the living room and sat down. They wanted to tell their father what their mother said but he told them he heard everything.

"Well, your mother was correct, the first coup happened early January after people had just finished celebrating New Year and getting ready to resume activities for the year. It was just then that the coup happened and sent the country in disarray.

However, the coup was not a complete success because all the leaders were eliminated. Let me start from where I think was the beginning of the whole conflict so you can understand the story better.

I'm not telling you this story to infuse hate in you; I don't want to hear that you engage in any tribal movement, are you hearing me?"

"Yes sir," they replied.

"Don't be partial, don't treat people based on their ethnicity, treat everyone equally. Again, I'm telling you the story for knowledge sake, and so that you people will stop disturbing me, and also that no one will poison your mind."

Chibuzor and Chigozie sat upright and leaned forward listening intently to what their father was saying. Mr Okafor sank into his chair crossed his legs on the small wooden stool in front of him and looked up and sighed as if he was watching something in the ceiling. The once bright rechargeable light started dwindling in intensity.

"Lord Lugard, a British man in the year 1914 annexed the northern part and southern part of Nigeria; he merged two very different people to live together as one. That was the genesis of the violent conflict that ensued.

In 1960, Nigeria got her independence on a platter of gold; however, the British were still interested in the enormous resources embedded in Nigeria. Being independent, Nigeria was free to rule herself. But perhaps the people were too free, political leaders began to abuse power.

The Northerners and Easterners deferred in so many things like religion, system of government, culture and values. The British from the onset didn't like the Igbos because they were not easy to manipulate. The Igbos did not have a unified system of government like the northerners, they were diversified, though there may be kings or Chiefs but every man regarded as the king of his own home.

The British found the Hausas easier to control. The Hausas and Fulanis had a system like that of an empire in which there were Emirs who served as their political and religious leaders.

Let me illustrate a simple distinction in the attitude or mind-set of the two. If a leader in the north told one of his subjects to walk from here to there, the subject will obediently do it with no objection, but if a leader from the east tells his subject to walk from here to there, that subject is likely to question why he should walk from here to there.

So the British left the northerners in charge so they could easily have their way in the so-called independent country.

Rigging in election did not start today; elections brought conflict between the two groups including the west which was the other part of the south. There was corruption in the government among the leaders, people complained and protested, overall, there was unrest throughout the whole nation.

The situation of Nigeria then and even now is just like when a well that was dug for three people to use but one being bigger than the other two, monopolized it, allowing the other two to use it only when he pleases – almost like he was doing them a favour.

The Northerners rarely gave any strategic position to the Igbos though they proved most competent. The army was filled with northerners because the British made more available slots for them like a quota system tilted in favour of one.

Most of the money gotten from the resources in the south was used to build the north leaving the real owners deprived. The northerners were good farmers, they had the groundnut pyramids, the cattle and so on, but from the time crude oil – the black gold – the cursed blessing was discovered, farming was abandoned. Everyone wanted to enjoy the money coming from crude oil.

Sorry, the story is not going sequentially, I'm just telling you as I remember," Mr Okafor said as he stretched and yawned.

"Ahmadu Bello one of the most influential northern leaders was asked why the Northerners seemed to be so much against the Igbos, and he said the Igbos always wanted to dominate, that any place they entered, they always wanted to be on top.

According to him, if you put him in a labour camp within a year, he'll try to emerge as head of that camp. He also said he wouldn't allow an Igbo person to be put in an important position. He would rather put a foreigner on contract if there was no northerner, or any other Nigerian.

His argument was that no northerner was employed in the south, but it was not possible to employ someone that was not competent when they were more competent people.

The strife grew worse, the discord grew wider, and the contrast between them was more lucid and vivid like the difference between black and white placed side by side.

The coup led by Nzeogwu which was meant to eliminate all the leaders including Igbo leaders that were assumed to be corrupt was not successful. They ended up killing only the Northern leaders like Tafawa Balewa – the Prime Minister, Ahmadu Bello – the most prominent Emir in the North and other people. They didn't kill Nnamdi Azikiwe who was the president majorly because he was on vacation outside the country and it seemed like he knew about it.

Also, they didn't get to kill Aguiyi Ironsi the head of the army at that time, though it was said that he didn't go home after he had finished drinking at a bar with other army officers. Instead, he went to another bar to drink because he was not satisfied yet. The mutiny soldiers went to his house to kill him but they didn't see him there. Okpara who was the head of the Eastern part of Nigeria wasn't killed either.

Nzeogwu and his gang were later captured when Aguiyi Ironsi took over but they were not executed as expected. Northerners saw this as a plan to install Aguiyi Ironsi – an Igbo man, as head of the new junta. Murders, massacre and mass killing of Igbos erupted in the North spontaneously as a result.

Igbos were ebullient and enthusiastic, most of them like water had moved to the length and breadth of the nation to make money anywhere they could see it like somebody had said; "If there is money on Mars the Igbos would be there."

"Like one of my friends said, when Igbo boys look at Iron Man's suit, all they see is spare parts," Chigozie said and laughed.

"Shut up let daddy finish first," Chibuzor said to his brother.

"Resultantly, crisis broke out in the northern part of the country; Igbos started running helter-skelter back to their homeland to escape death. Around the 29th of July that same year the northerners retaliated with a successful coup.

I don't know exactly how Aguiyi Ironsi was killed, some people say he couldn't be killed with a gun so they had to tie him to the back of a vehicle and drag him, driving him to his death. I can't tell how true that is, it's probably fabricated.

When the Northerners took power, the northern citizens probably got more violent, killing the Igbos, robbing them, assaulting and assailing them and so on. My Father was in the North hustling to get money, my mother was back in the village with my two elder sisters suffering, they stayed in the house of my grandparents.

My mother was maltreated by my grandmother and my father's sisters majorly because she had no son. Unknown to them she was pregnant of me," Mr Nnamdi Okafor sighed and squirmed in his chair as if disturbed by something.

"Daddy what happened?" Chigozie asked inquisitively, Chibuzor slapped the back of his head lightly.

"Can't you see daddy is trying to remember something or has remembered something painful?" Chibuzor whispered to his brother loud enough for their father to hear. The night was silent, so silent that the silence seemed noisy.

In the apparent loud silence, someone jerked up from the bed in their room and rushed to the restroom. It must have been Osinachi who usually rush to the restroom from sleep like someone was pursuing her.

"So the next year Odumegwu Chukwuemeka Ojukwu, who was now heading the Eastern part of Nigeria, had a meeting with Yakubu Gowon who was now Head of state after the last putsch. Ojukwu was supposed to be head of state because he was senior to Yakubu Gowon in rank but Gowon was made head of state in his place.

They had a meeting in Aburi, Ghana to discuss the fate of Nigeria. Ojukwu complained that Gowon did nothing to stop the onslaught and assault of Igbos in the North.

I don't know fully what happened in the meeting but from what I heard, Ojukwu asked for restructuring and placed other demands of which Gowon accepted. But on coming back to Nigeria, Gowon and his people breached the contract.

My father's shop was robbed and destroyed. Seeing that, my father fled the north very early in the morning when it was still dark with his Peugeot car he used as taxi. He escaped the North with his life in his hands and heart in his mouth together with other Igbos in his car.

My grandmother would send my mother to trek miles to fetch water to cook food. When she had finished cooking my grandmother would put a small amount of the food in a plate for my mother and my sisters to share. Sometimes she would be asked to pound yam, and she would not taste of it.

She washed all the clothes in the house including that of my father's sisters. My grandfather did not approve of the maltreatment but he did not really do anything about it. My mother had to send my sisters to hawk to survive while my mother sold things in the market just to have sufficient food for her and my sisters.

My grandmother did not approve of the marriage of my father and mother, and her dislike increased when my mother had no sons and when she discovered that she was pregnant she assumed it was going to be a girl again.

So my mother's work load doubled, even going to farm with her pregnancy. My aunties treated her like house servant, one of them was way older than her but she had not gotten married probably because she wasn't too good-looking coupled with her poor manners.

The other one was younger than my mother; she was beautiful but haughty, with no regard for my mother whatsoever.

My sisters became errand girls for her. They blamed my mother for making my father leave to the North again to keep working in search of greener pastures because my father came back home after the first coup but he returned to the North just before the second one.

They thought my father had already been killed by the brute and violent Hausa mob that had great animosity for the Igbos even though there was no way to ascertain this. Only rumours of what was going on and of war were widely heard around the country.

"My father was my grandparent's only son and they loved him, his sisters loved him too, not only that he was the only son but he made them proud, he was a good son, obsequious to his parents until he met my mother, and was determined to marry her. Now, they assumed, she has sent him to his early grave leaving them with no posterity to carry the family name.

TWENTY

THE BOOK written by Chinua Achebe entitled; *Man of The People* seemed to have foretold the coup, so he became a target of the Nigerian army but he was able to escape by fleeing Nigeria.

For a reason unknown to me, Wole Soyinka was arrested and incarcerated. Perhaps, he was linked to the ownership of a private radio station broadcasting against the military as an advocate of democracy and the Biafrans being autonomous.

On 13th May, 1967, Biafra officially seceded from Nigeria. General Ojukwu declared Biafra a republic – an independent country, telling Igbos all over the country to return to their homeland since the federal government did nothing to stop the onslaught against them.

Ojukwu was a full blooded Igbo man, very optimistic and enthusiastic, a confident and audacious person. He was unwavering like an iron peg drilled into a frozen ground, immovable.

Perhaps he was too confident and obstinate as many thought of him having come from a background of affluence. His father was a very rich man who started out with one vehicle he used for transportation and grew it into a very reputable transport company.

Ojukwu's father sent him abroad to have his tertiary education. When he returned, he decided to join the army. His father did not like the idea, so he used his influence to prevent him from easily joining the army. But Ojukwu determined, started from scratch as a recruit and rose gradually in rank and became Ojukwu "The War Lord".

"My father, your grandfather ran out of fuel when he was about to leave Kogi on his way back from the North to Ebonyi, with no other option, he and those with him abandoned the car and started running.

It was already getting dark when they left the car to run down the East; this was the same day Ojukwu declared secession of Biafra from Nigeria and encouraged every Biafran to come back home.

By this time, I was about one to two months old, the maltreatment of my mother had come to an abrupt stop because my grandmother was exhilarated that her grandchild was a boy, and so was my grandfather.

My mother told me I was her saviour because she could have died before my father arrived. My father arrived the next day; he had been running all through the night. When he saw my mother he fainted, my mother had no idea what caused him to faint.

After taking his bath and having a meal, he slept until my cry woke him up the next day; he woke my mother who was by his side asking her whose child I was. When she told him I was his son he nearly fainted again being overwhelmed with joy.

I can't remember anything but my mother told me the story over and over again that it seems like I was there when it all happened."

"But daddy, you were there," Chigozie said and sniggered.

"Oh my God, why can't you keep quiet like your brother, you know what I mean but you just want to talk, let me explain so your teenage brain can comprehend." Their father said which made Chibuzor laugh, laughing at his brother.

"I was a baby then, I didn't understand what was going on. Understood?" Mr Okafor vociferated, and his wife woke up and staggered to the living room, drunk with asleep. She balanced herself by placing her hand on the wall, and then she rubbed her eyes.

"Are you three still awake? Don't you know tomorrow is Sunday? Sugarcane, allow them to go to bed please," Mrs Okafor mumbled.

"Itetewo?" Mr Okafor asked his wife, meaning *have you woken up?*

"Mbanu, I'm still sleeping," His wife replied sarcastically. Mr Okafor and his sons laughed.

"Ice-cream, it's your sons you should tell to allow me to go to bed, besides I would soon finish the story," Mr Okafor replied.

Chibuzor and Chigozie watched their parents, they knew they call themselves those names mostly when one wanted to persuade the other, which was happening regularly these days.

"Has your father reached when his mother gave birth to him?" Mrs Okafor asked her twin boys. Their Father had skipped that part of the story, because he wanted to finish up quick and he didn't want to talk about it.

His grandmother had sent his mother to the stream which was far away, to fetch water; she was accompanied by his sisters. She was in labour by the time they reached the stream and gave birth to him by the stream with the help of an elderly woman who also came to fetch water.

They stayed in the woman's house that night before returning home because the house was not as far as hers.

"Daddy has passed that side; he is in the place where his father found out that he had a son," Chibuzor said.

"He did not tell you how he was born, right?" She asked and they nodded.

"So Mummy, you have heard the story before? Which time did daddy tell you?" Chigozie asked. Mr Okafor was just looking, waiting for the answer his wife would give him.

"Do you think your father and I started talking to each other when we gave birth to you? What do you think we have been doing to pass time even before your sister was born? I don't think there's any story about your father that he has not told me and me him.

Sugarcane better tell them the story of your birth, so they will know why your father did what he did and quickly, it's getting very late, it would soon be early morning," She said and chuckled to herself as she found her way back to the room to their bed with no light.

Mr Okafor narrated his birth story to his sons, because they were now curious and he saw reason in what his wife said.

"About a month's time from my father's arrival, my father opted to join the army though his parents, his sisters, my sisters and mother begged him not to. The Biafran army was already recruiting young men as soldiers to join the army.

My mother did not tell my father how she was maltreated and how and where she gave birth to me. She had forgiven my grandparents and aunties' shortcomings that were no longer forthcoming because she gave birth to me. Though he tried to inquire, wondering why his wife and children had emaciated so much.

He asked his mother, she was dumbfounded out of guilt, and he asked his father and sisters; none of them gave any tangible answer or reason until my sisters let the cat out of the bag. They narrated all they knew vividly to my father without the knowledge of my mother.

My father exploded with rage against his parents. My mother begged him to forgive them even as my grandmother begged him for mercy. My grandfather felt guilty but he was indifferent. He told my father that he did not do anything against my mother. But my father made him know that doing nothing to stop someone from doing wrong and covering it up is the same thing as committing the act, that's why accomplices are arrested.

"My father did nothing tortious to his parents but the mere fact that he was unhappy and disappointed with them made them shiver with guilt especially my grandmother.

My grandparents had begged him to hide so he wouldn't be recruited; my grandmother threatened to kill herself if he joined the army but he was adamant and told her to take care of her grandson if he dies in the war. On hearing that, she burst into tears.

They began to pamper my mother but that did not placate his anger against them. Additionally, he was also angered by what he suffered in the north as a result of the animosity of an averaged Hausa person against the Igbos by robing and burning down his shop like they gave him even a Kobo to build it up. He also remembered how the Hausas slaughtered his friends like ram they would use for Salah.

He got ready to leave like Odysseus left his family for war when his child was born. My mother came to him carrying me with tears rolling down her pale red cheeks begging him not to leave her again. He took me from my mother's arms and turned his back on her because he couldn't stand her tears.

My mother said that he said to me; "I am going to fight this war so that you my son would not be treated as a servant or a second class citizen in your own land by people who you are better than. And so, your mother would enjoy and not be exploited of what is rightfully hers."

He turned with tears cupped in his eyes, returned me to my mother, he cleaned the tears still rolling down from my mother's sorrowful eyes down her cheeks with his big fingers and kissed her for the last time and touched the tip of my nose. When he did, my mother said I started laughing but suddenly started crying when my father walked away.

My touching childish cry made my mother lie she was pregnant, not knowing she was actually pregnant then. My father stopped walking, it seemed like what my mother said was too much weight for him, which made him to sit down on the floor. She thought that would deter him from going but she later on realized that she gave him more reasons to fight.

I delivered my mother from oppression but I couldn't save my father from death," Mr Okafor said sadly. He took a deep breath and sighed, and then he told Chigozie to bring water for him to drink. Chigozie who was almost in tears, rushed to the kitchen cleaned his eyes and started gawking.

He searched for cup in the dark kitchen which had a little ray of moonlight through the curtain-less window. He found the cup and also found out that the bucket storing their table water was having little water mixed with dreg. He came back and told his father there was no drinking water left.

Their father complained, asking them why they did not buy water from local water vendors. They told him the price was jacked up because the borehole owner used generator to pump the water because of blackout, so they decided to manage the one in the house till the next day.

"More than fifty years since independence and almost fifty years from the war which aim was to keep Nigeria in unity because we would be better off together and an average citizen can't have running water in his house while our politicians can have milk running from the tap in their houses.

You people should better find water for me to drink if not just forget about the story and go and sleep, after all we would be going to church tomorrow."

The two of them started hustling for water, just then light was restored.

This happened around one o'clock in the morning when people would be asleep and rarely use it.

Chigozie noticed Osinachi's schoolbag lying on the floor by the side of their dining table. Osinachi had left it there after doing her school assignment earlier that day. Chibuzor had told her countless times to find somewhere to hang it, since she came back from school the previous day.

By the side of the bag was her Eva water bottle which was fortunately almost filled up. He stealthily carried it to the kitchen so his father will not know, and poured it in his father's cup and brought it for him to drink. Mr Okafor drank it and told him to switch off the kitchen and dining lights as he returned from keeping the cup in the kitchen.

"That water tastes like it has seen life, where did you get it from? Don't bother telling me where," Mr Okafor said thinking of the worst. He decided not to know where it came from because he had already drank the water.

"Let me tell you this, boys, we can't change the past; we can only change the future. Don't dwell on your past mistakes when you can only control your present. Don't cry over spilled milk but start thinking of how to get a cow because there's no medicine after death, except that medicine is made by God.

"My father stood up from the ground and walked away; my aunties finding out he was leaving, hurried to stop him but to no avail. My grandmother locked herself in her room crying and blaming herself for my father's decision. My grandfather tried to console her but to no avail.

Not long from my father's departure to join the army, my mother woke up one early morning from gunshots and bombs. Fortunately my grandparents had gone to stay with my grandfather's brother who resided in Enugu.

This was the beginning of the man hunt for the Biafran dissidents; my mother, my sisters and aunties, everyone ran for their dear lives.

Those who had cars, very few of them, could not use them because of strafing. Instead, everyone was in the bush running and hiding. People died on the way mostly old people, some out of hunger, exhaustion, fear or panic.

My mother said that in the night you could see bullets flying like tiny rockets in a projectile motion. She said someone could dodge the bullet if the person saw it and was fast enough.

Times came when my mother was persuaded to throw me away, because I used to cry so loud which could bring attention to where my mother and others were hiding. She admitted that the thought of throwing me away had crossed her mind, however, for the love of my father, the thought vanished.

She said her and my aunties became closer than sisters, they were looking out for each other, and they started taking care of my mother when they discovered she was pregnant. They slept in the bush for weeks, ate in the forest, ran and hid in the jungle.

Everyone became as still as logs of wood anytime a Nigerian plane flew over them, if not bombs would be sent from the air to the earth by the heartless Nigerian army, killing civilians, destroying lives and property.

They bombed hospitals, destroyed schools and market places. My mother said she jumped over carcasses, with my horrified sisters. The ground was littered with corpses, cadavers of someone's son, daughter, father."

Mr Okafor swallowed his saliva that seemed as viscous as phlegm, his expression was like someone that swallowed a bitter medicine without water. "Mother, sister, brother, grandfather, grandmother, uncle, aunty, cousin, friend, wife, husband, son-in-law and daughter-in-law, infants, little children, babies, people abandoned their babies for fear of their own lives.

"Refugee camps were full. Afikpo had fallen; because the Nigerian army passed through Ndibe beach from Cross River, completely surrounding the Biafrans.

I don't know if Calabar people betrayed us because they let the Nigerian army pass through their land and they had easy access from the beach to invade and pervade Afikpo. My mother and aunties searched for shelter, but before they found a house to shelter them, my auntie – the younger and beautiful one went to fetch water by the stream, and she was apprehended by two soldiers.

One of them went to ease himself, according to the witness that told my mother and aunty, he said the other soldier was forcing himself on her, struggling on the floor trying to free herself she grabbed a dagger that was attached to his trousers and stabbed him by the side of his stomach, then she stabbed him on the neck. The other soldier did not know she had killed him because he was backing them a distance away.

The witness said he tried to call her whispering loudly that she should run; but it was like she was in a trance, she couldn't move, she stood there looking at the man she killed; her hands were vibrating, her entire body shivering.

As she dropped the dagger the other soldier turned and in a split second shot at my aunty and missed, the loud sound brought her back to her senses but before she could run he shot again and killed her. My other aunty on hearing what the man said wanted to run back but was withheld.

"My mother, aunty and sisters ran from village to village, the soldiers raided from village to village killing and plundering, assaulting women and assailing men. Finally they came to the house of one Mr Ikechukwu whose house was already filled with people hiding, they begged him to let them in, and he explained that his house was full and that he had no room to accommodate them. However, their persistent plea made him have pity, seeing my mother was now heavily pregnant.

He said he would let her and my sisters in, exempting my aunt, but my mother said she can't leave my aunty, that if she was not allowed in that she too wouldn't come in. The man after trying to persuade my mother, making her more aware of her pregnancy and the dangers, seeing that my mother was adamant about it said so be it.

But as he watched them walk away and saw my mother walk with difficulty, my aunty carrying me and my sisters tagging along, he called them back and let them in. My mother said my brother was her second saviour; that it was because of him that they were saved that day.

But my brother was one out of thousands if not a million children that died out of starvation and malnutrition. She said he died a day before the war was over."

Mr Okafor cleaned his eyes making sure the tears that had filled his eyes didn't roll down because he couldn't be crying in front of his sons. A tear or two rolled down Chigozie's face which he quickly cleaned, his brother was numb showing no expression.

Chibuzor behaved like he was not there, like a tortoise in a shell, unmoved, motionless – he just kept listening.

"Daddy what about your father?" Chigozie agitatedly asked cleaning the other tears that flowed from his face. Mr Okafor wriggled in his seat, took a deep breath and looked up staring at the currently fluctuating low-current-yellow bulb.

"Hmmm, my mother said that a man met her about three months after the war. The man told her that her husband my father saved him, taking a bullet for him which left his arm broken. They were running from approaching infantry, my father could not run with his broken arm dangling so he told the man he took the bullet for, to take care of his family after the war.

He gave him my mother's name and location in Afikpo, the man refused to leave him but my father persuaded, telling him that he would try to stall the fast approaching soldiers; telling him to run away with the fleeing Biafrans.

The man capitulated and fled, but after the war which was not so long from that time, the man came back to the area only to see that my father had been mutilated. He said he had been looking for them since the war ended.

My mother attacked the man, loading him with slaps, blaming him for my father's demise, my aunt and grandparents tried to calm her down — the man feeling guilty did not try to defend himself though it was not his fault.

When my mother was sober, the man said my father told him that he loved his son, and daughters and that my mother should please forgive him for not returning.

My mother started sobbing, she wept all day long. That man was a father figure to me and my sisters up to the time when I was a juvenile but he died later on from chicken pox.

"Biafrans had the opportunity of invading and taking over Lagos which was the capital of Nigeria before Babangida, after escaping a coup moved the capital to Abuja. The Biafran army was heading towards Lagos during the early period of the war, but their plan was foiled because the person leading the invasion was a Yoruba man who put the mission to a halt.

From what I heard he made contact with the Nigerian army informing them about it because he thought he would be made the sole ruler of the Yorubas. Its hearsay though, but the fact is that he betrayed the Biafrans. Well there was no way he would lead another tribe against his own people. He would be a squalid traitor to his people if he did.

Well I think I've said everything about the Biafran war," Mr Okafor said and sighed with relief putting his legs down from the wooden stool.

"Daddy, you did not tell us what Biafran soldiers did and how the war ended," Chibuzor said.

"Yes, it is true daddy you did not tell us about them," Chigozie said, wanting the gist to continue.

TWENTY ONE

"YOU KNOW Yakubu Gowon was a Christian, his father was an Evangelist. He declared after the war that there was no Victor and no vanquished then he introduced the three R's, Reconciliation, Rehabilitation and Rebuilding, though in a speech after the war he said the Rising sun of the Biafrans on the Biafran flag is set forever.

General Yakubu Gowon frankly speaking was not totally a bad person though they said he had a hand in the assassination of Murtala Mohammed the person who overthrew him in a bloodless coup later on when he postponed the handover of the military rule to civilians.

"Obafemi Awolowo did a malignantly draconian thing, being the Minister of Finance; he made a decree giving all the Igbos a trivial amount of about twenty pounds, mindless of how much they had in their accounts, nullifying the Biafran currency, saying they knew nothing about it; postulating that Nigeria could have gone bankrupt probably because our currency was so valuable.

Well, later on, he too became part of those who were demanding for federalism of the Nigerian state; something that we're still talking about today. The ruthlessly cruel idea of stopping the passage of food to Biafra though it was an excellent strategy to end the war, wiped thousands of children including my brother I never knew who died of malnutrition.

"Have you two heard about Usman Dan Fodio who through Jihad conquered the northerners converting them to Islam, he was conquering coming down to the south but he was withstood by the Tivs. Now you hear of Fulani herdsmen killing Tivs and people in Benue because of cows, their conflict did not start today. Although you people said I should tell you about the Biafrans but you have to understand the story of Nigeria.

"Gowon said that if the Igbos succeed in seceding, it would make the country to scatter bringing divisions here and there, so in order for the country to remain one, they had to fight the Biafrans to have a united

Nigeria, they even made a slogan saying; *"To keep Nigeria one is a task that must be done."*

Even Gowon's name was made as an acronym for emm *"Go on with one Nigeria."* I think that motivated more Nigerians to fight against the secession of the Biafrans. The Biafrans saw this as propaganda; seeing the real aim of the fight as attempt to completely annihilate the Igbos.

That was why the Igbos fought with everything they had with the mind-set that if they surrendered, they were as good as dead. Mind you, oil was also discovered in Biafra and they couldn't let the wealth from it go to the Igbos just like that without a fight leaving the Biafrans with the question; *is the oil not rightfully ours?*

"This is one of the reasons the British heavily supported the war against the Biafrans urging Nigeria not to let the Biafrans go because they knew they would no longer benefit from the oil if the Biafrans were independent.

You see, Nigeria now sells crude oil to be refined abroad, and then buys the refined oil for local use because there are no functional refineries in the country, and the government has not done anything to build a functional one.

So the Nigerian government assumed propaganda made Nigerians to support the war against Biafrans, and the supposed propaganda of the pogrom of Biafrans and evident suppression made the Biafrans fight back defending their lives, their freedom and their posterity.

"Boys in your age group were recruited into the Biafran army, some forced to join while some volunteered like my Father, and expatriate mercenaries joined the army as well. A locally made weapon called "Ogbunigwe" popularly called *"Ojukwu's bucket"* killed so many people at once.

I heard some small impudent and smart children were sent to espionage the location of the Nigerian army by Biafran soldiers, I don't know how true that is though. Planes bringing aid materials, weapons, mercenaries and Journalists came in the night so that they won't be seen by the Nigerian army.

The runway was lighted with fire so they could see where to land. There was no electricity. Some starving children and other people were flown back, when the plane was departing.

People's legs were amputated because of gangrene mostly as a result of injuries; arms too were amputated. Adulation songs were sang to Ojukwu the saviour of Biafrans, he was praised for fighting for the Biafrans even though he didn't have to.

Nigerians didn't expect the war to last as long as it did; it was a shocker that the Biafrans could stand for that long with limited resources. The Biafrans had insufficient army, most of the fighters were new recruits, they had no effective air force, and they used few out-dated world war two, planes.

According to some people, if the Biafrans had up to half of the resources and ammunitions the Nigerian army had, the story would have been different. But the fact is that the Biafrans were fighting for their lives. It takes common sense to know that the way you run in a racing competition is different from when you are running for your life.

When Ojukwu could fight no longer, he moved out to the enclave of Ivory-coast leaving his second in command, Phillip Effiong, in charge, who then surrendered to the Nigerian army.

Gowon made sure that Nigerians did not retaliate or continue the onslaught on the Igbos, but some things are inevitable, people's properties were confiscated. The National Hero General Yakubu Gowon who ended the war did well not to victimize the Igbos. Rather, he started rebuilding places in the enclave and other things.

He also introduced the National Youth Service Corp (NYSC) scheme as a tool for national cohesion to help youth blend better with people of other cultures. Well I don't know if it is as effective now as then. Yakubu Gowon did some really good things.

I can't tell you everything, many things happened in the war and after the war. It's only what I remember I can tell you. But know this, both the Biafrans and the Nigerians had a hand in the war; you can't blame one side solely for the war. Understood?!"

"Yes sir." The twins chorused back.

TWENTY TWO

"Dike, are you *now* scared? Jump! Don't tell me you are shaking with fear now," Olamide said sarcastically.

"How many times have I told you to stop calling me Dike, especially when we *are* carrying out our morning chores? Call me sweet bitter leaf, is that clear?" Dike shouted.

"Guy, are you mad? Why are you shouting? Don't you know it is night time when a small sound would sound loud, *or* you want people to liaise alarm before we even start the job? Me, I don't want to go *plison* again because of you guys with small blains, last time *it* was because the *porice* guy was my man so I could *blibe* my way out of *tlouble* even though it was just chicken change. But he sternly warned that next time he may not be able to help me out. Nigerian *plison is* different from *Amelican plison* in terms of welfare. In Nigeria a two year sentence could last up to five or more years if care is not taken because you could be forgotten in jail," Amaechi said in undertones. Dike and Olamide burst into laughter forgetting they were in front of a compound in the dead of the night holding weapons.

"Guy, this is not funny at all, your Igbo pronunciation is something else, you're just mixing L and R anyhow," Olamide said. "And you Dike which kind of name is sweet bitter leaf?"

"Can't you see how handsome I am, but I'm robbing people. I finished school with second class upper, just about o.3 more would have given me first class, yet two to three years after that, there's nothing to show for it. Sadly, to get a job nowadays you'll have to pay money before you are employed. Does it make sense to pay someone who would start paying you after that? This country, if you no get connection you would be disconnected from progress. My parents are now depending on me to provide, because they sent me to school leaving my younger ones at home. I'm the only hope of my family but have become a shame and torment to families I rob. Do you now understand why my name is sweet bitter leaf?" Dike said mildly.

"Hmmm..." Olamide sighed. "I *have* heard you, but the name is too long, I will be calling you SBL instead. If I tell you my own story eh..."

"Which *stoly?* ..." Amaechi cuts in. "Is it this night you people want to use for *stoly* telling? See we are *lunning* out of time. You people should jump this wall so we can start the *lobbery* before dayblake."

"Ah, see those people's house in front of us, it's like they are still awake. Let's rob them first so they don't raise alarm," Olamide said panting after jumping over the wall into the compound.

"Guy, you are very stupid, you want us to rob people that are awake, how are we going to enter their house, if they hear noise they'll start shouting, you know we have only one bullet in this gun, and we're not shooting anybody, we'll just shoot up to scare them.

"First of all, wear your masks well; if they *lecognize* you, face it alone and if they catch you don't even call my name, I would just deny you, besides let it be clear I've never seen you guys in my life. We're wasting time let's *lob* the house with lights on I bet they have money, they are the ones that own this fine Sienna," Amaechi said and the three of them scurried towards the lighted house.

Chigozie and Chibuzor were battling with their eyes to keep them from closing so they could finish reading their Bibles as their father instructed. Their father had left them in the sitting room and was on his knees praying in his bedroom. He was praying for his sons; praying that God will speak to them and channel their hearts on the right path. His wife was deep asleep on the other side of the bed, she was awake a while longer, listening, after she had met them in the parlour earlier that night. Chigozie had dozed off on his Bible while Chibuzor was struggling not to sleep until he had finished reading Romans eight, the chapter he had started, when they heard a knock on the door at the back of their house. Chigozie jerked up, his brother stood up too out of fear, wondering who would be knocking on the door by that precarious time of the night. They slowly walked to the kitchen, asking 'who is that?' their father had finished praying and also heard the sound at the back door, alarmed, he walked circumspectly towards the kitchen where the back door was.

Unknown to them the uninvited guest used that as a decoy to guile them, swaying them towards the back door so that they could break in from the front door. The unknown guests had sneaked up their veranda and peered into the house through the partially opened curtain, they could see clearly because the light inside was on but they could not be seen because there was no light outside which was pitch dark with phlegmatic moon rays.

While Mr Okafor and his sons were busy now boisterously shouting 'who's there? Who's that? Who goes there?' Olamide left Amaechi at the backyard who was still knocking in slow successions like a cadence— to meet Dike who was at the frontage, on the veranda waiting for him so that they could strike.

As he came, their initial plan was to threaten them to open the door, or break it open. When Dike was about to break the door open, Olamide told him to just try opening it normally in-case they had forgotten to lock it. Alas the door was unlocked.

"So you two didn't lock the door as I told you to?" Mr Okafor asked as he rushed to the sitting room on hearing the door open, shouting back at them that they should quickly lock the back door. Amaechi at the back on hearing their father, quickly opened the back door pushing Chigozie who was about to lock the door, he would have fallen to the ground but his brother wedged him, being at his back.

"Raise your hands! Oya move to the parlour, and don't shout, except you want to meet your maker this night! Move!" Amaechi said pointing a bullet-less gun at them. They met their father and the other two masked personalities, one pointing a gun at him and asking him where the money was.

"I'm sorry to ask but did you noble people give me any money to keep for you?" Mr Okafor asked with all seriousness. Chigozie almost laughed but couldn't, it would be anachronistic. He and his brother had never experienced a robbery before. The thieves were shaking guns that were pointed at them, if the armed robbers mistakenly triggered the gun out of anger or frustration, they would just die and they would not come back to life even though it was by mistake.

The humour Chigozie perceived from his father's talk was no longer humorous, they could be dead and whatsoever money or possession they had would be useless. But if their Father gave the robbers the money they had, there was no guarantee that their lives would be spared.

"This man thinks we *are* joking here! Oga, don't play with us! We can waste your life right away; you better bring all the money that's in this house and the key to that fine Sienna outside there. Like right now!" Dike shouted, clenching his teeth behind his black mask. Chigozie and Chibuzor started begging the robbers to have pity, that their father had no money, and that they had not eaten since morning.

"Seliously! This people think we are here to pray, sweet bitter leaf show them the "load" to follow; show them what is in your hand," Amaechi said gesticulating.

"Wait wait guy, no knack that trigger," Olamide whispered trying to tell Dike something with his eyes through the hole on his black translucent mask, that looked like stretched leggings, Dike deciphered what he meant and tried to tell Amaechi who was at the other side of the room.

"My friend, if I shoot, there would be no other bullet to threaten other tenants, you know it's just one bullet, and without it they could overpower us," Dike said to Amaechi in Igbo unknown to them that Mr Okafor understood everything, his sons partially. Dike then told Amaechi to go inside the room and search for money and the car keys and every other valuable as he pointed his gun at Mr Okafor, while Olamide threatened his sons with a dagger. As Amaechi entered the room he put on the light and saw Mrs Okafor as she jerked up from the bed trying to clear her vision, she shouted "Blood of Jesus" on seeing the masked face in her room. Amaechi shouted *"Lock of Ages"* pointing the gun at her. Olamide scurried to the bedroom on hearing them shout, while Dike warned Mr Okafor and his sons not to move as he pointed the gun at them

"Ma I'm not Jesus oo, so I advise you not to shout," Amaechi said to her, then hollered. "Man, see gold, just look at her skin, Asampete! Your husband must be enjoying *in* this house." Ameachi said putting one hand on his head, licking his lips and blushing repulsively.

He gawked at her like a hungry salivating dog; about to eat a pot filled with meat. Mrs Okafor tightened her wrapper very well. She was confused, thinking it was a nightmare, but reality struck in as another masked man rushed in asking the man who was lackadaisically pointing a gun at her why he was shouting after partially bowing to greet her.

"Please where is my husband? Who are you two? And what are you doing in my house?" She asked raising her shaking voice.

"Ma I've warned you not to shout, just show us where the money is. If not I'll do what's in my mind; I will like to taste what your husband has been enjoying," Amaechi said still licking his lips and smiling cynically behind his black translucent mask. Mrs Okafor was scared but didn't show it.

"I bind you in the name of Jesus!" Mrs Okafor proclaimed.

"This house is full of comedians, I just said *bling* money, and you are busy binding me instead of *blinging* the money, do you think we are "praying"?" Amaechi said.

"Playing, he meant. Madam, we don't want problem, just bring the money and the car keys and we won't touch you, if not madam you can see my friend is hungry, I won't be able to stop him," Olamide said trying to convince her.

Mrs Okafor was busy praying in her mind, she knew where the car key was, but had no idea of where the money was. She knew her husband was trying to make ends meet because since they came to Abuja things have not been easy with them. Her husband had told her he was even planning to sell their car in order to raise money for their sons' school fees. If these thieves took the car, it would affect them in so many ways; it would be hard to transport the whole family to church, with the countries current economy. Her husband used the car to taxi people going the same direction with him in order to get money as he goes to work every day.

Unfortunately her husband had withdrawn money from the bank to pay his tithe, and it wasn't month's end, he had told her he wanted a miracle from God, she had once pestered him for money to buy foodstuffs because they were running out funds and he was not expecting any money until the end of February.

These thieves had come to steal the seed they were yet to plant; how would they harvest without planting? God had declared; give tithes and see if He would not open the windows of heaven and bless magnanimously. She asked God why He had allowed such a thing to happen to her husband who did his best not to do anything that would displease Him. She kept asking *"God why?"*

Osinachi had woken up as usual and sprinted to the toilet to ease herself, she had heard Olamide threaten her mother, she tiptoed back. She quietly woke her elder sister Amaka who was deep asleep. Amaka and Osinachi were now busy peeping through the curtain to the sitting room not knowing what to do, not knowing who to call, 911 doesn't work in Nigeria, anyone who calls would be told that he was on the line and should wait, an everlasting queue that didn't seem to end, that's if the call is picked in the first place.

Amaka then remembered that John their neighbour had literally begged her for her number and she was very reluctant giving him, she did not want to have anything to do with him, he was too forward. But she was glad now that she had capitulated, he had not stopped calling her though they were in the same compound and she was older than him.

She groped silently on the bed in search for her phone, Osinachi also helped to look for it. Osinachi found it and gave her. The phone was switched off, as she switched it on, a piercing sound came from the phone, it seemed very loud because it was night and silent. She tried to trap the noise by covering the speaker of the phone and pressing it hard into the depressed bed, making it more depressed.

Luckily the hungry burglars were too busy making demands for what wasn't theirs, they heard nothing ostensible though Olamide heard a sound but he ignored it, caught up in the moment. As soon as the phone was on Amaka started calling John, the phone kept ringing till the end and he was not picking the phone, he was probably sleeping she assumed, but she kept calling. John wasn't sleeping, he was actually using his phone as the incessant call kept coming, he did not want to pick immediately because he didn't want her to know he was awake by that time of the night and he was wondering why she would be calling him by that time of the night.

"Oga better tell us where your money and car keys are, so we won't scatter this house. Just bring it gently and hand it over to us so we can leave. You can save your fellow tenants; we won't have to rob them if the money is enough. My guys, is it not so?" Dike asked, and his accomplices replied, 'it is so' whilst pointing their weapons at them.

Olamide and Amaechi had forced Mrs Okafor to the parlour to join her husband and sons. Mr Okafor and his sons were commanded to kneel down, Chibuzor and Chigozie succumbed but their father refused.

"If this man doesn't talk now I will touch his wife where he won't like, in front of his Children. This woman's body will be sweet," Amaechi was saying when Mrs Okafor installed a tremendous slap on his face, jamming his lips against his teeth, he began to bleed. He was about to retaliate but stopped. Mr Okafor was threatened not to move, Dike was holding his gun to his head, Olamide was holding his dagger at the back of Chibuzor and Chigozie who were still kneeling down.

"Madam I am respecting you oo, I'm not a small boy, I would wound you, if you *tly* that thing again, this gun I'm holding is not for "pray"," Amaechi said touching the blood that sipped through his permeable mask.

"Don't you dare talk to my wife like that," Mr Okafor shouted.

"Or what?" Amaechi asked.

"Honourable and wise men, you wouldn't want to touch the apple of God's eye. You may leave here unscathed, but you would inherit endless problems. I cannot do you any harm but my God would fight for me and you would unequivocally live a miserable life," Mr Okafor said trying to control his anger.

"Pastor! Have you finished your sermon? We've robbed pastors before and nothing happened, and I know you're not a pastor. You're just wasting our time, but it's you that will suffer it in the end, go and bring the money, if not my guy go handle your wife, it seems like you don't understand.

Very well then, Amaechi show her the way," Dike said, grinning mischievously. Amaechi who was holding her by the arm pushed her to the floor. Mr Okafor lost control, he ran towards Amaechi despite the threat by Dike that he would shoot, knowing fully well that it was just one bullet.

Chigozie and Chibuzor who had been communicating with their eyes, at the same time struck Olamide's knees with their elbows, the shock to his knees made him loose the grasp of his dagger.

Amaka who was in the rest room with her sister had finally made contact with John telling him the situation, fortunately he believed her. Dike was about to pull the trigger when NEPA took light, he was aiming to shoot Mr Okafor to stop him, but he missed because of the darkness and had shot Ameachi on the part of his shoulder closest to his neck.

Seconds later NEPA brought the light again, Amaka and Osinachi rushed to the sitting room on hearing the gun shot. Mrs Okafor hit her kneel as she was pushed, she was rubbing it as Amaka and Osinachi came to the living room with the smoke of death that seemed to be hovering, they thought she was shot because she was sitting on the floor. Mr Okafor who was already on motion had already gifted Amaechi a punch immediately after he had been shot.

Amaechi was on the ground gasping for air and shouting *"who off light?"* Though the light was back on, Chigozie and Chibuzor had already held Olamide to the floor. Dike was still standing pointing the gun at all directions threatening them not to move or he would shoot again and not miss. Mr Okafor walked back towards him, knowing fully well that he had already planted the only bullet in the gun in his partner's body.

"Drop the gun, take your friends and run for your life, I would spare you, but the Nigerian neighbours I know would not, most of them must have woken up from that gunshot. I advise you to run," Mr Okafor said.

"My father said you should run, so run!" Osinachi said as she ran to meet her father leaving Amaka who was now massaging her mother's knee.

"We know there's no bullet in that gun, so better run," Chibuzor said as he carried the dagger from the floor, while Chigozie carried Olamide's legs hooking them up his armpit, in a way that Olamide's head and hands rested backwards on the floor.

Amaechi was still on the floor holding where he had been shot, he was bleeding profusely and blood was soaking his shirt. Mrs Okafor on seeing him told Amaka to take Osinachi and go inside the room.

"They can't run anywhere, John would soon be here," Amaka was saying as John, his father and other male neighbours banged their door open. The neighbours holding all manner of elements, from pestle to sticks, stones, knives, shovel, machete and so on.

"Please don't kill them," Mr Okafor pleaded.

Only Mr Okafor and his sons went to church that Sunday morning but they arrived late. Mrs Okafor wanted to still go to Church despite what had happened earlier that morning but her husband had convinced her to stay home and rest. He did not want her to stress her hurting knee, telling Amaka to take care of her, Osinachi was still asleep by the time they were ready to leave.

The thieves were mercilessly beaten though Mr Okafor tried to prevent it, he didn't want them dead. They were flogged and beaten by the neighbours and security men of other compounds before the arrival of the police that morning. Amaechi was beaten too, more so when they realized the bullet just bruised him, though he was losing blood – they cared less.

The anger of most of the people beating the thieves was that they were poor too but did not result to illegal ways of getting money, and these thieves came to rob them who were trying to make ends meet. When the police came, the broken-down-bleeding thieves were baled into the police van and carried away, Chigozie doubted they could be bailed.

Chigozie and Chibuzor kept replaying what had happened, in their minds over and over again. The event mixed up with what their father narrated to them made so much impact on them and it instigated controversial thoughts.

Chibuzor who thought the Igbos who were victimized during the war and were the only benevolent people in Nigeria with a just course changed his concept towards the matter, realizing there were good and very bad, corrupt people everywhere in Nigeria. While Chigozie's perspective of what happened earlier in relation to the story his Father had narrated was that the Igbos were so marginalized in the country and it had forced some of them to result to any crudely bale means to make ends meet or even to just survive.

TWENTY THREE

FUNKE WAS watching the *Crazy Rich Asians* for the fifth time, she loved Rom-com movies, and this movie seemed to interest her as much as *Pride and Prejudice* did. She was rich but not a crazy Asian but a sane Nigerian incarcerated in her own home. She had been grounded by her father, and her mother was incredulously in support because she had lied to them earlier during the week that she wanted to go shopping and her father had given her the money she needed to go shopping, but she actually went for a party, which spanned from day time till night time, and she kept lying that she was in traffic when they started calling her number.

Her father did not want her to go shopping, because she would just waste money, she already had all she needed but her wants were insatiable with her mother on her side, she persuaded her husband to let their daughter go. She had often said; "what is the use of having money if not to spend it?"

Funke finally came home accompanied by her closest friends, Aisha and Adaora whose cousin brother Buchi piloted them, Abike was also one of her closest friends, but she was dropped off before her.

None of them were in the University yet; they were a clique in a private secondary school popularly referred to as the 'A cube and F' because of the first letters of their name but most of the students insinuated it to be their grades in their academics which happened to be ironic because Funke was more brilliant than the rest but they became friends majorly because of their status and also being classmates.

"They were all rich, rather, their parents were rich and they all refused to go to federal universities, planning to go to the same private University. Her father had sternly warned her to stop hanging out with them especially Aisha and Adaora because he considered their fathers to be corrupt with their wealth almost tripling with the coming of the new regime. He knew they were working at strategic positions in government where they could siphon money and hardly get noticed and easily pay off or even silence whoever wanted to make a farce about it.

They offered people jobs so they would pay them a certain amount of money when they start working and most of the time they collect the money before giving the person the job or even acknowledge that they would do something about it.

Abike's father, on the other hand was in the petroleum business, there was no ambiguity that a person in such a business would make money, whether he cut corners or not. Abike's father was also into farming and Funke's father was acquainted with him because he had a business that was farming related also.

Funke knew her father wouldn't consent to her going to the party knowing fully well her clique would be there; and she was not certain if she could go through her mother, her mother was spontaneously unpredictable and sporadic at times so she didn't tell her. The reason she was in support of Funke being grounded had nothing to do with her attending the party but because Funke failed to trust her by not telling her about it.

Adaora had orchestrated the plan, for Funke to go to *Next Cash & Carry* Supermarket so that they'll come to pick her up from there in her cousin brother's father's car. Aisha funded their scheme while Abike tagged along with her furtive undergraduate boyfriend who vacated the party because she refused to do the lasciviously vile thing he wanted her to do.

Abike was in the same Church with Funke but they were in different branches, she was a sanguine and did most things just to feel belonged but she had standards probably inculcated in her by her parents and Church. She knew there were lines she should not cross but she jumped over boundaries sometimes. Abike felt depressed after her boyfriend left her. It was then she started drinking and dancing until she could dance and drink no more.

When the party was over and they were driving home she delayed them by frequently asking them to stop, so she could vomit, the reason they had to take her home first before Funke who was supposed to be the first to be taken home as far as their direction was concerned. The time spent on the road aggravated her parents worry and anger.

It was now Saturday and her mother and father had gone out to vote leaving her alone at home. The maids were busy arranging the house, cleaning everything cleanable and washing what needed washing. Stellar was almost done sweeping her room after arranging it.

"Stellar, what did my mother tell Okoro to cook this morning?" Funke asked the tired looking maid.

"She said Akara and pap and it's Bisola that's on duty" Stellar answered as she packed the dirt which was majorly dust.

"Is it mandatory that every Nigerian must eat Beans cake and *Akamu* every Saturday morning? And Akara would surely take time before its ready. I'm hungry," Funke said overwhelmed.

"I think it's because nobody use to go out on Saturday, so everybody can wait, unlike work days when people are rushing so, they eat the fastest food available like bread and tea," Stellar said. She was standing beside the room's exit door.

"I know but there are other things apart from Akara and Pap to eat; to make the Akara now, you will pick beans, wash it, grind it, then you would start putting ingredients before frying. See, the way I'm hungry eh I would have died before they finish cooking. What you will help me to do is to quickly cook Indomie," Funke said as she lay backwards lightly placing her hands on her stomach and sinking into her very big and soft bed.

Funke's room was almost half the size of Chigozie's whole house, the room was painted majorly with pink then purple and white. Her father had assumed that his daughter would like pink or pink would be her favourite colour because she was a girl, so he had her room painted pink and white but later on realized that purple was her favourite colour. So, he had purple painted on more than half of the side painted with white.

Her room was coloured with patches of aesthetic designs with little of other paint colours. She had a section of the room where she put all the framed pictures, which was majorly of herself, her family and some relations. Besides, the shelf of pictures was a wall paper of herself which she changed yearly as she grew.

On the ground beside the shelf was an open box filled with cut coloured papers with printed memorable quotes from the Bible. Her father had told her to pick up to five of them and read in the morning when she wakes up and in the night before she slept anytime she was unable to read her Bible.

Her room was cosy, soothing and always air conditioned. Her wardrobe which was beside her aesthetic restroom was filled with gorgeous clothes, attires and elaborate number of shoes ranging from high hills to flat, to sneakers and canvass of various colours. There was a shelf close to her bed filled with books, there were: textbooks, novels, motivational books, biographies of great people and so on.

"Hmmm... Sorry, so sorry, I can't cook anything for you," Stellar said.

"Eh? Is that a joke or what? ... Is it April yet? If I may ask, why can't you cook for me? Are you resigning?" Funke sputtered as she sat upright, puzzled by Stellar's statement.

"Your parents said that you should fast, I think it has to do with the party you went for. They instructed me and the rest not to cook any food for you till they vote and are back. I know that would take a while, a long while ma." Stellar said sympathetically, she had worked for the family longer than most staffs of the house – since Funke was in primary school.

She knew how things operated in the house but had not seen Funke deprived of food in the name of fasting. She acknowledged the labelled punishment was for a good reason but the method didn't seem to be that good. Funke was a comely child and she liked her though she could be petulant at times but Stellar loathed her mother because her mother practically despised her for no just reason.

"You must be joking, how would they starve me in the name of fasting? Is the house arrest not enough? What did I do that was so bad to deserve such treatment?" Funke lamented hugging her soft pillow, then she threw it away, wriggling her leg on the bed as if pushing back something, then picked another pillow and covered her face.

She was not accustomed to fasting, she rarely even fasted during the church regular prayer and fasting which always took place at the beginning of every year though her father was fully involved while her mother also fasted but broke her fast any time she felt like. Stellar just stood by the door holding the broom and watching her with a bit of lethargic disdain. She understood her pain, she knew that Funke was not used to such treatment but her reaction didn't seem to be worth it.

"Wait first, my parents are not around just quickly cook the Indomie before they come back, and you don't have to tell them," Funke said removing the pillow from her face, fantasizing her hopeful idea as she stood up and rushed to the window opening the curtain which had a pretty valance, as if to see and confirm that her parents were not coming.

"I would have loved to do that for you but other maids especially Bisola would report me to madam, your mother. I don't want to get in trouble with your mother again; the last time she almost threw me out like a waste bin, if not for your father I wouldn't be here. My family depends solely on me, though my parents are working but they are doing petty jobs and are poorly paid."

"Oh my God!" Funke cut in. "I'm not ready to start hearing stories I just want to eat I'm hungry, I didn't finish my food last night," Funke said blocking her ears then squeezing her pillow as if the more she did that, the more her hunger would abate.

"I'm sorry, I would leave now." Stellar said as she turned to leave carrying the broom in her hand and dustpan.

"Wait, wait, wait; I didn't say what I said to dismiss you, sorry about my hissy feat," Funke said.

"I took no offense; I think I understand how you feel," Stellar replied.

"You seem learned; you've been to school right?"

"Yes." Stellar replied.

"Hmm nice, I can tell from the way you speak, you speak better English than the others who mostly speak pidgin and Yoruba. I've known you almost all my life and I don't really know much about you," Funke said. "Can you tell me how you started working for my Family?" Funke asked.

She had called her back because she knew boredom would increase her hunger and she also wanted to know why a learned person would be working as a maid and getting a meagre salary which seemed to be more than what her parents were getting.

"My life story is not so interesting and I doubt you would enjoy it, it's very short. Do you still want to hear it?" Stellar asked.

"Yes of course, I don't know much about you. Is Stellar your full name?"

Funke asked.

"No, Nwokoye is my surname. Stellar Nwokoye is my full name, and the Stellar is with an R.

"Oh, so is not just S t e l l a?" Funke asked spelling out the name.

"Yes." She replied.

"Hmm, such a peculiar name, and you said Nwokoye, is that not an Igbo name?"

"Yes it is?"

"Wow, I thought you were Yoruba, you even speak Yoruba fluently with the other maids, only your radiant fair skin says otherwise. Hmm I didn't know you're Igbo oo," Funke said surprised.

"I'm Igbo oo, but I grew up in Lagos. Well the thing is that I don't know my real father and my mother died when I was very young, so it's my grandfather's name I'm bearing."

"Ah ah, so who did you now grow up with?" Funke cut in, puzzled.

"My parents," Stellar replied knowing she would be confused.

"Which parents are you referring to then? I thought you said you don't know your father and your mother died when you were young. So which parents?" Funke asked completely perplexed. Stellar laughed, getting what confused her.

"Yeah, sorry I get your point, it's not that complicated though. My mother was staying with her uncle before she died. He was too busy to take care of me, so he gave me to his son and his wife who had no children since they got married. They became my parents; they're my real parents because they brought me up. So my surname is still the same because my present father is bearing the same surname as his father who is the younger brother of my grandmother. Do you understand?" Stellar asked hoping she understood because she didn't know how else to explain it.

"Yeah... Yeah, yeah I think I do" Funke said looking up and moving her head as if she was linking dots together. "But your grandmother supposed to be carrying your grandfather's surname, right?" Funke asked reasoning it.

"Yeah that's true, that's the funny part. According to my granduncle, my grandparents had the same surname before they got married, that's why he has the same surname as my grandfather who is not his brother," Stellar explained, with a subtle smile.

"Wow, that's incredulous; I've never heard such a thing like that. And you said there's nothing interesting about your life." Funke said with a questioning expression like The Rock raising his eye brow; and Stellar smiled sheepishly, she had not thought about it. "But how? Won't there be a lot of confusion?" Funke asked, surprised that there was something like that.

"Yeah, I was baffled when I heard it too. But it is what it is; I also asked questions but my parents had limited knowledge about it," said Stellar.

"But have you met, or do you even know your grandfather – the real one?" Funke asked wondering why he was a passive actor in the story.

"Well, I don't really know him, when I asked my granduncle about him, during one of the times he came visiting, he told me to forget about him that it was better I didn't know him. It seems like my grandfather had a problem with my mother that caused them to separate. From the little I heard from my parents," Stellar explained as she thought about it.

"Hmm, I wonder what kind of problem it was. So about you, how did you learn to speak so well?" Funke asked, curious.

"Emm, I was actually a brilliant student back in school as the only daughter of my parents," Stellar winked and Funke smiled getting what she meant. "They said I was an answered prayer. I was double promoted when I was in primary school. In secondary school apart from JSS one and two I topped the class throughout, and by the time I had finished writing my WAEC, I was still fourteen entering fifteen years.

I wrote jamb, and I did well, I scored emm around two ninety-something but I didn't get admission mostly because of my age; I was to be at least sixteen years before I could enter the university. So my parents sent me from the village to come and work here.

Your Father knew my father when they were still young, and they maintained a long distance friendship because of locations. So the plan was that I would work here for just a year then I would register for jamb again, by then I'll be almost sixteen years and able to get the admission.

But things weren't going so well for my parents; which was part of the reason they sent me here in the first place, my mother was not working, my father was the one providing for the whole family from where he was working. It was at the work he was doing that his colleagues conspired against him by framing him up for stealing something.

As a result, he was incarcerated with nobody to bail him. But your father intervened and bailed him. Since then my father and my mother started doing menial jobs, and I have been working here to support them.

So my hope of going to school was dashed, and there was nothing I could do about it, but I've been reading, making use of your library," Stellar said with a suppressed glitter in her eyes.

"Wow, now I see, I had no idea of your background and it seems like you love to read," Funke stated.

"Yes, I do," she affirmed, facing the large mirror attached to the glass door in Funke's room.

"How on Earth is it possible to postpone the election on the Election Day which they've been making plans for since last year, what kind of country is this? And they expect people not to think that they have something malicious up their sleeves," Mr Adefarasin vociferated from downstairs as he and his wife walked into the house.

He had been hearing that some set of people from a particular area or tribe had mischievous plans but he didn't know how true it was, it was probably false, some people may have instigated the treachery to ridicule the government though Mr Chukwueze, Stellar's father and some other people he knew had told him that they had been trying to get voters card but to no avail.

Funke and Stellar heard his voice from upstairs and Funke stood abruptly, and grabbed her robe to wear. Up until now, she was only wearing a camisole and pyjamas trousers. She rushed down stairs, and almost tripped on reaching the ground floor.

"Don't fall oo, I don't have another daughter," Her mother said as she sank into the couch. Mrs Ade was skimming through channels on the TV set. She had just checked Telemundo but they were repeating *Iron Rose* – the programme she had watched during the week, she now switched over to Zee World. It had just finished previewing scenes of *King of Hearts* which would be aired the next week.

"Mummy I'm your only child and you want to starve me," Funke said standing at the back of her father's seat

"Who told you that? It's your father that brought the idea of fasting," Her mother said facing the TV and backing her husband and daughter.

"Daddy, why do you want to starve me? Please I said I'm sorry, I would not do it again," Funke said as though she wanted to start crying as she bent to hug her father from the back of his chair.

Her father was still disturbed by what the postponement of the election meant, what was really going on apart from the supposed ruse declaration that equipment and tools needed were not available or sufficient.

Still focusing on her movie channel, Mrs Adefarasin muttered as she changed the channel; "This Roshni sef, how many times would Siddharth prove to her that he can do anything for her? But she will just be there doing anyhow. This one is just showing that they're just making the film long so that they'll make more money".

"Eyaah Daddy! You're not answering me oo? Remember, I still remain your only pretty little daughter," Funke said dragging her voice.

"Yes, you're my only pretty daughter. I wanted your mother and I to fast on your behalf but your mother disagreed, she said you committed the offense so you should pay for it and fast for yourself and your future.

I supported it because it would be good for you. You know I love you," Mr Adefarasin said as he held her hands and drew her to sit by his side on the arm of the chair. "You know I love you right? All I do is for you alone."

"So all you do is for her alone, right?" Mrs Adefarasin cut in.

"I do what I do for you too, you are my flesh and bone, my wife," Mr Adefarasin said as he was playing with Funke's hand.

"Story, story... story," Mrs Adefarasin said as she stood up abruptly, leaving the sitting room and walking up the stairs clapping her hand as if she was dusting dust from them.

"You literally forced me to marry you," Mr Adefarasin mumbled as he trailed his chick cheeky wife walking upstairs. Mrs Bolanle was fit and energetic, she was always cautious about maintaining her shape.

"Daddy, you say what?" Funke asked fully hearing what he said.

"Don't bother, it's nothing serious. Wait! are you not up to eighteen years? You are supposed to vote," Mr Adefarasin said as he turned, looking up to his daughter who was now staring at their curved Samsung LED TV which was about fifty-five inches wide. The TV looked like it was plastered to the wall or in the wall like a drawer in a cupboard. She stared with her lips pursed as if she was sulking but she heard what her father said.

"Daddy even though I'm twenty, I don't think I'll ever participate in voting or election practices; it's just a waste of time, and I cannot go and waste my time and energy in the name of civic duty," Funke said standing up to leave.

"Funke, wait. Where are you going to? Bring that chair here and sit down and tell me why voting is a waste of time," her father said pointing at the Windsor chair.

"Daddy if I tell you, you'll allow me to eat, and my imprisonment term would come to an end," Funke said smiling, as if asking.

"Hmmm, when you tell your one and only father, I'll reduce your feather fasting from five to four."

"So Daddy you wanted to starve me till evening?!"

"Funke, bring that chair here and come and sit down, and tell me what I want to hear."

"Yes sir!" Funke said and saluted her Father, putting her right hand to her forehead and down knowing that he was serious but she replied that way to ease the almost taut atmosphere. She did not want to aggravate or displease him. She brought the chair and sat down facing him.

"Daddy, democracy is a farce in Nigeria, the democracy Abraham Lincoln posited in his speech over two hundred years ago of the government of the people, by the people and for the people is not working here in Nigeria. Nigeria democracy is government of the government by the government and for the government, and perhaps a few elite connected to the government of the day.

Nigeria has an oligarchy system of Government which is heading towards fascism; most of the leaders are there to embezzle money for themselves and their cronies. The law doesn't work on them and they're licentious. To some extent the rule of law is in the grave because so many people are above the law. The word impunity must have been created because of Nigerian leaders.

The law punishes the poor and justifies the rich. Most people that were in PDP are in APC, so who are we going to vote for? What will be the difference? The winner of this election has already been predetermined. Tell me which ruling government gives up the government for the opposition party if he has not completed his tenures?"

"Former President Goodluck Jonathan did so," Mr Adefarasin said.

"Goodluck Jonathan was a good man, he didn't want violence just like Mandela who didn't retaliate on the blood sucking Apartheid government who not only took over their land but oppressed them and deprived them of their legitimate rights to be humans.

Goodluck knew if he did not hand over, there would be bloodshed, but there was still bloodshed but I'm not certain of it I heard some people of the party that won killed some of the opposition while celebrating their so-called victory at the poll.

Daddy from the time M.K.O Abiola was denied of winning the election and was killed because he wanted justice to be served; Nigeria's democracy with all certainty and no ambiguity has been filthy, completely soiled, though fortunately there are some very good outcomes by God's intervention. So, daddy, I don't see the use of going to vote when the results has already been predetermined," Funke said waiting for her father to talk.

Mr Adefarasin sat back in his chair, sighed and looked up like Aguiyi Ironsi while talking.

"You said by God's intervention there are some good outcomes. Do you think God is sleeping or God doesn't know what is going on in this country? But how do you want God to work if you don't play your own part? We have to play our own part and let God play His own.

God is not a magician, you should understand that. If we all sit down at home and fold our hands, do you think there will be any change for the better? Most of the things you said are true but some are ambiguous, I wonder where you heard them from. Be careful it's not everything you say outside. Politics is an incendiary topic; it tends to cause fights to break out."

"There's this one I heard, that in the north they pack underage children to go and vote and some people even say they add animals too," Funke said.

"Just imagine; that's ridiculous!"

"Daddy Nigeria is ridiculous and it's ludicrous, we're probably one of the most endowed countries in Africa, with numerous mineral resources, yet dwelling among the poorest in the world," Funke cut in.

"But listen, how would they carry animals to vote? You say they carry underage children to vote, if the votes are already predetermined why would they need the under-age to vote? And see you and others like you that are of age don't want to vote."

"Daddy it's possible that they use them to meet up with the number they have already calculated." Funke said protruding her two hands forward, palms upwards and bending her neck to one side.

"Foolish sayings can put you in trouble, don't say what you don't know or not certain of."

"Daddy you said I should tell you why voting is a waste of time and I've done that. Now I'm going to go and eat." Funke said and stood up to leave.

"Come and return this chair to where you took it from, I wonder how you know about Lincoln and his postulation of democracy and all those other things you were saying."

"Daddy I went to school, and in school there are books and I read."

"Hmmm, thank God the money for school fees was not wasted." Mr Adefarasin said and Funke chuckled as she walked towards the kitchen after relocating the chair. He then walked a few steps to where his wife was sitting before she went upstairs and picked up the remote. When he sat back on his chair he started skimming through news channels then Sport channels. He switched to one of them and they were about to start replaying a football match he had missed. Then suddenly, with no prior notification, the lights went off.

"Gbenga! Gbenga! Put on the gen," he shouted in Yoruba.

TWENTY FOUR

"ANYONE GULLIBLE enough to be duped by Harry deserves it."

"How can you say such a thing? That's preposterous. How Harry hilariously helped Happiness hid her hideous habit that was why she succumbed."

"I told you, she deserves it!"

Two people were busy acting that they were arguing on the TV as Mrs Hannatu sat in her sitting room, watching the soap-opera while Joseph was resting his head and petite torso and hands on his mother's lap watching the TV but pretending to be sleeping. His mother had always sent him to bed whenever that particular soap-opera was about to start.

It was Wednesday; the election results took over three days to be collated. INEC had been adding up the results from the Saturday the previous week. Mr Habib had warned his wife not to vote for anybody if it was not the candidate he had told her to. Mrs Hannatu who did not want to bring strife and did not want to lie decided not to vote at all because she knew her husband would ask her who she voted for.

She prayed and fasted on the day of election praying that God's will be done in Nigeria, peace was better than war. She had heard different prophecies from different men of God on the outcome of the election. In Churches, even in her church she was surprised that there was division on the person to vote for, it baffled her. But she later on realized that some people started prospering during the current regime, some were connected to someone that was connected to the people at the top, so they could do anything for that connection to remain as it was.

On the election-day she heard that some people were not able to vote because the Card Reader could not verify them. She heard of crises in some states as people came out to vote. During one of the electoral debates the two main party leaders were not present; one came but decided to leave when he discovered his major opponent was not present.

Many people saw this as an opportunity for the opposition to have an advantage but after the collation of results were done; they were roundly defeated. She wondered if the country which seemed to be coming out of recession would enter another one since the person who had brought the first recession was the winner. Her heart seemed to beat faster while her breathing slower anytime she thought about the nation. She knew what she passed through during the last recession.

People had said that the former president was the reason for the incessant bombing by the Boko-haram but the Boko-haram harassment had not stopped, though it had reduced. Some said it had reduced because the new government had a hand in it to debase the former government but under the present realities she was lost on what to believe. Some pastors were clandestinely open about who they supported while other pastors encouraged their congregation to pray for the will of God to be done.

"What are you doing? You're busy watching TV; do you want me to starve?" Mr Habib said walking into the sitting room and blocking her from viewing the television. He was facing her bare chested and was also waving his hands.

"Can't you see I'm watching something, can you please move away?" Mrs Hannatu asked.

"Don't you know who our wonderful president is, it calls for a celebration," Mr Habib said raising his hands.

"Be careful! See the fan," Mrs Hannatu said quickly.

"I know, I have eyes," he said as he started dancing and chanting the President's name and turning round, doing his best to obstruct his wife who was bending left and right to keep watching.

"Come and join me and dance, I know that you know how to dance, one of the many reasons my brother fell for you. Come on, Allah gave you those magnificent hips for a reason," Mr Habib said grinning at his wife, gesturing that she should come.

Mrs Hannatu looked at her husband's beautiful dentition, he looked so handsome especially when he was happy, which was rare because of his constant outbursts. Part of the things he used to woo her was his scintillating dance steps. But now she was not in the mood to dance, the state of the country made her uncomfortable, unhappy with no real reason.

"I don't want to dance, just let me be," Mrs Hannatu said in apparent frustration, still trying to view the TV despite her husband's obstruction. Mr Habib took the remote placed on the table and tried to switch off the TV but could not. Riled, he flung the remote to the chair beside him and scurried to the connecting socket to disconnect the TV.

"Come now!" Habib shouted.

"Please stop shouting, you might wake Joseph, he needs to sleep, he has been awake until lately. By the way, I can't dance with you because you're angry, I'm going to bed," Mrs Hannatu said as she tried to stand up, lifting Joseph.

"You're not going anywhere, if you wouldn't dance go and cook our celebration dinner, I'm hungry I've not eaten this night," Mr Habib vehemently said.

"Haba! Habib, it's too late to start cooking now. I came back home late and I've been working since morning, now I'm very tired and need rest. Please you can eat that remaining Tuwon shinkafa and the Miyar Kuka, your favourite; I'll warm it for you."

"No, I want something different and fresh."

"But I'm really tired," she said.

"You're tired, and you sat here watching film, I know you don't care if I die or not. In fact I know you have been praying to that your God to kill me," he paused then chuckled. "But I will not die no matter what you do, better go and prepare the food that I'll eat this night, I don't want to hear story."

Mr Habib tried to put on the TV forgetting that he had disconnected it.

"It's disconnected," his wife said, he then hissed and went to connect it back.

"Habib, you've been here since afternoon, couldn't you cook what you wanted to eat, I've been working all day and I'm also hungry. Couldn't you help me cook just this night even though it's just for yourself?" Mrs Hannatu said with a wistful tone, hoping to persuade him.

"This your Christianity has made you mad. You have forgotten your place in this house, how do you expect me, your husband to go and do women's work. Better go and start cooking, I wouldn't sleep on an empty stomach when you're here and there's food in the house. You are my wife and you must cook, I'm the man of this house," he sputtered.

"Couldn't you help me cook?" He mimicked her as he plugged the TV back and cleaned imaginary dust from his native trousers. He walked back to the same chair and sat down and crossed his legs.

"If you're the man of the house, act like the man of the house," Mrs Hannatu said in undertones but her husband heard it.

"What did you just say?" Mr Habib asked standing up. "Are you talking back at me?" Losing his temper Mr Habib swung his hands to slap Hannatu his wife. Although he wanted to refrain on realizing what he was about to do, but his hands were already on motion, so he slapped her but then became remorseful.

"Habib, you slapped me." Hot tears flowed down her red pale cheeks while her mouth became so heavy that she could not close, leaving her lips ajar. She was in shock; her husband had never slapped her before. She knew Habib; he was not that kind of person, that abuse physically, though he maltreated her but she had never imagined him laying his hands on her.

Was the prayer she had been praying for her husband to repent and stop maltreating her like adding fuel to the fire for becoming worse each time? She stood there mouth ajar trying to massage her cheeks.

"I'm sorry," Habib said, as he moved close to touch her. He didn't intend to hurt her because he really loved her. The trouble was her Christianity.

"Don't you dare touch me," she said as she stepped back, talking with an authoritative voice, she didn't even know where it came from.

"Don't you dare talk to me like that! I'm still your husband never forget that. Now go and prepare my dinner! And don't let me run out of patience. I'm waiting!" Habib said and sat down. "Bloody Christian," he mumbled as he switched from channel to channel sitting on his Channel T-shirt, not really seeing what he was doing, he just kept changing the channels.

Mrs Hannatu turned to look at Joseph; he was still sleeping. She was happy he was not awake to witness what had just transpired. But more tears came down her eyes seeing her cute son hugging a chair pillow. She carried him and walked to his room and tucked him in bed, switched off the light as she left his room.

"Submit! Submit!" kept ringing in her head, being words of counsel she had received from Mrs Adaeze. But this time she was not going to listen to such. Rather, she was determined to end it all.

She walked briskly to the kitchen and checked where she kept a pesticide she bought recently to eliminate cockroaches. The cockroaches seemed to multiply when killed. One of her friends had suggested the Sniper would work in exterminating the voracious vermin which seemed to survive on almost anything and even nothing.

She had spent some time one Saturday trying to clean up and eliminate them. Though after that day it seemed like they were gone forever but some nights later she came into the kitchen to get something and as she switched on the light she saw a multitude of them running to hide.

It seemed insurmountable. The sniper she bought seemed to be working after applying it for some nights; she would see dead cockroaches lying breathless in the morning. Now she was going to use the Sniper to kill a bigger cockroach.

Mrs Hannatu started cooking. She decided to quickly cook Jollof rice since there was grinded fresh tomatoes in the fridge and enough rice but no meat. Her reason for using dry fish had to do with her husband's like for dry fish stew, although she was using it this time around for Jollof.

"He'll still like it anyways," she thought as she angrily sliced the onions while her husband was having the fun of his life in the sitting room – having high pitch-laugher, probably from what he was watching on TV.

She wanted to blend the crayfish but as she switched on the blender, lights went off. "Habib! how are you enjoying this incumbent government?" She shouted in her mind, too angry to talk. Then she circumspectly found her way to the sitting room where the rechargeable lanterns were, switched them on and carried the Smaller lantern to the kitchen while her husband still sat there operating his Samsung phone as though nothing happened.

She rinsed her mortar, poured the crayfish inside and started pounding;

just then, lights were restored back.

"This government is awesome!" her husband voiced out from the sitting room as if he heard what she had said in her mind earlier. Mrs Hannatu sighed heavily, and started pounding the crayfish viciously.

"What's wrong with women of nowadays?" Mr Habib blurted. "Can't you see that there's light? Make use of the blender and stop making noise with that thing!" But Mrs Hannatu hit the mortar harder as if she heard nothing. She started sweating profusely, getting inundated with it.

"Hannatu what is wrong with you, why are you punishing yourself when the person who needs the punishment is there enjoying himself. Calm down and cook his food, the last food he will ever eat," Hannatu thought to herself then she calmed down.

She then put down the pot of rice she had parboiled, poured the rice into a colander by the sink, under running water. She put groundnut oil in a frying pan and put on the fire again. While waiting for it to heat she tried to defrost the frosted tomatoes. It had started to thaw because of the hot water she had put it in earlier.

She brought out the sniper from where she kept it, beside her waste bin close to the kitchen's exit door to the backyard. After holding it for a while she decided to drop it back and wait till she had mixed the rice and fried tomato sauce and it was boiling. Rushing to get done with it, she poured the poorly sliced onions, and then sprinkled a spoonful of salt, then added thyme to it, waited for a while then poured the partially thawed blended tomatoes.

When it had fried for a while, she sprinkled Star Maggi, she preferred it than the rest of the seasoning cubes because it always brought out the taste in the food. Knorr seasoning cube was also one of her favourites but it had finished, if not she would have mixed the two together. After that, she poured the grinded crayfish and dry fish and then added some amount of curry, and stirred.

When she had mixed the tomato sauce with the rice, she heard her husband laughing and making jokes, he was on the phone with someone, probably his closest friend, Ahmed Salisu. They were talking politics and laughing, and it angered her more. How will they be discussing politics by this time of the night? She rushed and carried the pesticide, to kill the biggest parasitic pest in her life but suddenly refrained just when she was about to pour it.

"What of if this man tells me to put food for myself and eat? I'll just tell him I've eaten and I want to sleep. Who would eat the remaining food Hannatu? The man would be dead by then and I'll just throw the food away. But what of if Joseph eats this food somehow? I wouldn't let that happen. Pouring the sniper now may be complicating its better I just wait for the food to cook then pour the sniper. But wouldn't the sniper smell? I'll mix it very well." Mrs Hannatu kept asking and answering questions in her head.

She rushed and hid the pesticide and waited for the food to cook. She walked slowly to the dining room which was facing the sitting room and sat down on one of the wooden seats looking her husband with loathing eyes.

"Why are you looking at me like that? Has the food not cooked? I'm hungry oo," Mr Habib said after he had finished making the call, noticing his wife's steady gaze.

"Hmmm... It would soon be done my husband, I'm sorry that it's taking so much time to cook," Mrs Hannatu said in a calm and palpable voice. "The food would soon cook, my dear husband so you can eat and then sleep. Sleep forever or convulse to death," she said in her mind.

"Ehen, my beautiful wife," he said in Hausa. "No problem, I shall wait for your delicious food. I'm glad you now understand your place as a wife," he said and grinned at his wife who was faking a smile.

"The slap must be working, I'll try it often," he thought and chuckled. Turning his attention back to the television, he changed from Channels, a top news station in Nigeria to a movie channel. He then relaxed on the chair, and reduced the volume.

It was dark and silent outside their house because it was late in the night at the time. Mrs Hannatu scurried to the kitchen to see if the water had dried and the rice had cooked. She could wait no longer, her life would be better without her husband – very blissful with only her and her son. No more problems, abuse or maltreatment.

Her son would not grow up in a divided and belligerent home but a peaceful one. He would not grow up to be wicked, like his step-father but grow having good values like his mother, a murderer? She just realized she was about to kill her husband in cold blood. What of if her son asks her about his father and how he died when he has grown? Would she be able to justify her reason or reasons?

She also thought about what kind of Christian she was for killing someone? She had forgotten all Mrs Adaeze had said to her about being submissive and rather battle the agents of darkness that were turning her husband against her.

She was not the first Christian to marry a Muslim man but her case seemed different. She had to keep praying for her husband and loving him even though he despised her and did everything to subject her to a state of servitude, mostly because of her belief. She realized she could not proceed with what she was planning but rather make him to believe in Christ.

Hannatu rushed to her backyard holding the sniper. She flung it, projecting it far away from her house not caring where it landed.

"So someone cannot sit outside in peace! Who the hell threw this stuff?" a man shouted from outside, the voice sounded familiar. It sounded like the man who had no disabilities but he used to stand close to a junction begging for money saying; "I am hungry, please give me money to buy food."

She had given him money the first time she encountered him but have not given him again since then. She wondered how a grown up man, fully able, would be begging for money while some other people who had disabilities were working or doing one kind of business or the other.

The food was finally ready and she served her husband in his favourite plate. And while he ate she asked. "Why are you so excited that the president won knowing fully well that he doesn't know you, and you cannot really benefit from his regime and there's a possibility that things may get worse?"

"Why do football fans support different clubs, and argue on which one is better? They are happy when their club wins and sad when they don't. When the players in the club don't even know that they exist. Sometimes they even fight to defend their clubs. Why?" Mr Habib returned the question to his wife by using a different scenario. "Besides this one affects me, and there's this joy that comes when the person you supported, wins," Mr Habib said.

Mrs Hannatu was silent, seeing reason in what he was saying. After sitting for a while and watching him masticate and gulp down his food, she stood up to leave but her husband called her back as if suspicious.

"Where are you going to? Why didn't you serve food for yourself to eat? I thought you said you were hungry too."

"I don't feel like eating, I am okay, I want to go to bed I'm feeling sleepy," she replied.

"Hmmm, what of if she poisoned my food, because she's acting like nothing happened earlier and she didn't serve food for herself. The only way to find out is to ask her to eat from my plate. If she refuses, there's every possibility that she poisoned the food, she must have been fed up. And if she did, I'll kill her before I die," Mr Habib thought.

"At least come and eat from my plate, even if it's just two spoons so that you will not sleep on an empty stomach," Mr Habib said gesturing for her to come. Mrs Hannatu wondered, had it been she had actually poisoned his food, she would have fallen victim of her own evil. Proving what the Bible said that anyone who digs a pit will fall into it.

"I really don't want to eat I'm okay and I'm tired and I want to sleep," she stood there for a while, and watched how her husband looked at her with suspicious eyes. "Let me just take one spoon," she said and took a spoon of rice from his plate and ate and swallowed it in front of him then drank water from his cup.

"Thank you very much my hubby, I would have eaten more but I really want to sleep," she said having a comely tired face. She then traipsed to her room knowing that he was watching her.

"Jesus! Jesus! Jesus!" Mrs Hannatu uttered in undertones in the restroom in their bed-room in their two-bedroom flat kneeling down, with tears in her eyes. *"Oh God please forgive me for conceiving and conjuring such a malicious evil in my heart and mind. Lord, I pray you have mercy on me; I have sinned greatly against you. But you are too good oh God, you saved me from my deliberate foolishness, you delivered me from staining my hands with blood,*

taking vengeance, when it is yours to do. Father as it is in your word that you do not want anyone to perish, God please don't let my husband perish, have mercy on him and forgive him for he does not know what he is doing, though he lets the evil one use him. Thank you oh Lord, thank you for saving me; and also for forgiving me for my abominable sin. O my Father, please change the heart of my husband, I really do love him, I sincerely do... Let him come to know you, let him come to love you like his brother, my late husband, let him repent and turn from his evil ways, deliver him from the shackles of the evil one, show him mercy, mercy oh my God, mercy..."

TWENTY FIVE

"I ALMOST killed my husband," Mrs Hannatu said.

"What!" Mrs Adaeze shouted; unconsciously releasing the chilled glass of juice in her hand, it fell and shattered. Fortunately, none of them got hurt.

"What do you mean by you almost killed your husband? How can you say such a thing? What manner of joke is that?" Mrs Adaeze uttered as one of her maids rushed in to see what occurred, then rushed to clean it up.

Mrs Adaeze gestured that Mrs Hannatu follow her to her sitting room. The sitting room was large and well furnished with fine wooden furniture, it had linen curtains, cosy rainbow coloured rug at the centre that left a footprint when stepped on. There was a wooden exotic round centre table covered with glass looking like a mirror.

The sofa, couches and armchair were white and wood-brown in colour; they were sleek, snug and immaculately clean. There was a very big air conditioner at the extreme end of the sitting room which was close to the stairs leading to a dining space. But there was no television in the room and that captured Hannatu's attention. She wondered why but realised she wasn't there to banter.

But Mrs Adaeze perceived what she might be thinking, so she decided to answer her thought. Most people have had the same expression when they saw no TV in a house of this nature. "Well you know, I don't really like to spend my time watching TV, so I moved the TV to my other sitting room, but we're not here to talk about that. Please explain to me what you meant by what you said earlier."

"Ma'am, I don't know how I would explain this to you. You have always been there to encourage me and instruct on what I should do to keep my marriage and win my husband for Christ. You have told me how to do it, what not to do; you told me what to expect, and you told me it would take time to overcome it and that I should be patient. But ma, I grew out of patience." Mrs Hannatu was already tense with emotions with eyes full of tears.

"If out of patience then enter long suffering," Mrs Adaeze retorted softly.

They sat on ivory chairs opposite each other separated by a dark glass rectangular table in the elevated dining room was beside the sitting room. The air coming from the AC in the living room was chilling the tense atmosphere.

"I'm sorry, I just have to be a bit hard on you; if not, if I begin to sympathize with you, you'll be weak. But I feel your pain, I understand what you're going through, it's not an easy task that is before you. Take heart, be strong. But you have not yet explained how and what you mean that you almost killed your beloved husband," Mrs Adaeze said empathetically, relaxing on her snug armless chair to hear what Hannatu had to say.

"Ma God saved me; I cannot stop thanking him, my husband slapped me."

"Why did he slap you?" Mrs Adaeze cut in sitting upright.

"I questioned him. I questioned his authority as the man of the house."

"Ah, you know, you shouldn't have done that, that's like telling him he's dead; it's like tearing his dignity into pieces like a cloth and setting it on fire. Men like to feel on top, to dominate and so on. They have this ego in them even when they don't have *ego* – the Igbo word for money. I know something must have instigated it, please continue."

"I think he wanted to apologize but I'm not sure, I was infuriated, I carried my son to his room then I went to the kitchen to cook for him, because he had literally commanded me to do so, though I was unwilling because I was drowsy."

"So you decided to poison him; right?" Mrs Adaeze cut in.

"Yes ma." Hannatu replied and sighed, sunk into her seat and stared into nothing, tears began to fill her eyes again. "I was about to put the sniper when the food was almost cooked, that's when God brought me back to my senses, I had truly lost it."

"Don't cry, stop punishing yourself, at least you listened and obeyed God. Stop feeling guilty, you didn't kill him, I'm sure God would be proud of you for overcoming such a huge temptation because your husband, from what you've said is like a thorn in your flesh; cheer up God has forgiven you."

"Don't let guilt hunt you, it has no right. You did nothing wrong but something great, we are made stronger each time we overcome a temptation. But apart from that day how has he been? Was he acting better?" Mrs Adaeze asked.

"That was the day he was even more liberal and jovial compared to other days, he was overjoyed by the result of the election. Apart from that day he has been very difficult to live with, and it seems like it gets worse every day. Ma I'm really finding it hard to even be a Christian when I'm at home, sometimes, I feel like exploding," She said as she started crying, putting her hands and head on the table, sobbing.

A tear or two rolled down Mrs Adaeze's face, which she quickly erased, leaving no trace. She didn't want to cry there, it would weaken Hannatu, it would break her down; Hannatu depended on her as the strong one and comforter, not a weakling. If Hannatu saw her cry, it would demoralize her and deteriorate her already pitiable situation. She stood and walked over to where she was sitting.

"Hannatu please stand up, you need to rest, let me take you to a room where you can sleep, I know you're very tired and devastated. You need to rest." Mrs Hannatu obliged, stood up, still crying and Mrs Adaeze took her to one of her several guestrooms so she could catch some sleep. "When you wake up, we'll pray."

TWENTY SIX

"A PRINCE wanted to get married to a peasant, but the king, his father was pissed and disapproved it. The prince still intrepidly went ahead and got married to the lady. The father got riled and out of exasperation he stripped his son the prince of all rights and privileges he had and sent him packing out of the palace. Years later the king died, and the elders decided that the winner of the quest they created would be king of their kingdom. The ex-prince also participated along with other youths and he won the quest and became king."

"Chigozie! Chigozie!" Mrs Okafor hollered, ending the story he was telling his twin brother and Osinachi. He rushed to the room where his mother was. "What do you mean by you don't have cloth to wear to church? And they should buy you new clothes. Who is the they you are referring to?" Mrs Okafor interrogated, putting one hand on her hip and using the other hand to gesticulate.

Her knee was no longer paining her, weeks had passed since the arm-robbery took place but the trauma kept replaying in her head many days after. Sometimes she jerked up from the bed in the night because of nightmare resulting from the robbery. But now it seemed as though nothing happened except someone talked about it and of recent it was a joking matter.

"Mummy my clothes are already old, some are wearing out," Chigozie said.

"That means some have not worn out. Be wearing those ones to Church," his mother said.

"But Mummy those ones that are not worn out are undersized and so I don't like them anymore," Chigozie said crossing his hands at his back, looking around except at his mother.

"Look at me when I'm talking. Is it because you don't like the clothes that you don't want to wear them, eh?"

"Mummy the clothes are not fine and most of them are out-dated."

"Wow, wonders shall never end," Mrs Okafor said clapping her hands as if dusting them. "Wow, so you go to church to show off, to show you have the latest clothes. So as you don't have the latest and finest clothes, you will not go to church?" She asked looking at Chigozie who was now looking at the floor, behaving as if he didn't hear what she said.

"I say look at me when I'm talking to you. Is it not the same amount of clothes that you and your brother have, but he's not complaining, can you see yourself? How many clothes do you need, that you're here making a fuss about the clothes me and your father spent our hard earned money to buy. You don't even need plenty clothes you're a boy, boys can just wear one trouser and be changing their tops or T-shirts."

"But mummy you have more than ten laces. That is, different from other types of cloth that you have."

"So Gozie we have become mates? That we should be having the same amount of clothes, right? Chigozie! We're now age mates?!! You should even have more clothes than me because you want to show-off in church, you're asking for more clothes. I won't stop you from having more clothes, you're free to have them, just use your own money and buy them," Mrs Okafor said, and then continued folding her clothes into a box.

Chibuzor and Osinachi were listening to the whole thing from the sitting room but pretended not to. When Chigozie was approaching where they were, he became somehow delighted with the idea of buying clothes for himself but then realised he had no money. In the first place, he didn't really need permission to buy clothes; money has been the hindrance.

"Chigozie! Come back here," Mrs Okafor called. "Don't use any money to buy any cloth, because all the money you have, comes from either me or your father. Better wear the clothes you have; and I don't want to hear anything about that again. You will tell me whether we're picking money from the floor or plucking it from trees. Your mates are out there working, some are even giving their parents money, and you are here draining our meagre income."

Chigozie was speechless standing there and looking at his mother, not knowing what to say, he turned to leave. "As you're going, go and wash that bitter leaf that's in that big black bowl in the kitchen. Better wash it well," his mother said while trying to zip the box filled with her clothes.

Chigozie's heart sunk, he hated washing bitter leaf especially the ones that were not very fresh, they were harder to wash, and he had to taste every round to know how less bitter it was, he preferred to go to the market to buy foodstuffs than to sit down washing bitter leaf. *"Why did God create such a* thing?" he thought.

"Gozie please come and finish the story," Osinachi pleaded. Chigozie did not even deign to answer; he just walked to the kitchen to squeeze bitterness out of the bitter leaf. He wondered why the bitter leaf couldn't be cut and boiled until it was no longer bitter. In his head he questioned why it must be washed with hands?

A flood of thoughts filled his mind. He wondered why he didn't have money like other people his age; wondered if he wanted to marry, would he marry a person as poor as himself, would a rich girl like Funke look his way, was there hope of getting rich, if so how? Would he continue to live like his family did? They were breathing poverty now; would he have children and struggle to train them as his parents are doing? If not, what was he going to do to change it?

As he kept asking and contemplating in his head, he realised the harder the questions, the harder he washed the bitter leaf. Apparently, he was transferring aggression. But behold, after rinsing the bitter leaf for the first round he discovered to his disgust the bitter leaf was still crassly bitter. His neck seemed to grow longer, his tongue stuck out, he rushed to drink water.

"Is there anything bitterer than this thing?" he asked in his mind, as he walked back feeling groggy. Agitated, he started washing the bitter leaf more violently hearing his brother and his younger sister laughing in the sitting room while his elder sister took his place of storytelling.

She was usually resolute and reserved but could be extremely energetic and dramatic when she was in her mood. They were laughing and cheering, clasping their hands in excitement while he was busy washing the bitter leaf for the *Ofe-olugbo* soup that they were all going to eat from, a soup he wasn't really a fan of.

Chigozie reasoned that his mother had used the work for his sister to punish him for being meshugge. How would he say that he wanted new clothes when there was shortage of food, and they were trying to survive in Abuja, where everyone who lived in other parts of the country think all its inhabitants were enjoying just because they were living in the capital of Nigeria.

Why would he even compare himself to his mother? Saying she had more clothes than him, was it not her money she used to buy the clothes? And out of her money she used to buy the clothes he had. The therapy of punishment after the display of foolishness seemed to work all the time, as if it was planned by his mother so that he would rethink. *"Chigozie, you must make it in this life,"* he said to himself, silently though.

TWENTY SEVEN

"I AM DISAPPOINTED by your insolence and foolishness. How can you tell me, your father that you are ready to make money the fastest possible way? Mindless of whether it is good or not, and you were impudent enough to say you will never die poverty-stricken like me?" Mr Okafor said touching his chest with one hand while holding a mini box he used as a bag to carry files and other documents that were work related with the other.

"But daddy I didn't say you, or poverty-stricken," Chigozie objected, looking down, scared to look at his father in the eye.

"Hmmm, okay, what did you say?" Mr Okafor asked.

"I said I don't want to die always scratching for money, eating from hand to mouth," Chigozie replied fidgeting, editing some words, still looking away from his father's face for fear.

"Explain to me what the difference is in what I said and what you just wasted my time saying with that mouth of yours? You want to show me that you went to school and I didn't eh? Gozie!" His father vociferated. Mr Okafor only called him Gozie mostly when he was pissed with him while his mother called him that mostly when she was happy with him and his siblings.

"No, no, no sir," Chigozie replied. "Daddy, that's not what I meant, I was just trying to explain what I said earlier."

"Hmmm, it's okay, I've heard enough of it, I need to rest, I just came back from work and then this," Mr Okafor said as he turned to go to his room.

"Daddy please wait, I want to tell you something," Chigozie pleaded.

"Tell me what?" his father asked vociferously, getting impatient.

"Emm, emm daddy, even though we do no longer have money like before, we should not be acting like we don't have money."

"Who told you we are acting?" his father cut in and Chigozie was speechless for a while, reasoning it.

"But we can fake it until we make it," Chigozie said as if he just dropped the most brilliant idea at the moment. But too bad, his father was not going to take it.

"Gozie... What's wrong with you this evening? What's this about money? And what do you mean by fake it till you make it, you want us all to be living a fake life, living like we have what we don't have? What if you keep faking it and never make it eh? You'll be a life-hypocrite. I don't know why I'm talking with you, I don't have time for this, after all the work I've gone through today just to put food on the table; your action shows I'm not working hard enough, right?"

"No oo, daddy," Chigozie said.

"No! what? See let me tell you something, getting money by all means will get you into all manner of trouble, I'm not going to discourage you from making money, but I proscribe you from getting it through crooked means. It's a good thing that you want to make money, money is good, money can get you almost anything and take you anywhere but if you don't get the money through good means, what would be your gain? How would you enjoy it? It's just like passing an exam you didn't write or being applauded for something you didn't do, it's empty, nebulously void.

A passage in Proverbs says *"Stolen bread tastes sweet, but it turns to gravel in the mouth"*. I want you to value your name more than money. A stainless reputation should be your utmost priority. Go and read Proverbs thirteen eleven and be wise," his Father said and headed for his room.

Chigozie had read that scripture so many times that he could recite it even if he just woke up from sleep.

"But daddy," Gozie was saying.

"But what?" his father asked. *"I want to do business instead of going to school."* He said in his mind without voicing it out for fear of what his father would say. "But what Gozie? You still want to fake it till you make it?" his father asked in derision.

"Try sleeping this night without eating, in fact no food for you this night, let your stomach give you a preamble of what living a fake life looks like."

"Yes sir!" Chigozie answered and sat in the living room thinking about his life.

"Somebody that has already eaten," Mrs Okafor said as her husband entered the room, then she started peddling her sewing machine, she had been listening to their discussion.

"Hmmm, so he has already eaten; and he answered as if he has not, besides where are the rest of them?" Mr Okafor said as he sat down on his bed removing his shoes.

"They went for Bible study in one of our church branches which is not too far from that *Somto limited Pharmacy* building, you also find a shop owned by a woman who is also a member of the church close by," she said as she was trying to put the red thread into the needle.

"Yeah I know the place, is it not me that told you?"

"You? no oo. Anyway, I can't remember if someone else told me too," she said.

"It's me. So why didn't Chigozie follow them?" Mr Okafor asked as he removed his suit jacket, which was once fitted before but no more.

"That boy has been complaining that he does not have church clothes, and I was not in the mood to contend with him that time and I needed something from the market so I sent him. He has been saying that he's a man that he wants to start work and make his own money since he can't get money from, you know? That boy is something else," Mrs Okafor said and sighed. Mr Okafor sighed too staring at his sunken stomach.

"I'm very sorry, what we're going through is my fault, had it been we had stayed in Abakaliki, we would have been way better off than this. Mr Okafor said, distraught, standing at the back of the seat his wife was sitting on and she burst into laughter.

"Ah Sugarcane, you've started again. Didn't I support and follow you, or was it not you and I that planned to come here. You now want to take the whole blame. Please stop it. Don't worry God will see us through, He never fails. Besides it's not your fault but the fault of your boss, that want to kill you with work and take you away from me, but God will not allow it," she said as she looked up at him, then turned and continued doing what she was doing.

Tears filled his eyes; he said nothing as he walked to the bathroom. *"God what did I do to deserve a caring wife like this?"*

"That woman can dance. Come and see dazzling dance steps," Osinachi delightedly said as they sat in the sitting room. They had just come back from the Church.

"Its true oo, and she's also a prayer machine, she knows how to pray too, like mummy. See the way she was blasting in tongues," Chibuzor said as if he was still watching the woman pray.

"Which woman are you people talking about?" Chigozie asked; interested.

"Can you remember the woman we saw with her good-looking son at the wedding we attended – the wedding between that Hausa guy and Igbo girl?" Chibuzor asked hoping he remembered.

"Is it that woman that was sitting close to us trying to feed her son that was looking Asian with curly hair?" Chigozie asked trying to remember.

"Yes, yes, I think so. Yes she's the one, mummy too knows her, she was calling her Mrs Anna something," Chibuzor said.

"Mummy said her name is Mrs Hannatu," Osinachi said and pursed her lips.

"She's right, oya you guys should come and eat your food. Chigozie has already eaten," their mother said as she was walking towards the kitchen.

"I'm not eating," Amaka said as she stood up from where she was sitting operating her phone, and started walking towards their room.

"I hope you're walking to the kitchen to carry your food and eat? What do you mean by you're not eating? So the food should waste? I wonder how you're even adding weight when you're not eating anything. Better come and eat so you will reduce," Mrs Okafor blurted which made Osinachi and her brothers burst into laughter.

"Mummy, I don't want to eat Eba. I'm full," Amaka said trying to evade further persuasions.

"Ada, please I don't have time to be contending with you, let me not come out later on and see this food here. Osinachi and Chibuzor, what are you waiting for?" their mother asked after doing one or two things in the kitchen before going back to her room.

"Is it that soup that we ate yesterday? Me I did not like it for anything," Osinachi said as she sluggishly walked to the dining room.

"Yes, it's the same soup. If you people don't want to eat, tell me. Mummy has garnished it, and it is sweeter than it was yesterday, in fact it's born again," Chigozie said with enthuse as if he was the one that revamped the soup. Mr Okafor came to the sitting room and sat down waiting for them to serve him his own plate of food. Chigozie became placid when he saw him. In the end Amaka ate only a little of her food so Osinachi helped her devour the remaining.

Later on after their meals, their father, while relaxing in the sitting room, decided to watch news on TV. His children's favourite programme, *"The Johnsons"* was on but he wanted to know what was going on in the country, refusing to be left in the dark.

After watching Channels, he switched over to AIT which was also broadcasting news. Unfortunately, for Mr Okafor the lights went off. Mr Okafor was upset while his children felt justified in their subconscious mind, since they couldn't watch their programme, now nobody could watch anything. Amaka, who was not even paying attention to the television, but was busy with her phone, switched on her phone torch and went to her room. Osinachi located where the lantern was charging and switched it on.

"Well it's good the lights are off, technology has connected people online and disconnected people offline even in a family. You see your sister always with her phone chatting, posting, viewing status and so on," Mr Okafor said and received no reply or acknowledgement from his sons. The twins saw their father's statement was indirectly directed at them, as reasons why they had not been bought or given better phones, having requested earlier, in preparation for school.

"Daddy! When am I going to get my own phone?" Osinachi asked excitedly.

"Didn't you hear what I was saying; besides you can't have a phone now," Mr Okafor said mildly.

"Daddy, why can't I have a phone? Everybody has a phone." Osinachi said with chutzpah.

"Hmmm, you're not of age to have a phone," Mr Okafor retorted.

"Eh, when will I be of age to have a phone?" Osinachi asked, knowing there was no direct answer to that question. Mr Okafor was a bit perplexed not knowing the age that guaranteed, or was specified for a juvenile to have a phone in this fast mutating generation; it was obviously an Android she was requesting for.

"Hmmm... ... Ehen by the time you are able to touch the ceiling you would have been of age to get a phone," Mr Okafor said, feeling that would finally silence her since she was not tall enough to jump and touch the ceiling yet. Chigozie and Chibuzor were just watching what was going on, they had not gotten better Android phones and their younger sister is talking about getting her own, a new phone. They watched her walk towards the dining room thinking she was going to get something from the kitchen so they paid less attention to her.

"Daddy is it only during full moon that they used to tell stories in those days," Chigozie asked.

"Not really, but it's mostly during the full moon that children gather round to meet an elder or an adult to tell them stories, but nowadays all that seem to have vaporized, vanishing into thin air," Mr Okafor said as he cleaned measly dirt from his fingers using the fingers of his other hand with the lantern that was feigning brightness, which was just disconnected from the charger.

"I wish I was born during that time, when life was easy and I wouldn't have to be forced to go to school." Chigozie said.

"Daddy! Seee! I've touched the ceiling!" Osinachi bawled vehemently.

"What?" Mr Okafor exclaimed, while Chigozie and Chibuzor turned to see her at the dining room which was behind the couch they were sitting on. They saw her standing on one of the dining chairs which was now on the dining table. Her hands were stretched touching the ceiling. Mr Okafor couldn't see her from where he was sitting, and was still in disbelief.

"Daddy, she has touched it oo." Chibuzor said while Chigozie's mouth was agape in awe. It wasn't an impossible task but they never thought of her executing it.

"Osinachi, come down from there before you hurt yourself. Chigozie go and help her down," Mr Okafor said looking at his daughter, he was now standing. When she came down her father beckoned on her. She was breathing heavily.

"You're really a smart and sharp girl, I know you have touched the ceiling but what I really meant is that you'll get a phone when you are big enough to handle it and not get encapsulated by it like your sister.

Though your sister got her first good Android phone in her second year in the university, me I got my first Nokia button phone with no torchlight when I was already married to your mother, but for you, since the world is advancing, and you want to know when exactly, not a sine die time you'll get your phone when you're done with secondary school education and have passed your WAEC because I don't want you to be distracted.

But if things have changed and there is urgent need for it, you may get it before then," Mr Okafor said as he carried her and spun a little, then dropped her down. "My Osibaby." Osinachi grinned looking up at her father who was smiling, looking down at her.

"Hmmm, Daddy by the time Osibaby is in JSS three, her mates would be carrying phones bigger than what Amaka is using," Chigozie said.

"Till that time comes," Mr Okafor said, wanting the matter to die down.

"Eh Daddy, you said something like emm sign die, please what is the meaning? I've not heard it before." Osinachi asked and Mr Okafor chuckled.

"So you've not heard of that one before, well it's a good thing you asked. I know your brothers don't know and have no Idea. They don't know that it's by asking questions that people that know, know.

Ask questions like you're a fool who knows nothing and you will become full of knowledge. You guys should crave for knowledge and information, anyone who is not informed is deformed and a deformed person cannot perform therefore the person will underperform in any chosen field," Mr Okafor said looking at his sons. "Sine die simply means unspecified time, or an event that don't have a date. Understand?" Mr Okafor asked turning back to Osinachi.

"Ye... Yes sir," Osinachi said as she walked to sit down on the seat which was facing the dining table, opposite her brothers.

"Emmm, Chigozie, you said you wish you were born in the olden days, in the village just because you don't want to go to school. You think life was easier then and you think money was less stressful to get; I know that is the major reason you're making such a statement.

See; let me tell you what being a man meant in those days especially from our village Afikpo. During those days, boys in their teenage age, some even younger than you, would be carried from their parents when the season of initiation comes.

They couldn't refuse going, it was a must, it was mandatory, parents couldn't do anything about it, most of the men had already gone through the cult-like initiation. Without a boy going through it, he wouldn't be regarded as a man and therefore wouldn't be able to get married, he would be treated like he was a woman"

"*Chineke* mei, wonders shall never end," Chigozie said and laughed.

"The tradition was that strong then but it has stopped or subsided," Mr Okafor continued. "Thanks to Christianity, that that tradition has been abrogated, that Ogo fetish culture is not in vogue like before.

Christianity really brought about civilization all over the world, especially here in Africa. Jesus has really done a lot in our lives; you guys are free and not bound to conform to those things. Jesus has broken the yoke that caused men to fall for such mundane things.

Then during the initiation which lasts for about a month, women and girls were not allowed to go out to do anything, even boys that had not undergone the initiation process were not allowed. Then masquerades would be all over the village. The boys involved wore almost nothing, they just wore something to cover their emm."

"To cover their what?" Osinachi who was keenly listening asked.

"Time for you to sleep has reached, oya go to bed," Mr Okafor said swiftly.

"Ah ah, Daddy you said we should be asking questions," Osinachi objected.

"Yes I know, but it is time for you to sleep, so go to bed," Mr Okafor said in a diplomatic manner, not like a dictator so she would see reason.

"Hmmm; had it been I know, I would have kept quiet. Me, I will not ask questions again oo," Osinachi said, throwing a semi tantrum, dragging her legs as she walked towards their room while her father and brothers watched.

"Okay, come here," Mr Okafor called her. "You've watched *'the god's must be crazy* right?"

"Yes," she replied.

"You see how those men dressed, it was just something like that, and that's how the boys and men were dressing during the initiation and even in the olden days. Understood?"

"Yes sir," she replied.

"Now go and sleep, you have school to attend tomorrow," Mr Okafor said.

"God save you people," Osinachi said to her brothers and laughed as she ran to their room, having gotten what she wanted.

"Daddy, between you and mummy, which of you does Osinachi get her character from?" Chibuzor asked and Chigozie also waited keenly for answers like the question was on his mind too.

"Hmmm, I don't know oo. But it's mostly likely to be from your mother, and I know if you ask her she might say it's from me, so it's ambivalent. So as I was saying, those boys who were of age that were carried for the initiation slept outside throughout that period, masquerades organized the things they do. Anyone found outside during that period was pursued and sometimes flogged. These boys use to eat from the pot, with their..."

"Daddy we use to eat from the pot too, sometimes." Chigozie cut in.

"While the pot is still on fire, with your bare hands?" Mr Okafor asked and Chigozie was silent. "Yam was what they mostly ate, you know yam is regarded as the king of crops in Igbo land. So while it's still boiling in the big pot on fire, fire made from firewood they would start putting their hands inside the boiling water to get the yam. If you're weak or scared, hunger would be the consequence because that was the only food available.

Some crafty and cunny boys will try to snatch the yam as someone is bringing it out of the boiling water, arguing that it was theirs. They did so many rigorous things such as sleep under the open sky in the cold night with mosquitoes.

After the initiation spanning the duration of about a month period, a man now had the license to get married and do other things earlier prohibited. To get married was not an easy task. You had to equip yourself with money because the things one was asked to buy were enormous compared to the demands of nowadays.

The major occupation was farming, some were palm wine tappers, others traders. You'll trek miles to a farm, where you would work from morning till in the night before you trek back home.

Then, when Akpu was still Akpu from the real cassava, when you take it in the morning and with good soup, like oha, Ofeolugbo, Egusi and so on, the energy you will derive from eating it would enable you carry on with your task till evening. Strangely, these days, I don't know whether the cassava they use to make Akpu is fake because by the time you cough or laugh two times the whole thing you have eaten would just vanish away.

"Then men were men. We trek miles to school and still get punished for coming late, because most of the time we have to trek to far away streams to fetch the water we would use to bath and the water our mothers would use to cook, and the tendency to fight to get water was there because everyone was rushing and needed water for something.

Now to fetch water from well that is close by, you people see it as work even fetching water from tap is stressful for you. Now you guys have bus carrying you to and fro and money is even given to you to take to school to buy something to eat even after eating from home, yet you complain that it is small.

You people don't know the value of palm kernel; it was our snack then, a life saver. Then my mates in elementary school what you call primary school now were almost my age mate now. Hmmm you guys are really enjoying now oo, you now use electric bulbs to read, we used hurricane lanterns or candles.

You have fan now that is spinning and fanning you without you doing anything, then you have to fan yourself, well that's happening even now because of inconsistent power supply. There were so many rigorous things we went through that I can't talk about now. There were no phones then, anybody traveling was never monitored until he or she returns. There was no way to know how the person was doing while away from home. During my days, letter writing was introduced so one could communicate with a loved one who has gone to reside in another place. Now, with social media such as WhatsApp, as you're sending the message the person is seeing it and it would even show that the person at the other end is responding to you. Hmmm, you guys are really enjoying. Chigozie do you still wish you were born during that time, because of less work and stress?" Mr Okafor asked in a jocular manner.

"Ah no oo, things are better now," Chigozie said.

"Maybe that's why Solomon in the Bible said in Ecclesiastes that we should not say the olden days are better. But me I wish I was born during the time of Jesus, it would have made sense eh," Chibuzor said enthusiastically.

"Ha, you too? What if you were born during Jesus time and you were born in Africa, or you were a Roman, or from Palestine or any other country that was not Israel. Or what of if you were an Israelite but a Pharisee or among those who supported the crucifixion of Jesus, because you didn't know he was the Messiah... eh? What of if you were Judas? I'm not even ready to start talking or analysing that one now. Just thank God for your life and that you are a Christian," Mr Okafor said as he stood up and walked to his room while Chigozie burst into laughter.

"Your own is even worse than mine," Chigozie said. "Jesus time," He teased.

"How? Just how is it worse than yours?" Chibuzor asked feeling insulted.

"If you died not accepting Jesus then, you would have been damned forever," Chigozie said twitching and tweaking at the idea.

"God forbid!" Chibuzor bawled.

TWENTY EIGHT

"I LIKE THE way you talk to them as if you were their sibling or their elder brother, not like a draconian father, like my father was. I love the sonorous synergy," Mrs Okafor said as she pecked her husband on his cheek and walked to her side of the bed and picked up her Bible to read.

She had just finished sewing her first traditional bride's garb, she wondered what made the bride's mother to entrust her to sew her Ada's traditional wedding wear by just merely telling her after church that she is into sewing. It must be God's doing and maybe the pricing, times were hard.

She was reading Proverbs thirty-one which talks about a virtuous woman. She had obligated herself to finish the book of Proverbs every month while reading other books of the Bible.

"Hmmm, please don't say that, how can you say your father was draconian, and you turned out to be like this; so benevolent. If you turned out to be the way you are because your father was draconian, then I have to be draconian to have our children be like you," Mr Okafor said as he sat at the edge of the bed, expecting a retort. His wife always had the final say, she sniggered then chuckled, and about to talk.

"You must be joking, please don't try it oo. Ah... Just thank God for Jesus in my life; I may not have been as clement as you see me now. Well draconian may not be the right word to use though, but my father was overly pushy; he wanted me to be very ambitious as he was.

He wanted me to be the best at everything, and if I failed there were consequences. Maybe because I was like the only child, my twin brother died when we were still kids while my father disowned my elder sister when she was still in the university because of her relationship with a Yoruba boy.

He had no son so he tried to make me the son he never had. But he pushed too much, I saw everything as competition, I could do anything to win, I mean anything until Jesus delivered me. Sometimes I see those traits in Osinachi, I heard you talking about it. I pray the negative part does not become dominant.

My husband, my only husband please don't be a draconian father, it may bring the best in our children or surely bring the worst in them," Mrs Okafor said and paused for a while waiting for a reply but none came from her husband who was backing her. "Hmmm, it seems like I'm still far behind, I wish I can be a virtuous woman just like the one in Proverbs."

"King Lemuel's mother must have seen you when she was describing a virtuous woman to her son," Mr Okafor cut in. "You're the perfect example of a virtuous woman, an epitome of what she was trying to explain to her son. You're eponymous of virtue."

"What kind of flattering is this? Ah, please stop it oo, you have started again with this your carnal adulation. That's one of your bad attributes - good in some way though. You used it to woo me and I'm glad I fell; but enough of it, don't place me where I'm not."

"By no means dear, the fact is, I'm not saying what is not true. Ice-cream, the Bible says give honour to whom honour is due."

"Jesus said in Matthew, you Capernaum that has been exalted to the heavens will be brought down to hades. You're hoisting me; I don't want to be brought down to hades."

"Holy Ghost fire! God forbid, nothing like that will happen to my wife. Are you not a child of God? Capernaum was a city full of intoxicated sinners. But you are an angel and would not be brought to hades in Jesus name. Please don't say that again. The Bible says life and death lie in the power of the tongue."

"Yes and Jesus said that anyone who exalts himself would be humbled, and the scriptures can never be broken. Yes or no?"

"Hmmm, you're right oo; but you're not the one exalting yourself and you did not complete the verse, Jesus also said anyone who is humble would be exalted. Just like now."

"The Bible also says pride goes before a fall, if I take pride now in what you're saying, falling will be inevitable, besides God detest pride. I don't want to be proud."

"Hmmm, you're correct what you said is very true. You're not virtuous oo, you're not virtuous at all, *sam* sam. At least now I can sleep, I've committed a sin, a heinous crime by telling my wife the truth, an incriminating truth. I'm sorry, I wouldn't do it again," Mr Okafor said discontentedly as he sighed and dressed his part of the bed to sleep.

"Ah ah Sugarcane, don't be angry with me, I am only avoiding being puffed up, pride is one of the seven things God detest the most according to Proverbs, please don't be angry; I'm sorry," Mrs Okafor said waiting for him to respond but he didn't.

She became agitated and couldn't concentrate on what she was reading. "Papa Amaka, talk to me please, I said I'm sorry. I was just, just..." Tears filled her eyes, affecting her voice, she couldn't talk again she turned her concentration to the Bible cleaning her tears and sobbing silently, and still got no reply.

"God please help me to be a virtuous woman and wife, give me the right choice of words." She prayed in her mind as she tried to read the passage in vain because tears blocked her vision.

Mr Okafor who was giving a silent treatment to his wife could not stand her sobbing, lying down, he stood up from the bed and walked to the bathroom, jamming the door behind him. He walked and sat on the closed water cistern. As he sat, he wondered whether what he was doing was necessary or he was just being puerile, why would he leave his wife crying without comforting her.

"Mummy why are you crying, what did Daddy do to you," Chigozie was probing.

"Shut up! And go to bed!" Mrs Okafor commanded; leaving Chigozie astounded. He and his brother had been hearing voices from their parent's room, but were unable to decipher the words. He was confused at the ferocious outburst from his mother.

TWENTY NINE

"WHAT OF if Chigozie has no place to stay when he gets there?" Mr Okafor asked.

"Hmmm, I don't know," Mrs Okafor replied. Tables had turned since the night Mr Okafor seemed to be apathetic to her palpable words. Now as he sat by the dining table, she seemed to be prescribing to him her own doses of partial silent treatment.

Mrs Nwaozioma had been indifferent to him, not taking a stand in any decision making or even taking part in a discussion. There was a night she dozed off almost immediately, when he started narrating how his day at work went. There was a straining contrast between his work at Ebonyi and his work presently in Abuja, though he still had some difficulties back at Ebonyi but it had worsened in Abuja.

He was transferred to Abuja from Ebonyi because his bosses and colleagues were not able to smoothly corner money by inflating budgets, so they could get more money from the government. So they found a way to transfer him, now his present colleagues were determined to break his stand and bend his belief so as to corrupt his Christianity.

There were so called Christians too among them, but Jesus was not their Lord because they would choose what to do and not do for Christ. Money had become a serious challenge for him and his family. He had to sell the family's only car to augment the money he had at hand to pay for his two sons going to school.

"Well, Chigozie would just have to find a place to stay when he gets there— he would have to look for any Christian fellowship student to squat with till he's able to secure his hostel accommodation since the one we can afford is not yet available," Mr Okafor said and got no reply.

"I think Chibuzor's case is settled he was able to get accommodation in the hostel," He said and still got no reply. Mrs Nwaozioma continued doing what she was doing— cooking the food her sons would carry on their journey, it was still very early in the morning.

Mr Okafor now acknowledged that his wife was right when she said she was not a virtuous woman but trying to be, or was it him that removed her virtuousness. He was finding it very hard to cope with her new disposition. He couldn't hold anything against her but her indifference was too tangible to be ignored. He had to do something about it before it got out of hand, because he was now loosing grasp of the problem he had caused.

He thought that with time she would stop— with the notion that time heals, but time was not healing anything, it was rather getting worse, they were no longer together as before, instead they were becoming more distinct as time went on, widening the gap between them.

All their previous differences were ephemeral, they ended like a debacle with no casualties, probably because they were active and poignant disputes but this one seemed to be passive, too passive. Anytime he thought of apologizing or tried to talk about it, pride wouldn't let him thereby the words got stuck in his throat like pap stuffed in the mouth of crying babies. For him, pride was hard for him to swallow, preventing him from uttering any word concerning the matter.

Now he thought of the story of a haughty proud man whose shirt stank but refused to acknowledge it. He even declined a friend's offer of a spare shirt on their way to a birthday party. Now in the party, flies wouldn't let him be. Children sitting not too far from him were laughing profusely, pointing at him because of the flies. But pride still wouldn't let him deign to ask his friend for the spare shirt even though it was as good as the one he was wearing.

Mr Okafor decided not to fall prey to pride knowing fully well that pride goes before a fall. He thought about Solomon and all the women he garnered, he reasoned that Solomon must have been so adroit in crafting sophisticated rhymes and words to be able to woo them or was it his money?

But Solomon had wisdom first and ostensibly used it to sweep women off their feet. Being the wisest and one of the richest of all time, he had a record no living mortal has been able to break--- seven hundred wives and three hundred concubines at his disposal.

Mr Okafor couldn't even think of attempting to compare himself because he loved his wife that's all he knew and needed to get her back.

"What would I do?" He kept asking himself.

Mrs Nwaozioma dropped two take away plates of rice on the dining table and walked briskly to her room. Mr Okafor who was sitting at the dining room watched his wife walk away, the same beautiful girl he couldn't get his mind off, after seeing her for the first time more than two decades ago. He remembered how she playfully played hard to get, and decided he had to introduce the tactics he used to make her say yes.

He trailed her to the room while thinking and praying in his mind what to tell her. He met her sitting on the bed picking up her Bible to read.

"Hello... Hello..." Mr Okafor stuttered as he entered the room, leaving the door behind him half-closed.

"Hmmm, Hi," Mrs Nwaozioma replied placidly as she glanced up at him and turned her attention back to her Bible, flipping through the pages.

"Please can we talk?" Mr Okafor asked as he dragged a wooden chair to her front, sitting opposite her. The wooden chair she usually sat on while sewing.

"Talk? ... Like right now? As you can see I want to read my Bible."

"Ah, but you read your Bible when you woke up this morning."

"Can't we talk after I have finished reading?"

"Please Ice-cream, I've been postponing this talk; I'm sorry for intruding into your time but I need you to forgive me. Please," Mr Okafor said as he moved the chair closer to the bed.

"Hmmm, you want me to forgive you for intruding?" Mrs Nwaozioma asked.

"No not for intruding, well sorry for that but I need you to forgive me, I really don't know what to call it but I need my Nwaozioma back."

"I'm no longer a child," Mrs Nwaozioma said brazen-faced, hoping that daunted him, but it sounded like a taunt. Her name Nwaozioma meant *'Child of good news.'* She knew what he meant and she knew she would capitulate if she left him to keep talking; he seemed to have overcome the hardest part: trying to talk about the issue. She was already tired of what she had been doing and was ready to succumb but she wanted to see how far he would go.

"My *Obi* uto, my delight..." Mr Okafor continued, ignoring what she said; knowing fully well that flogging the matter would shatter the bridge he had started building. "You know, you are the salt of my life, you give my life sublime taste, my oasis, your smile quenches my thirst. Your candour dentition is whiter than the tip of an iceberg and your lips look so succulent like fruit salad choked with pineapple and watermelon.

If I was Shakespeare, I would write a library of poems for you. If I was Michael Jackson, I wouldn't stop dancing until I see you smile. If I was lecrae, I would rap for you. You scent like lavender so lovely and endearing. You're so irresistible, like a plate of pounded yam and Egusi soup to a weary hungry labourer. My love, you have the keys to the door of my heart, the password to my soul, after God it's you ..."

"What about our children?" Mrs Nwaozioma cut in.

"It's you I married and it's you I'll spend the rest of my life with. My Asampete, you have cheated age, you seem to grow younger every day. God must have been sophisticated with superfluous joy when He was done creating you."

Mrs Okafor did her best to ignore him, trying to read her Bible, whose words she was finding hard to align, and when she eventually did, lights went off and the room grew dark. She could hear their children scurrying as the sound from the spinning fan reduced— they were obviously getting prepared for their journey, the day was dawning and it dawned on her that they had to get prepared too, but her husband wasn't done talking.

"You're my oxygen, the air I breathe. Please don't avoid me so I can stay alive just to behold your immaculate face," Mr Okafor said wistfully.

"Please it's okay oo," Mrs Okafor said as she brought down her legs from the bed and stretched to open the curtain covering the window behind her to let in some rays of light in. She was backing him trying hard to hide her blushed face. "This your flattering is too much, I'm now finding it hard to stop smiling. Please can you stop?" Mrs Okafor said trying not to blush further.

"My Ice-cream, I'll stop when you forgive me."

"Forgive you for? I'm not holding any grudge against you."

"Then why have you been acting up and being so indifferent, these past weeks?"

"To please you; you seemed not to like me talking a lot, because you didn't even reply me when I was trying to talk to you. So I held my tongue," Mrs Okafor said, knowing fully well that was not the whole truth, but she didn't want to be repulsive now.

"*Eze* nwayi, my queen we've been married for years now, have I ever complained that you talk too much, besides you don't. Why would you think such, eh? Omalicha."

"I really wanted to discuss with you that night but you were silent, so I decided to get back at you. I'm so sorry; I need your forgiveness too," she confessed as she dropped her Bible and stood up to hug her husband.

"May God forgive us both," Mr Okafor said as he spread his arms to hug her.

"Daddy we are ready oo," Chigozie said entering the room.

THIRTY

CHIBUZOR WAS still in Kogi when he received a text message from his brother to inform him that he had already reached Minna, the city where his school was located. Chibuzor was sitting at the penultimate row, close to the window of the bus he was travelling on. Peace Mass Transit Company seemed to be one of the best most widely used means of transportation in the country especially from the North to the East and vice versa.

Before they took off from their departure terminal, a pastor preached and prayed in the bus--- a tradition at Peace Mass Transit Company. The passengers were receptive to the pastor's preaching including Chibuzor as they sang along when the pastor led choruses. The pastor alighted from the bus when he was done while they were still at Abuja. The bus had been moving smoothly with no issue.

Chibuzor, skimming through the passengers in the bus, had noticed two teenagers like himself; a boy and a girl, who he suspected were students, busy chatting. The boy would say something and the girl would giggle like she was tickled; it had been going on for a while.

The woman beside them seemed irked by their lackadaisical behaviour but feigned a nonchalant deportment, which she was doing a bad job at. He heard the boy say something that made him remember his journey to Enugu the previous year when he and his twin travel together to the state's university to write their post UTME.

They were accompanied by their Father who resented the idea of accompanying them. But being cajoled by their mother, to follow them, he eventually capitulated. She wouldn't have her only sons make such a journey all by themselves at that age to a place they haven't been before.

Mr Okafor's reluctance was due, according to him, to the fact that they were already men and could fend for themselves and they could start getting ready for the University through this type of experience but their mother wouldn't have any of such.

Chibuzor had put the Enugu State University as first choice and the one at Minna as second while his brother Chigozie did the reverse. Now, they both got admission to their first choice schools.

The three of them arrived at the school on a Sunday night. They came on Sunday so they would be in the school early enough and head back home immediately they were done writing the exam. But they started hearing rumours from some of the students that were still in school that the post UTME would be postponed because of a Salah public holiday they had no idea of.

Chigozie and Chibuzor had come with just one extra shirt, which they planned to wear on the day of the exam. After meeting up with some of the students in the boy's hostel, one of the boys offered them a room of some students who were not in school at Nsoo. It turned out the students were so hospitable.

On the Monday morning after they were done preparing for the exam, they went to the library where the exam centre was located; after a long time of waiting with few other people— they were informed that the exam had been postponed till Friday because of a Salah public holiday they didn't hear of implying they wait four more days.

 Chigozie and Chibuzor had no option than to keep using the same clothes they put on while making the journey in order to preserve the extra shirt for the day they would write the exam.

To them, it was adventurous--- an experience they would never forget. They had their baths in the small hostel bathroom, after fetching water from the tap. They had to go downstairs to join a long line to fetch water from the tap in the boy's hostel which they would then carry upstairs to bath and use for other things.

Now the bus Chibuzor was in was leaving Kogi towards Enugu. They had been in traffic for about thirty minutes with little or no movement. He began to wish he got admission in his brother's school which was by far, closer to Abuja than Enugu. Enugu was over four hundred kilometres from Abuja while Minna was less than two hundred kilometres from Abuja.

But he was overjoyed with the fact that he would be free to do whatever he wished and would be answerable to no one in school. The closest person who could follow him up was one of his aunties, his father's sister; but she lived far from the school.

Chibuzor didn't want to be too reserved like he was back home— in school; he wanted to be more sociable and jovial, even sometimes loquacious like his brother and also have lots of friends. He was planning to live life to the fullest.

The traffic situation eventually improved as the got less congested. A dark plump woman probably of the Yoruba tribe who was sitting at the front seat with the driver screamed "Jesu Olorun!" and almost all the passengers turned towards her, wondering why she shouted.

The driver was busy saying; *"I talk am! I talk am, chai! I know say that man go cause accident, see the way him been dey drive."* A black car on top speed wanting to overtake the bus that Chibuzor was in had entered the lane for the oncoming vehicles overtaking three vehicles.

As the black car was overtaking the fourth vehicle in front of Chibuzor's bus, before the car could get back to the lane a big bus which was on the oncoming path of the road obstructed it. The driver of the black car trying to avoid the big bus drove out of the road with great celerity. Losing its balance, it somersaulted and drifted upside down into the bush by the side of the road.

Several cars stopped to check for survivors in the car, the driver of the bus that Chibuzor was in, kept on driving and lamenting. Chibuzor's heart started beating heavily. He had never seen an accident so up-close before.

THIRTY ONE

CHIGOZIE, WHO was already in Minna, was in a tricycle, locally called Keke as he headed towards the school. The sun was blazing hot like white liquid metal, capable of liquidating flower petals, radiating like gamma rays and letting only dryness reign.

The Passengers clothes were almost completely drenched in sweat. Even the breeze was hot, making the atmosphere tensed up. Five people were in the Keke including Chigozie; three were at the back while Chigozie sat with the Keke driver at the front.

The Keke driver was busy moving to the beat of the song playing on his phone that was so loud, obviously China-made, he was busy mumbling lyrics he could not sing. It seemed like the driver had just finished smoking before carrying them.

Chigozie was sitting beside him discomforted and irritated by the song and the exuding smell of smoke from the driver, wondering how someone could smoke cigarettes under such a hot sun. *"For what exactly?"* he thought.

It seemed like the sun in Minna was different from the one back home at Abuja. While he was still wondering; he saw two small energetic dark boys, one topless the other on singlet run past a dark woman who was busy sweeping the front of her shop; as they were sprinting, one of them trying to avoid a bike that was on-coming ran into a girl hawking cold pure water, the whole tray of cold sachet water dropped to the ground, and the girl looked like she would drop dead. Chigozie could not see what happened next because the Keke accelerated further away from the scene.

Two of the three people sitting at the back seat were boys who looked like students too, having their loads and baggage in the Keke with them. The third person was a fat dark woman who was backing her baby that was probably asleep under her hijab. She was also holding a market bag, nobody could be certain if she was going to or coming back from the market.

The boy who was sitting at the edge of the left side of the Keke was putting on a white cap and backing a faded black bag, wearing native attire and an overused dusty black canvas was busy with a used iPhone.

He was so captivated using the phone that it appeared he was trying to show it off, while the other boy who was sitting at the middle and was better dressed was trying to mind his own business, but the other boy was trying to start a conversation. He was loquacious, making obvious statements and asking questions that had obvious answers.

Chigozie who was at times loquacious was taciturn now, trying to get used to the environment while the talkative boy hardly let anyone finish a statement before jumping in.

"Stop me for there," the fat dark woman said to the driver as she pointed to a spot by the side of the road ahead. But the driver didn't hear so Chigozie nudged him a little to get his attention.

"I wan remove me from za motto?" the driver shouted.

"No... No!" Chigozie stammered, wondering why the he would say such.

"I say make you stop me for there," the woman reiterated. The loquacious boy burst into laughter, watching what was happening.

"Guy, why are you laughing? What's funny?" The boy sitting in the middle asked.

"You no see wetin dey sup?" The other boy retorted. The boy sitting in the middle hissed and shook his head, not knowing what to do to silence him. The Keke rider had reached the spot the woman had pointed at, and stopped for the woman to come down, when she came down she gave him fifty naira, the driver refused to collect arguing that the money was not complete, the woman was saying that she didn't reach where she would have to pay the complete money.

The argument continued, they both started speaking Hausa and exchanging words probably insults. They kept arguing and the woman's baby woke up and started crying under the big hijab that also clad her feet touching the ground.

Chigozie had quickly moved to the back seat when the Keke stopped, escaping the odour he had been enduring. The boy in the middle trying to settle the matter wanted to pay for the woman, but the driver refused insisting that the woman must pay with her money.

Chigozie and the other boy, understanding the situation got infuriated and started shouting at the Keke driver to leave the woman and continue driving, the man refused. The Keke driver more agitated, flared up and came down from the Keke, telling them to follow suit.

"Oga it has not reach like that na," Chigozie and the boy in the middle started pleading. As they were pleading the woman walked away.

"Shet! Why *are you guys begging* him, is he the only Keke rider? *Abeg lets leave him, ee be like say him brain dey touch."* The loquacious boy said as he came down from the Keke and brought down his load.

"Na me I dey insult? I dey craze?" The driver said pressing his index finger to the side of his own head. He was short, so he was looking up to the loquacious boy who was taller. The boy laughed and carried his load to the side of the road to wait for another Keke, the other two came down and joined him. The Keke driver entered his Keke and zoomed off.

"Ah ah, I think say you go enter am, why you no fight with am?" Chigozie said as he reached where the boy was standing.

"Why I go fight with am, na beat I go beat am. But If I touch am, he fit faint for here and I no want this Hausa people problem this afternoon," He replied as he removed his was white cap, smoothed his hair and put it back on.

"Me ma sef, I thought you would fight oo, thank God you did not fight, all of us would have entered trouble. This is the first time I'm seeing a Keke driver behaving like this," The boy who was sitting at the middle said.

"That's how all of them are," Chigozie said. He had taken all northerners as the same, having the same language, behaviour and religion. He was scared at first to apply to any school in the north because of the news of Boko haram and terrorism going on in the north, but his brother and he had planned to apply for schools the way they did.

The story about the Nigerian civil war fuelled the fears and disdain he had for the north and northerners though his father had tried to quell it. He also took them to be foolish and incapable of being understandable, to analyse situations objectively, or even being considerate. He labelled them "intransigent bigots" there was no room for compromise or tolerance even among themselves and anyone who faulted was like a rebel to them and needed to be silenced.

He had heard that some Muslim youths killed a youth like them who was not fasting during their annual fasting. He had also witnessed what happened during one of their Friday prayers; they had blocked the road which they normally do anytime they were about to pray and it was within a commercial area to avoid disruptions and movement— a woman who's destination was within the enclosed area explained to their security personnel that where she was going to was within and she could not follow another road which they advised her to. Running late, she decided to get in either way, since they refused to ken her situation, as she attempted doing that, a young man withstood her carrying her up and pushing her back, this was a grown up woman, possibly a mother.

"All of them are not like that oo," The other better dressed boy said emphatically.

"The guy didn't even collect money," Chigozie stated. The three of them kept standing waiting for another Keke to board. Later on Chigozie found out that the name of the loquacious boy was Abiodun and the other boy's name was Joel.

THIRTY TWO

"FUNKE! FUNKE!" Mr Adefarasin shouted his daughter's name as he sat at the balcony of his room staring at his German shepherd and his wife's white haired Chihuahua playing. He remembered when they bought them; they were sworn enemies always ready to rip each other apart even while they were still puppies. Now they were play-fighting for a big bone.

The beagle they had bought for their daughter died as it was run-over by a car, the sight was traumatizing for Funke, she never requested for another dog or any pet at all after the incident, besides she hated cats probably because of the mystic stories behind them. Mr Adefarasin after waiting for a while and receiving no reply, stood up to call Funke. But as he stepped out of his room he saw Stellar dusting some furniture, he then told her to call his daughter for him.

Stellar rushed to Funke's room to call her, she found her busy listening and dancing to music on her headphone. She stood by the door hollering and waving her hand to catch Funke's attention but it was in vain, so she walked in to call her.

"Funke! Funke! Funke!" Stellar hollered till she touched her, which made Funke jerk away as if scared.

"Whoa! ... You startled me" Funke exclaimed.

"I'm sorry, your father sent me to call you, right away and your mother said I should tell you not to forget to do what she told you to do, before she left."

"Alright, I've heard you," Funke said placing back the headphone on her ears, and continued dancing.

"But your father..." Stellar was saying when Funke cut in waving her hands to acknowledge that she knew what she was about to say and that she would do so. So Stellar walked back to her Boss's room and told him that Funke would be with him shortly. So Mr Adefarasin settled down on a brown armchair in his room that was close to the balcony to wait for her.

Five minutes passed and she was not still there, piqued he went to her room. The door was half open when he came and he saw his daughter dancing, facing her window, backing him, her room was upside down, completely scattered.

"Funke! Funke!" he shouted, seeing she couldn't hear him, he walked towards her. But before he reached where she was standing, she turned.

"Hey daddy!" she exclaimed removing her pink and blue headphone.

"Didn't Stellar tell you that I was calling you?" Mr Adefarasin said in an angry tone.

"Ye ... Ye ... Yes ... I was coming, I just," Funke stuttered.

"You just what? For more than five minutes you're still coming, eh?"

"I'm sorry daddy, I'm very sorry."

"Just take a look at your room, so messed up. Everything is where it is not supposed to be except for your bed because you cannot move it. In fact give me that earpiece," Mr Ade said and Funke knew fully well what her father meant but she brought her earpiece that was on her bed to give him.

"Why are you giving me this? Give me the big one, this one hanging on your neck."

"Daddy nau... Pleeeese, I wouldn't delay next time when you're calling me and I'll arrange my room right away," Funke pleaded. Her room was usually arranged by the maids and her father knew that, but he had warned her not to be scattering her room and waiting for a maid to come and arrange.

"I know; that's why I want to collect this big earpiece now so that you will hear me when I'm calling you next time; so hand it over."

"Ah, daddy it's a headphone, not an earpiece. Earpiece is that small one I wanted to give you," Funke said as she reluctantly handed over the headphone.

"Ehen ... So the name is headphone, thank you for correcting me. Now this headphone is going to stay longer with me so that I will know the name," her father said as he pulled it out of her grasp.

"Daddy please ... what will I be using to listen to music?"

"Ask me again, by the way what kind of music are you listening to?" he asked her as he brought the headphone closer to his ear. "When did you start listening and dancing to unholy music, this kind of secular music? Since when did this Satan glorification start?" Mr Ade thundered and his daughter shuddered.

She had not seen her father this infuriated towards her before. She wondered if something was bothering him and he was now transferring aggression or her messed-up room and delay to answer him had started the fire he was now breathing.

"Daddy they are just normal songs, they are not glorifying Satan or anything," Funke replied.

"What's normal about this song? What is normal about *'shake that body, shake what your mama gave you'* in this song?"

"It's just a motivational song, encouraging people to dance and not be depressed."

"Are you depressed?"

"No, but ..."

"But what? Don't you know there are Christian songs of all genres, even rap for youngsters like you, who are always intoxicated with inexhaustible energy? You said that this song doesn't glorify Satan, who then is it glorifying?"

"I just know it's not glorifying the devil. It's a motivational ..."

"Motivating you to do what? To serve who? See let me tell you something, if you're not serving God you are serving the devil either directly or indirectly. There's no middle ground, it is either you're in or out, in darkness or in the light, black or white no greys. Just as it's impossible for a rat to give birth to an elephant, so it is impossible to serve Jesus and the devil.

I know in your mind you'll be thinking of songs we all sing that doesn't necessarily glorify God like our national anthem, nursery rhymes and some other songs like that, see it would be poignantly incorrect for me to tell you that you should not sing any song that doesn't have God or Jesus in it besides there are some soiled squalid songs that God is mentioned in— or to tell you not to sing any song that is not gospel, because there are various good songs that are not necessarily gospel.

You have a conscience, if you listen to a song and you hear things in it that are contrary to God— that is against the teachings of Jesus Christ, please I beg you don't feed yourself with such songs, songs that motivate you to do nonsense, like aphrodisiac or amorous songs. I would not always be there to tell you this, it depends on you. You can decide to do or not to do. Your heart and mind are there to judge you. Are you hearing me?!"

"Yes ... Sir," Funke slowly answered.

"Now for the reason I was calling you; don't you want to further your education? You are not getting any younger Funke. A whole year has passed since you graduated from secondary school and you have been at home doing nothing."

"Ah ... Daddy I've been writing a book that can be published."

"That is not my point, what I'm trying to say is that you have to be in the university this year. You wrote post UTME in that school in Minna, wouldn't you check if you got admission?"

"Ah, Daddy na, I said that I don't want to go to a federal university. I want to go to a private university like Covenant University; it's one of the best Universities in Nigeria and it's even a pastor that owns it--- Bishop Oyedepo."

"I know, but do you have any idea of how expensive that school is?" Mr Ade asked.

"But Daddy we have the money, it's not so big compared to what we have."

"Wait first... Who is the "we" you are referring to? I'm the one that has the money not you. Don't forget that, and it's not because of the money that I don't want you to go to that school. I went to a federal school, and there were a lot of things I learnt there that I want you to learn and experience, which I know you wouldn't experience in a private school. So you have to go to a federal school.

"My only daughter is not going to any federal school. She can't, in fact she won't," Mrs Bolanle cuts in, as she walked into the room sweating.

"She can and she will and on this matter you are not going to have the final say," Mr Ade retorted.

"Ah, ah, is that so," Mrs Bolanle sniggered. "So you are trying to tell me that my daughter, my only daughter should go to a common federal school, school meant for mere plebeians. See Adekunle, your mates, people in the same class with you and even lower class, are sending their children abroad; outside the shores of Nigeria and Africa as a whole to study. But you, I don't know what is your problem, you too like suffering, is enjoyment too hard and difficult for you?" Mrs Bolanle said as if bewildered.

"Why do you talk to me like this, like I irritate you? What ..."

"Yes ... You most of the time disgust me, your method of reasoning is unreasonable."

"Ah ... Iya mi, please don't talk to Daddy like that," Funke said sympathetically.

"Olorun ... See this small girl of yesterday, you that I used to bath and wear pampers. You have now grown with wings to instruct me on how I should and should not talk abi? Funke! We're now age mates; that you can now talk to me anyhow."

"If you like be disgusted combined with irritation, what I said still stands, Funke is going to go to a federal university. My word is final," Mr Ade said authoritatively and walked out of the room to his room.

"Jesus! Did I commit a crime to marry this man, a man that prefers poverty to wealth, and to be wretched than affluent. Funke! Why is your father like this?" Mrs Bolanle said turning to her daughter and putting her hands forward as if to collect something from her. "Eh? Funke why?"

"Mammy, you're overreacting, daddy has his reasons for saying so, though I don't want it, but I have no option. Daddy is the one paying the fees so he makes the laws."

"Funke... Keeki baby you know I love you, you're my only daughter. But next time me and your father are talking don't put your small mouth inside our big conversation especially when you're supporting your father. Are you hearing me?"

"Yes ma, I'll try my best not to."

"Try ke, try ni. You'll do as I say. See me here trying to help your life and you're here, telling me you'll try. Come and give Mummy a hug.

THIRTY THREE

HABIB HAD pervaded her mind; Hannatu could not concentrate on her work anymore. Her husband had been coming home very late for the past few weeks. Some of her bad and also her well-meaning neighbours had mentioned that they've been seeing her husband with a nubile woman obviously younger than her.

When she heard these reports the first few times she neglected it. She did not believe it or she refused to believe it but she had a lot of doubts about her husband's integrity, and her neighbours were grooming it.

She started having nightmares, imagining things, creating pictures in her head of her future with her husband and how the future of her son would be like if all she heard were truly true. She decided that it was better to put an end to issue before gets the worse.

"Emu! ..." Mrs Hannatu called her sales girl. After waiting for a while and getting no reply, she stood up from behind the counter which was close to the exit door. Only a paltry number of customers had come to her grocery store that day.

Some of them had come and gone without buying anything, some came picking different things and bargaining for each commodity, trying to beat down the price and ended up not buying anything.

The day was running out, it was now dusk. Mrs Hannatu wanted to go home early so she decided to tell her employee Emu, that she was leaving. It was a Tuesday, a day dedicated for Bible study in her Church. But she did not plan on going because she was frustrated and tired, mostly from over thinking.

She opened the door to leave her shop and saw people on the street, every passer-by was a potential customer, she smiled and greeted a group of ladies passing her grocery store, and they responded and kept walking; unhappy she walked to her cloth shop— on reaching the door she saw her sales girl Emu snoring loudly.

She remembered what Emu's sister had told her some time ago when she accompanied Emu to the shop. She had said; "My sister is either walking and talking or sleeping and snoring, the fact is that her mouth is always open." Which proved to be very true, Emu was loquacious but very good at her job she used her mouth to bring customers and make them patronize her Madam, Mrs Hannatu.

"Emu!" Mrs Hannatu called. Emu jerked up from where she was sleeping and stood up.

"That material is five thousand naira but last price na four eight, if you no fit afford am buy the other one that is three five; na the last price be that, I no fit remove anything from that one, my madam go sack me ..." Emu babbled all this, loud enough for Mrs Hannatu to hear. She was busy cleaning her eyes as she sat down, gabbling other things her Madam couldn't decipher.

"Hmmm, her sister didn't tell me she sleep walks and talks too," Mrs Hannatu mumbled. "Emu! Wake up."

"Ewo ... Madam, I'm sorry I slept off," Emu said as she stood up abruptly.

"Hmmm, you're sleeping on duty. What if a customer comes in, and seeing you sleeping leaves the shop. Please don't sleep during work hours. Are you hearing me?"

"Yes ma." She replied.

"But you've been doing a good job, keep it up, don't stop now. You are still looking like you want to sleep," Mrs Hannatu stated.

"I'm very sorry Ma; I wasn't able to sleep last night. My Father is distraught with me, he quarrelled, making statements like "how would he spend years spending money to train me in school only for me to end up a sales girl." He was really sad, and I can understand with him.

I don't want to be a liability but an asset to my family but I seem to be more of a liability than an asset." Emu said with apparent sad tone staring at the floor, full of tears in her eyes, but she quickly cleaned her eyes and started smiling trying to belie her true feelings. "So I was up almost throughout the night thinking about my life," she said and Mrs Hannatu felt pity for her, but didn't know what to do.

"So you are a graduate, what did you study in school?" Mrs Hannatu asked inquisitively, she knew she was a graduate but had not given it much thought. She was now wondering why a graduate would be a sales girl.

"I studied microbiology in school, although I actually applied to study medicine so I could be a doctor, but was denied it, though my score was above the cut off mark, and in school I saw other students who I did way better than studying medicine.

I didn't sit for JAMB immediately I finished school because the resources were not available to send me to school, so my parents told me to wait till the next year. The following year, I sat for JAMB, but didn't get admission though I passed; so I had to wait for another year and that was when I was offered Microbiology, I couldn't forfeit it because I was way behind my mates," Emu explained as if she was lifting a burden off her chest.

Mrs Hannatu stood looking at her understanding what she was saying because she had heard stories like that before but had not seen a victim of such circumstance.

"But what did you graduate with?" Mrs Hannatu asked to find meaning to her current situation.

"Hmmm Ma, unfortunately I graduated with a first class."

"Wow, you graduated with a first class? But why did you say unfortunately. Is first class not supposed to be a good thing?"

"Yeah. Yes Ma, it's supposed to be, but it's more like a cursed blessing; because there are virtually no companies or firms that employ microbiologist in Nigeria, research firms here are so few, I don't even know the few. So I had to look for jobs at other places. Some tell me I'm overqualified, while others..." She said in a slow low tone.

"Some bosses wanted me to offer my body; which I can't. I haven't been able to get a job mostly because I don't know anybody that knows somebody that know somebody that can help me. I have no connections," Emu said, surprised at how she poured out everything about herself to someone she did not really know. "I'm sorry ma for plaguing you with my personal problems."

"It is okay, I wish there's a way I could help you but I don't have that kind of connection either. You are really good at business and commerce, why don't you delve into the market and do business; you're really good at it. You've really made a substantial contribution to the stability and progress of this business. You are way better than my previous employees.

Besides how did you become so good at marketing?"

"Well ma, it started in school, I used to buy and sell things because I needed the money to pay for some necessities. So I had to market them whether sun or rain, my parents were not rich and are still not, so I had to help myself."

"See Emu, the Nigerian government doesn't appreciate people of value but people that know people that know people in high places. The elite keep getting lit with money and the poor keep descending in indigence sometimes with celerity.

See my advice to you is that you don't wait for the perfect job whether government or private. You can start something on your own, mostly on what you are naturally good at, use your marketing ability. I truly like you here, I know I shouldn't be telling you this but I have to; you'll do way better on your own than working for somebody. I'll be here to support you in any way I can when you want to start something," Mrs Hannatu said.

"Ha... Ma, Thank you so much. Thank you for your advice and your willingness to support me. I really do appreciate," Emu said with joy.

"It's really the least I can do to help you. Please lock up this shop and stay at the grocery store; I'm leaving now. I'm feeling lethargic right now; please don't forget to lock the grocery store when you're going," Mrs Hannatu said rubbing her forehead thinking of how she would drive home in her listlessness.

"Yes ma, I won't forget," Emu replied as she stood up to lock up the shop.

THIRTY FOUR

ON REACHING home, Mrs Hannatu discovered that the door to their house was still locked. Her husband was supposed to be home before her. His closing time was an hour or two earlier. But she ignored it, maybe it was because she came back home early. Then she realized her son would still be at her neighbour's house.

The neighbour also had children going to the same school as her son, so it was arranged that her son would stay at their house until Mr Habib her husband came home. Mrs Hannatu rushed to their house to carry her son, and as suspected he was still there; she thanked them and also apologized for the delay.

When they got home she arranged the house, cooked dinner, fed her son, helped him with his assignments and tucked him in bed after they had taken dinner. Mrs Hannatu after taking her bath, remembered one of her friends that lived in Yola, Adamawa State that had told her that Yola was so hot that you could be bathing and still be sweating and she had heard that states like Bornu were even hotter. She thought her friend's statement was an exaggeration but now it seemed possible.

"Have you heard the story of David and Goliath?"

"Yes!" Joseph shouted. *"They have tell us the tory in church, plenty time."*

"Hmmm, what about the tory of Jonah?" she said 'tory' mimicking her son.

"Yes... big fish sallow missonari Jonah," Joseph said as he cleaned the beaded sweat from his forehead with the back of his hand.

Mrs Hannatu chuckled; she had not seen Jonah as a missionary before. Then wondered which Bible story she would tell her brilliant son that he had not already heard of.

"Hmmm, I doubt he knows it," she thought out loud. "Do you know who Othneil is?"

"No, who is hotnel?" Joseph asked inquisitively sitting up on the bed and his mother chuckled.

"Ha, I guessed as much. His name is Othneil. This is how the story goes; after God finished plaguing Egypt. You know Egypt right?" He nodded.

"Where Joseph…" As he mentioned the name he blushed because it was his name. "…the dreamer who moved from prison to palace and turn from slave to saviour of the Egyptians and the whole world."

"Yes that's right my son, your teachers are doing well and you're learning fast," she said and smiled.

"So after God harassed and humbled the Egyptians with plagues through Moses showing them that He's God, making a spectacle of Pharaoh even though he was not bespectacled, by sealing the marriage of no divorce of Pharaoh and foolishness. Pharaoh pursued the Israelites to recapture them after initially letting them go."

Mrs Hannatu paused for a while realizing she uttered words she doubted he knew but he seemed to understand and was anticipating what happened next in the story. *"Well if he doesn't hear such words, how would he learn?"* She thought.

"The Lord God Almighty, Yeshua Hamashiach, blasted the red sea, the breath from His nostrils parted it," *"Figuratively,"* she said in her mind while dramatizing and gesticulating like she was narrating a story that she witnessed.

As she did that she remembered a black American pastor she had watched on television, T.D something, she couldn't remember the complete name— the way the pastor was sweating profusely like she was now, with evident exhilarating passion, and after every statement of note, the keyboardist would hit a note, it was so melodramatic, but the words spoken really gave thrills.

"The sea parted to the left and to the right. The ground was probably dry like the land in Sahara desert under a midday sun, because they did not have difficulty walking by. The water on each side stood like glass walls, no shark or wicked fish was able to come out to bite anybody.

So the Israelites may have seen fishes swimming, eating taking their bath and so on," Joseph laughed hysterically, probably imagining just how. His mother laughed too and continued. She wanted to make the story as epic as possible so that he wouldn't forget it, not that he had forgotten any before though.

"The children of Israel left the sea unscathed and the Egyptians entered unscathed too, I mean without wounds. God in his unfathomable wisdom fooled the fool and his gallant *"follow follow"* soldiers— into the middle of the sea. Probably, as they were still running, the water in front of them grew tired of standing and with God's permission and Moses' obedience collapsed in front of them.

Pharaoh looking towards Moses and God's people, the Israelites from afar, begging and shouting for mercy forgetting he himself was merciless. The waters at the back and middle fell too and met each other again drowning the wicked Egyptians in it, as Moses stretched out his hand over the sea."

"Mummy what about Othneil, did he survive," Joseph asked and she chuckled.

"I think Othneil was yet to be born, but his uncle Caleb must have been there with Joshua the successor of Moses. Well the Bible didn't say exactly that Othneil was Caleb's nephew. It said something like Othneil the son of Kenaz the younger brother of Caleb," Mrs Hannatu speedily dashed to her room to her Bible to confirm. She didn't want to tell her son the wrong thing, because things children hear for the first time when they're small usually stuck like engraving into the surface of a rock.

"The same blood running through Caleb also manifested in Othneil," she continued when she came back to the room after confirming. "But we've not reached there yet, I want you to get the background story. The Israelites started their Journey to the Promised Land which would've taken them about forty days, eventually it took forty years because of their unbelief.

Moses met God and God gave him the Ten Commandments. God fed the children of Israel with Angel's food that is Manna in the wilderness, God also commanded a kind of bird I think "quail" not to fly so high so the Israelites could catch them and eat. God made bitter water sweet through Moses. God led them with clouds by day and a pillar of fire by night.

The children of Israel saw all these wonderful miracles first-hand, not hear-say. God even made the walls of Jericho that were very high probably as high as six big giraffes filing up, standing on each other's head. You know giraffe right?"

"Yes, that long neck animal," Joseph replied.

"Exactly, the wall was also wide enough to house houses. God made the walls of Jericho to fall down without the Israelites touching it; it fell down flat before them like a slave falls down before his king."

Joseph was listening with keen interest; eyes wide open with all his attention on his mother. "Before then Caleb, Othneil's uncle was chosen from the tribe of Judah where David and our Lord Jesus Christ came from, to spy out the land of Canaan with Joshua and other men from the other tribes.

When they came back only Joshua and Caleb were confident in saying that if God delights in them He would give them the land and the giants that they fear would become like bread to them. But the other ten gave a negative report saying that they were like grasshoppers to the inhabitants of the land.

So the Israelites feared, for this reason God did not let anyone of them who were twenty years old and above to enter the Promised Land, because they didn't believe in God after all the miracles he displayed before their eyes.

Do you know something Joseph? We're the same as the Israelites anytime we doubt God. We see him perform miracles every day," Mrs Hannatu talked to her son like he was an adult, and as if she was also talking to herself.

"For every breath we take we indirectly express miracles, and even when we don't deserve it God serves us big portions of blessings. Joshua fought a lot of battles with Caleb at his side, Joshua ordered the sun to stand still, and not to move an inch towards setting until he and his warriors have defeated the enemy. Othneil's uncle Caleb at the age of eighty said he was still strong enough to go to war."

"Wow!" Joseph exclaimed, baffled.

"Yeah, wow. So finally, Joshua and Caleb and the Israelites who were less than twenty entered the Promised Land that God promised Abraham over four hundred years ago. Joshua died, Caleb as well, and that generation passed away and a new one came, who did not know the Lord.

They sinned against the Lord their God; not repenting after countless warning. God who knowing the end from the beginning didn't let them completely destroy the nations around Canaan so that he might test the Israelites to know if they would obey and keep his commandments.

As expected they didn't. Just like us, when we are blessed by God, we most times forget Him and do our thing, transgressing His precepts, we let the devil in. God uses things like that to make us come back to our senses to turn away from our evil ways and sometimes we do and sometimes we don't.

"The children of Israel sinned against God, by serving other gods. So God let them fall into the hands of a pagan king. They were slaves to him. Othneil when he was a boy must have listened to stories from his uncle Caleb how God parted the Red Sea, fed them in the barren wilderness and did so many other miracles.

The Israelites began to cry out to God to have mercy on them, they had been serving a heathen king for eight long-cruel years, and God so great in mercy heard their prayers. Othneil summoned the courage he didn't have before, because the spirit of God came upon him.

Filled with the spirit of God, he began to show unusual courage. Othneil rebelled against the evil king. So Othneil delivered the Israelites from the hands of the wicked king. Othneil the saviour of Israel judged the people of Israel, and there was peace in the land until his death. That's the end of the story. Now you can sleep."

"Momma please tell me another one."

"You have school tomorrow, you have to sleep."

"Good night momma."

"Good night my son," Mrs Hannatu said to Joseph who was now looking sleepy. She pecked his forehead and left the room switching off the light.

It was passed eight and her husband was not yet home. Mrs Hannatu was getting agitated; she was wondering why her husband had not yet come back home; she had tried to call him but his number was not connecting.

She had called one of his co-workers to find out if her husband was still at work, wondering why her husband would still be at work by that time anyway. His colleague informed her that they had closed since and that he was already at home, saying that her husband even left the office before him.

Fears of her husband's safety crept into her mind.

"Habib, where are you? Why are you not home yet? God please protect my husband; let him not fall into the hands of the evil one. What of if he had an accident? Oh no, no, no. Hannatu remove that thought from your mind. God please bring my husband back safely. Oh God please I can't lose another husband, my son can't lose a father again.

What if he was kidnapped? I don't have millions to pay. What if he got into a fight? What if he got murdered?" Mrs Hannatu shut her eyes, holding her head tightly with her hands, as if to remove the incessant unpleasant thoughts from her head. But it was like squeezing a dry cloth to remove water; her efforts were not yielding results.

She was now insecure, acting paranoid. Then she heard a sharp rapid knock on her door, she jerked out of fear, breathing heavily as if she had just finished running a marathon, when she calmed down she rushed to the door instinctively to know who it was. On reaching the front door only to see nobody, then she heard someone talk, the voice came from below. It was her neighbour's son, a small energetic boy, shorter than his age.

"My Mummy say that I should give you Joe's lunch-box." The small boy said as he stretched his hand to offer her the lunch box. The boy was her neighbour's son, at whose house Joseph stayed.

"Thank you very much Daniel, tell your mother thank you," Mrs Hannatu said. The boy was about to leave when she called him back and gave him biscuits that she rushed to get from her kitchen.

"My Mummy will beat me," said the Daniel.

"Why?"

"She say I should not collect food from strangers."

"Am I a stranger? Ok just take the biscuit when you go home, give your mother and tell her it's from me."

The boy took the two packs of biscuits and ran towards his home. Later on Mrs Hannatu heard the boy crying. She guessed his mother beat him because he ate one of the two biscuits before entering their house, she watched him sprint to his house and he spent a lot of time outside the house before entering. She couldn't really see him eat it because it was dark but she suspected so.

"Hmmm children. We can only caution them when we see them or find out what they've done, we can't know the things they do when nobody's there. God help us, God please help me guard and guide my child," Mrs Hannatu thought and then prayed in her mind as she sat down and put on the television to distract herself from over-thinking about her husband and child.

While she was still browsing through the channels on the TV to see what she would watch, the lights went off. Distraught and tired she just lay down on the chair and dozed off.

Kon! Kon! Kon! Mrs Hannatu jerked up from the sofa, standing up alarmed, as if slapped from her sleep to reality. She was trying to see clearly when she heard a voice.

"Come open this door!" Someone shouted from outside probably the same person that knocked so loudly on the door. Mrs Hannatu quickly tightened her almost loose wrapper and strained to look at the clock hanging on the wall in their siting room and discovered it was passed eleven o'clock. She walked circumspectly almost tip-toeing towards the door.

"Please who are you?" She asked because she did not recognize the person's voice.

"I say open the door!! I don't need to be interrogated to enter my own house," the person replied. As she heard *'My Own house'* she recognized the voice, realizing it was her husband she opened the door quickly; she also realized the door wasn't even locked and wondered why he didn't just enter.

On seeing him, he looked impossible. His trouser was dirty and sagging off, his shirt was so rumpled, as if someone chewed it, half buttoned, even some buttons missing, and he was smiling weirdly, he smelled like cocktail of beer. When he opened his mouth she almost became high. *"He must have been smoking, but he doesn't usually smoke,"* Mrs Hannatu thought. Her

Husband looked like Lil Wayne having a veisalgia.

"My love," He said and staggered towards her trying to kiss her. She moved away and closed the door behind him and locked it. She was exasperated yet placated that he was safe, such a bipolar feeling. She turned and looked at him as he used the armrest chair to wedge himself. He looked like he had been thrown out of the bar where he must have been drinking.

"You stupid and wicked man, I'll kill you myself. How can you leave me and your child to starve at home while you went out clubbing and spending all the money on beer?" A woman shouted from the television which was on *African Magic Epic* Channel.

"Habib, what's going on? Where have you been? I've been worried about you, What happened?" Mrs Hannatu asked with pacified panic in her tone.

"Can't you see? I've been having fun, and we're *gonna* have some fun this night," Mr Habib said smiling like a klutz.

"Habib... You promised me you would stop drinking before we got married... Now you're completely drowned in drunkenness. You need to take your bath and sleep and rest your head," Mrs Hannatu said calmly, remembering all the promises he made to her before they got married. Then the scripture came to her head again *'Do not be unequally yoked with an unbeliever.'*

"Let's have fun, just you and me honey all night long," Mr Habib said smiling waving his hand up and down like a child asking for sweet. He then raised his hands up and started twisting his waist whilst trying to find balance.

She sighed heavily shaking her head. *"Oh God what have I gotten myself into?"* She said in her head then she walked passed him to their room. He tried to touch her as she passed but she shoved him off and he laughed as if he had just seen or heard something very funny.

She entered their room, unknown to her that her husband was following her. She bent by the edge of the bed to pick up her phone, and he grabbed her from behind. On turning to see, Habib pushed her down on the bed, trying to raise her wrapper up, he forced himself on her.

Hannatu face down, struggled to free herself, screaming while he was pressing her down. In her restless writhing she hit him with her elbow by the side of his head. He fell off her and rolled to the ground from the bed. She stood up hurriedly tying her wrapper well; she stood beside him hoping she had not killed him because he didn't move. He suddenly raised his hand beckoning her with it while smiling.

"Oh baby... Come to me... Come to papa." He said nodding his head as if dancing to a beat; he had probably heard the statement from a song from the bar. He looked like someone in a delirium with lucid hallucinations.

Tears filled her eyes, and gently rolled down her pale cheeks. She tightened her wrapper and hurried out of the room to her son's room which was opposite theirs. She locked the door behind her, with thoughts in her head. *My husband almost raped me. But is it rape? He's my husband. But it still is.*

THIRTY FIVE

"TO PIQUE Pique is a waste of time he takes pique in his skills," said Wole, one of Chigozie's roommate, leaving Chigozie in a conundrum, because he had just finished talking about how much he knew about football and how he cleared his English WAEC papers, getting an *A1* which was really rare, especially for a science student.

"Do you know that his wife is Shakira, the one that sang zaminamina ei ei waka waka ei...e... ei?" Chigozie said to swerve from Wole's statement like a lawyer giving finesse, as he took another spoon from the pot of hot, *cut and join* jollof rice nicknamed *concussion rice.*

"Ehen nau, maybe that's part of why he's so pique, I mean full of himself," Wole said to elucidate what he meant.

"See something, reason the song, as if she know Minna, she said Minna Minna, waka waka," Chigozie said.

"True, as if she's telling Minna waka," Wole said and both of them laughed.

Just then one of their roommates rushed in who had an acrid stench, which was poignantly acerbic like spoilt egg mixed with sour milk. He rushed to the bathroom without saying a word, though Wole and Chigozie tried to inquire.

The smelling roommate Abiodun Sowore who they now called Sabio because he talked too much and used to claim to know everything was followed by his friend Zadok into the house who was laughing profusely.

He was the one that explained to them that Abiodun was mistakenly poured beans water by one of the indigenes of the place and that he was already sweating from trekking under the scorching Sun when that happened. This Abiodun is the same loquacious boy Chigozie met in the Keke the day he was coming to school.

"Abeg I go chop oo?" Zadok said as he sat down on their stacked mattress while Chigozie and Wole were sitting on the white-tiled floor. The apartment they were in was like a self-contain that had a small kitchen and restroom in a compound having other flats filled with students mostly first year students.

The sun was blazing hot resulting to severe heat as usual. Wole was sweating, though shirtless, he was wearing a pair of shorts and eating opposite Chigozie who was hanging his already drenched shirt on his shoulder.

"Enter the kitchen and carry spoon, but don't touch anything there oo," Wole said to Zadok who was watching them eat."

"Ah! so there's no water and you guys did not tell me," Sabio shouted as he came out of the restroom wearing only boxers.

"You suppose to know na, over sabi sabi," Chigozie said sarcastically. The other two shouted *'Sabio!'* and started clapping and laughing.

"You guys should not finish that rice oo. It's my pot you guys are using," Sabio said.

"Oga go and bath, don't you know you smell? Your stench can change the taste of this food," Zadok said coming out of the kitchen after taking the spoon. Chigozie burst into laughter while Wole was silent, he was the one that cooked the food and it was actually tasteless, but food eaten when hungry always taste sweet.

"How do you want me to bath without water?" Sabio asked derisively.

"Tor stay like that. But enter the toilet your body odour is pervading this room," Wole said without looking at him.

A very slim, tall fair guy walked into the room hanging his one hand bag across his shoulder. He was a two-hundred level student called Akachukwu, but Chigozie usually called him Omekagu meaning behaving or doing like a lion because of the way he saw him pray, during one prayer and deliverance service at Christian Student Fellowship (CSF).

Chigozie, Abiodun and Joel the boy that was in the Keke with them— met Akachukwu when they were at the post office; a kind of cybercafé hub for the school, mostly used by first and final year students during the registrations exercise.

Akachukwu with other CSF members were there to invite new students to the fellowship. That was how Chigozie and Abiodun started squatting in his room waiting for the old hostel to be available but Joel had already paid for accommodation in the new hostel that was about eighty thousand naira, far more expensive compared to the old hostel.

The student that was staying with Akachukwu had moved to the new hostel, so he was the only one in the room.

During the first week of Chigozie's arrival to school he had been walking up and down like other students from one office to another looking for either his level adviser, Dean, H.O.D or one lecturer to direct him to another lecturer.

From pillar to post, he trekked under the hot sun. He and Abiodun had trekked to the school clinic to get their medical record only to find out that each department had their own day when they would be attended to.

Distraught because he needed it to complete his registration to be finally done, before going to the senate building to get his school I.D card, all this was stalled because the day he went to the Clinic was not the day for his department.

Lectures had started but lecturers were still doing introduction lectures, nothing serious had started but he had been hearing news of how people failed the previous year despite their seriousness.

"But this thing doesn't make sense oo," Wole said.

"What?" Zadok asked as he was using his spoon to scratch the burnt part of the rice that was glued to the bottom of the pot.

"Somebody will pay to write JAMB, pay to write WAEC, you will still pay to see your result. I can't really complain about that one, but the fact that when you write post UTME and get admission, how will they still tell us to pay acceptance fee, that is we would pay for them giving us admission after we passed the exam we paid for.

It doesn't make sense; had it been the money for the acceptance fee is small there would have not been problem but the acceptance fee is more than sixty thousand naira. If you calculate how many students they admitted, times that amount, the money would be in millions, yet ordinary school gate they cannot revamp.

Why am I even calling it school gate something that looks like door to a dog cage," Wole said and all of them burst into laughter.

"Dog cage door, haba guy that is ridiculous, but welcome to Nigeria, a lot of things don't make sense here in our country," Chigozie said after laughing to satisfaction.

"Like this rice. It's only pepper I'm tasting," Zadok said taunting Wole, Chigozie burst into laughter again, Sabio didn't know whether to laugh or not because he was hungry and the food was almost finished.

Wole didn't take the joke lightly; he stood up without saying anything, took his shirt and walked out of the room.

"The way you talk eh, it's like you're hungry for slap. The rice doesn't make sense, yet you're scratching the pot and eating like chicken that has been starving for many days." Sabio said still distraught that he didn't eat. "Oya Zadok, you may now go to your apartment. You've eaten my night food, therefore, you owe me lunch tomorrow."

"If you see Wole, better apologize oo; you've made him to lock up, before he talks again, hmmm maybe Jesus would have come back," Sabio said loud enough so Zadok would hear him.

"Ah ah, you did not see any other thing to use as an analogy, there's no logic in what you said, that's over exaggerating," Chigozie said as he carried the pot to wash.

"Jesus is coming soon right? But before Wole would talk to him again, it would not be soon, it will be a long time. The last time I teasingly made a joke of that small tribal mark on his face, that's how my guy just lock up, *Wole no talk to me for almost two weeks.* Two!" Sabio said adjusting his now dried boxers.

"I've been trying to hold it since, Abiodun *abi* Sabio why does your body smell like this?" Akachukwu asked squeezing his face in disgust as he dropped his bag.

He was just a victim of circumstance.

Now to your unwarranted exaggeration; if you use to read your Bible you would understand that it's not a lie or something to make a joke about; of how long it has taken for Jesus to come back when the Bible said He's coming soon.

It is recorded in the Bible that a day to us would be like a thousand years to God and a thousand years to us will be like just a day to God. Jesus died and rose again over two thousand years ago. In the light of that scripture, it may just be like two days to God.

So don't be saying or joking about what you don't know," Chigozie said. He had recently read second Peter chapter three.

"Hmmm, that's right but you're talking like you don't believe it," Akachukwu said and got no reply. "Well you guys are just starting; there are many things in this school that will not make sense, especially in your academics.

You guys should better start preparing for your e-test, so many people failed last year. Read like there's nothing like prayer and pray like you've not read anything," Akachukwu said, sorting out the clothes he wanted to change to, he was just coming back from a lecture. "Why didn't you guys come for the prayer service yesterday?"

"Me, I was already tired, after trekking up and down for registration. Sometimes those photocopy people at that post office will just make you to print things that are not needed so they can make more money, I even forgot about the meeting," Chigozie said as he lay down. He actually remembered, but he was tired and he didn't like prayer meetings.

"Wallahi even me too I forgot," Sabio said as he carried their white bucket to go fetch water after putting on his half damp jeans trouser. The tap was close to the first apartment closest to the gate. The apartment was made up of three separate bedroom flats like theirs, owned by different tenants which were mostly students.

There were three Apartments like this in the lodge. The Apartments were in rows adjacent to each other. The students named it 'Wakander lodge' deduced from a Marvel movie of a Black Superhero named *Black Panther*.

"Tomorrow is Wednesday; you guys should better come for Bible study," Akachukwu said as he was changing his clothes.

"I will try," Chigozie said stretching himself on the mattress. It was already getting dark and there was no light.

"By God's grace," Sabio said as he left the room only to see Wole running towards him.

"You guys should come and watch fight oo! They're fighting where they're fetching water," Chigozie jerked up from the mattress.

He liked anything that was energy-related. He heard what Wole said and followed them running to go and see. Akachukwu remained in the room. By the time the three of them reached there, a large number of people had gathered, some trying to allay the issue others trying to aggravate it.

Chigozie reaching there and seeing no fight but berserk noise accentuated what his father had told him and his brother before: that the length of a snake seen by one person is not as long as the stick the person compares the snake to when telling others.

It was dark and Chigozie couldn't really pick the faces of the people contending for the space to fetch water. Just then lights were restored which was a rare happening off Campus— compared with inside the school where lights really goes off.

In a matter of seconds everyone dispersed, light made fiends friends just like watching the world cup made adversaries amigos. Chigozie was baffled.

THIRTY SIX

THE NEXT day, Chigozie and Sabio were trekking from their lodge to school. From their lodge to the school gate was more than a kilometre, while the distance from the school gate to their faculty buildings was nothing less than three kilometres. It was still early in the morning; they had just passed the school gate.

Wole was not having lectures till later in the afternoon while Akachukwu had already boarded a bike to school. As they were trekking Chigozie remembered the first day he had lectures, he woke up early in the morning and put on his best wear as if going for an interview.

That day he climbed a bike because the money was available, and it was his first day, he couldn't be trekking, so he thought. But in school he still had to trek, walking up and down with other students to finish their registration.

From that time on he hadn't worn that attire especially the shoe except he had nothing else to wear. Now his dress was so casual, he was putting on a normal polo collarless shirt, blue jean trousers, black socks to prevent dust and an aging slipshod. He has been using it since he was at home because it was still usable, he couldn't get a new one.

His fashion sense had changed. He saw people with impeccable immaculate raiment that made him wonder if it was the same school they were attending, if they were using the same road, under the same sun or if they even had any challenge at all.

Display of wealth was also real and evident. *"But people say there is no money in this country,"* He thought. Now he was trekking with Sabio who was busy listening to music via his earpiece and trying to sing out its lyrics. By now, the sun was rising, warming up to start tormenting everyone, especially those trekking.

It was such a long line of trekkers, students were walking behind them and some in front, some in groups and others alone, most walking as fast as they can, only a few were slow.

"Sabio add leg, let's walk fast we're getting late," Chigozie said as he picked

up speed.

"You calm down na, Gozie where are you rushing to?" Sabio asked, but when he received no reply from Chigozie he walked faster.

Chigozie was thinking of how he would upgrade, from his penury situation, when he remembered a story his father told him about a man who was complaining about his life, to a pastor, saying he wanted to throw in the towel because he was completely frustrated.

The man had a car and the pastor told him that they should go on a ride and go to the slowest lane on the road. The pastor told the man not to speed, and kept telling him to reduce his speed, until they were moving painstakingly slow.

The man told the pastor he couldn't move any slower, then the pastor made known to him that at his slowest velocity he was still faster than some cars on the road. Then the pastor said no matter how horrible and terribly frustrating your situation might be, you're still way better than so many people, and people could trade anything to be in your position.

So cheer up he told the man. Chigozie questioned that there are so many ahead of the man as well why should he compare himself with those behind him when he could compare himself with those ahead of him and be better off.

Chigozie was always nursing the idea of showing off especially to the people who had taken him for granted because of his almost indigent status. What hurt him most was that some girls treated him like that too, it pissed him off. His antithesis happened to be what most girls posit, he thought good looks and intelligence was what really mattered but now found out money answers all things. He was determined to make money and command respect.

When his money was running out, the friends he thought he would trek back home with, would take Keke and wave him good bye; it was ridiculing. From then he's set of friends changed mostly to the rickety, both in money and brains. But what could he do to change it, he had no other source of income apart from what he got from home, he knew what his parents were passing through to get money just to send him and his brother to school.

But why would he come to school just to suffer when he could have just started business at home, he reasoned that if all the money that his parents had been using to pay his school fees since secondary school were used to set up a business for him, their family would not be in the state they were in, they would have been eating the fruit of the investment. Education was really a long time investment that may even end up not yielding good fruits. *"Business was* philoprogenitive," He thought.

"Nnamdi... Nnamdi... *You are not Azikiwe oo, no dey do pass yourself, you could land yourself inside serious trouble! Trouble dey sleep Nyanga go wake am,"* A student shouted, talking to his friend or course mate in the congested class. The class was packed full of students. There was no space vacant in the big auditorium; there were students on the stairs, desks, windows, even on the rostrum where the board was, close to the exit door. Students were standing everywhere.

The heat in the hall was terrible. Two or more students were sharing a seat, almost all the students of all the departments in that faculty, of the same level, were present because the lecture they were about to have was MAT III. It was a general course having three unit credit load, everyone had to pass the course. It would morbidly affect anyone's CGPA if failed.

The place was choked up even before time and the lecturer wasn't present yet. Students were all talking, some making gesticulating others were laughing surreptitiously, some superfluously. The noise in the class was incomprehensible; there was so much energy, probably because over ninety per cent of the students were having such freedom for the first time. Some were now showing their true colours, some concealing it, some were ostensibly naively wide-eyed.

"Abeg, forget that thing. I can do it, let them pay me well, I go run am," The supposed Nnamdi replied. They were sitting on the next row from the back where Chigozie was sitting. Suddenly there was a great hush in the auditorium. It was so silent that someone could hear a dead person breathe.

The MAT III lecturer had entered the hall and had already sent two unruly urchins as he called them out of the class. The sending out of the two unfortunate unruly urchins had drawn everyone's attention, no one else wanted to be sent out.

It was the third week already, since the resumption and they had not received any lecture. The lecture was aborted the first week, the second week they waited for the lecturer till the lecture period was over. The lecturer who was casually dressed stood without saying anything.

"How would he wear that kind of palm slippers on the podium to lecture us," a student whispered to his mate sitting beside him. The person refused to reply, but the other student kept whispering.

"Guy please keep quiet ..." the silent one replied.

"Hey! You! Stand up from there and get out of my class!" The lecturer growled pointing at the student who was trying to hush the whisperer. The boy tried to protest that he was not the one talking. The whisperer was silent like he didn't know what was happening.

"So you're still sitting down there, give me your Matric Number, it's like you want to see me next year," the lecturer said. The boy had to stand up and leave the class, meandering through students that were sitting on the stairs that led up to where he was sitting.

The lecturer watched the boy walked out with his face as rigid as a hardened stone. His expression changed as the boy left, like he was a different person. He sniggered maliciously and started talking.

"My name is Alhaji Usman Abdullahi, everybody knows me in this faculty. Go and ask your level advisers, your Deans and H.O.Ds they all know me. If you're ready to pass you will pass but if you want to misbehave I'll help you to miss B and A and you will not see C but you will see me again next year, by that time when you're serious you can get D for door or E for exit, so you can leave this class with your serious Juniors, if not, you will keep seeing me till you graduate, some carry overs from last year and last two years are still here.

If you were here last year wave your hand." No one did and he laughed. "I know they will not wave, because it is a thing of shame, you have yourself to blame if you follow in the same footsteps.

I know most, if not all of you watch football or have watched football. You see, that the referee in any game has the final say; he is like God on that pitch, what he says stands. The same thing here, do as I say or face the consequences," The lecturer kept talking and talking before he came to what they had to do for that day.

"We are going to be starting with *Set*, then *mapping and function*, then later on we'll do Binomial, *partial* fraction, *quadratic equation* and so on," the lecturer said.

Immediately the lecture was over and the lecturer left the class, students scattered like cockroaches when light is switched on at night on the surface of a sink of unwashed plates in an unkempt kitchen. They scampered to the next hall where they would be having their next lecture.

They were all rushing so that they would get a seat to sit, especially those who stood up throughout the MATiii class. Only for them to reach the hall for their next lecture which was opposite the current hall to see that other students were still having lectures in the class. They all stood at the entrance of the lecture hall waiting.

Some students were already negotiating with other students seated in front to keep their seat for them. Chigozie was busy trying to maintain his position close to the door, only to see Sabio already in the class.

Sabio was in a different department from Chigozie but the same faculty. Sabio had climbed upstairs and sneaked into the class through the back door while the lecturer was still lecturing, just to secure a seat. Nobody wanted to sit on the stairs or stand.

There was still jostling and balancing among the students outside, and the lecturer inside came and warned them to be silent, while he was backing the class and shouting at the students at the door, more students who were at the back entrance upstairs slipped into the class.

Chigozie decided to go upstairs to the back, leaving his position that was very close to the entrance. On his way upstairs to the back, the lecturer ended his lecture, and forced his way through the throng of students who were trying to enter the class. Chigozie on his way up, came down so as to follow the front door, because students had already crowded the way leading upstairs.

On reaching down, the students in the class were also struggling to come out making the movement rather too slow. Students, as soon as they entered darted for seats, some students got a seat for themselves and kept seats for other students probably friends that were still outside, this brought some minor arguments between them and other students. Chigozie at the entrance was calling Sabio to keep a seat for him. Sabio didn't even see him; he was busy laughing watching the drama that was going on.

One girl threw her bag on a seat before reaching the seat and a boy already there was about to take the same seat, the boy removed her bag and sat down. When the girl arrived at the seat, she questioned him but before he could answer she rained insults on him.

He stood up in a state of discomfiture, perplexed not knowing how to manage the situation; he just walked away, while the girl was still talking. Watching him walk away she said *"You for wait make I change am for you, nonsense, see as you short like kelvin hart younger brother."* Then she hissed loudly and turned to her friend by her side who was already sited and started laughing.

THIRTY SEVEN

"... You look like a tired tyre
Begging to retire
Your tummy is so plummy
Yet you look so hungry
Should I call you a glutton?
Or you're okay with fluffy gallon
You call yourself king of rhymes
That's too sad
Cuz your rhymes are so bad
Like parallel Fs in a report card....."

"Wow!" The surrounding crowd exclaimed, clapping and chattering including Chibuzor who was drawn downstairs to the hostel's common room by the noise he was hearing from his bunk on the hostel's first floor. Two people engaged in a game called Parody, a verbal melee.

The game was basically about two people jousting, aspersing each other using rhyming words and statements; it was more or less like a rap battle but slower. So the winner was whoever dropped the most devastating punch-line leaving the opponent speechless for a period of time without retorting.

"See who is... talking
You're an example of big for... nothing
Trying so hard to be good at... something
But you can't be good at... anything
Your parents sent you here to... study
God knows they wasted their... money
Cuz your brain is so supine and... lazy
Probably at the state of ... atrophy
Failure and you are ... synonyms
You mediocre... dummy

Take this... dictionary (the person speaking said mockingly trying to give him a book he just grabbed from a student)

And check the blatant... meaning (the other person shrugged)
Oh, I'm so sorry
You can't read, cry baby
But I hope you can descry royalty
So you can see
Who's the real king
The main Obi
In this rhyming industry
You were spitting trash
About my rhymes
And you have no cash
Compared to mine
You're a candid sordid trash
Full can of squalid ash
You dirty sash
Please don't cry
When your crush becomes mine
Cuz by the time
I'm done with you
No doctor could treat you
Victor, you're analogous to defeat
When last did you eat?
Constant failure has made you thin
Slim like Spaghetti ... ."

And the whole place got rowdy, students started shouting, some were hailing him, shouting K.O.R! ... K.O.R! Meaning king of rhymes; his opponent Victor was dumbfounded, the noise from the crowd seemed to lock his mouth.

Obinna, the apparent winner, full of pride, paced around with his right fist up with his belly protruding, taunting Victor who was speechless. After Obinna was declared the winner by the MC, the students began to disperse, as twilight approached. Chibuzor had watched with amazement, he didn't really like the insulting but enjoyed the play on words.

Some girls were inside the boy's hostel as well at the ground floor by the common room which was close to the entrance. Chibuzor wanted to participate in word fisticuff, which was conducted by one four-hundred level student named Kelechi--- known mostly as KC the MC by students.

He was well known; mostly because he was the usual MC for most parties, and was the director of socials when he was in three-hundred level. He was both famous and infamous mostly because of the scores of girls he had as girlfriends, and girls still kept falling for him like every floor he shared with them was slippery, he was tall handsome and intelligent.

He wasn't the best in his class but was more like the benchmark for excellent students. He captained his class soccer team from hundred level till three-hundred level when he became director of socials. He stopped being captain because it affected his results negatively, dropping from over 4. to around 3.6. He was in the same Computer Science Department with Chibuzor.

The Parody was held almost every Saturday. The winners usually collected a certain amount of money. For a student to participate in the word fisticuff they had to register, it was more or less like a tournament. Chibuzor was captivated by the idea of spitting rhyming words, manipulating sentences, shooting punch-lines, in a competitive setting.

The opportunity of being like his brother, to show off and make a name; caring less about the price for fame. The end justifies the means had become his new motto. Walking back to his room upstairs he caught the gaze of a girl that he had perceived to have been staring at him in the common room during the contest.

She abruptly shifted her gaze when his eyes caught hers, she then called her friend who was busy talking to Chibuzor's roommate Ifeanyi, signalling that they should leave probably to their hostel. When she looked his direction he quickly turned and picked up pace heading upstairs. She too, walked briskly towards the exit, leaving her friend who was giving farewells to Ifeanyi.

As Chibuzor climbed the stairs he cogitated on the girl's appearance. The girl was a bit tall and fair; she was pert and fitly endowed. Her hair was short, the top part was partially desert-dust coloured, it was oily and curly, almost frizzy. He wondered if she dyed it because it looked like it was recently barbed though it seemed natural.

Her deportment since he noticed her was loudly tacit, that it looked like she feigned her composure. Her equanimity faded briefly when Obinna finished lambasting defeated Victor, when there was a lot of cheering and the ambience was *boisterous.*

"Hmmm, what a girl; what level and department would she be in?" Chibuzor thought as he evaded jamming a student who was busy chatting on his phone while walking.

It was getting dark and his room was a little bit hot. He could hear the noise mosquitos made audibly and felt their remorseless stings on his exposed skin as he lay down on his iron bunk, twisting and turning, waving away what he could not see, clueless of what to do next.

He had a reverie of the tall, short-haired girl, he wondered why he couldn't get his mind off her; she wasn't the most beautiful girl he'd seen at Enugu. Beautiful Igbo girls were everywhere, of all classes and ages and types: big, small, tall, short, fat, slim, sleek. None had caught his attention like this girl. He patiently waited for Ifeanyi to come back to bombard him with some questions.

They were five in his room though one of them, a four-hundred level student Chidi, scarcely slept in the room because he had a place off campus; the remaining three were, Ifeanyi who was in two-hundred, Alex a three-hundred level student and Chima a hundred level student like him.

Only Alex was in the room with Chibuzor, he was busy reading with his phone torch, he had been reading since the second week of their resumption and they were in their third week by this time. He read like he was having test the next week.

Chibuzor did not see any reason to start reading anything when most of his classes were cancelled during the first week and the classes that held were just introductory classes. There was nothing salient enough to read.

Alex was taciturn, he's physique seemed diametric to his disposition. He was well built with his hair very full; Chibuzor had tried inciting an exciting discussion with him but to no avail. He even behaved platonic and looked like a devout catholic. Chibuzor wondered why so many Igbos were Catholics and why he could hardly see Catholics from other tribes like Yorubas and Hausas; maybe it was because he was in the east, he thought.

Hunger began to set in to make him uncomfortable in addition to the menace of mosquitos. He had not eaten anything since the hundred naira Okpa and garri he drank that afternoon. He had not been able to cook mostly because his gas was exhausted and he did not want to beg or even ask any of his roommates for their cylinder, though he had seen them do so among them.

He knew asking would give them license to ask him later, and he was not ready to start sharing gas or any other thing with his roommates yet, he was still getting to know them; he did not want any disruptions on how he had already planned to live.

"How far Alex, were you in the hostel last session?" Chibuzor asked from the top bunk looking down at Alex who was sitting on a wooden stool by the plastic table he was reading on.

"Yes I was," Alex replied placidly. Chibuzor was distraught by the plain answer but was bent on having a conversation, normally it used to be people trying to talk to him and him replying like he had limited words.

Chibuzor wanted to talk with him to distract himself, if not he would be pressed harder by hunger to buy something to eat, and he didn't want that, he had been spending so much lately and when he calculated his remaining money it wasn't enough to serve him till the time he would be eligible to call home to ask for money he knew was not readily available.

"So you've not stayed off campus before?" Chibuzor asked wanting him to say more.

"Yes," Alex replied flippantly, flipping his hand-out to the next page which almost piqued Chibuzor.

"Hmmm, nawa oo, you're just too quiet," Chibuzor mumbled and Alex burst into laughter, dropping his pen and slapping his arm, as if attempting to kill a mosquito.

"I wish you saw me in hundred level; well it's a long story. I have to finish this hand-out first," Alex said and Chibuzor was surprised at the sudden outburst, he never expected or thought Alex could become so animated.

"Wow, this is becoming interesting. So this reading has a reason," Chibuzor said as he came down from the bunk. "Let me allow you to read, *hunger want to kill person.*"

"I have small rice remaining in my pot, you can eat it."

"Ah... don't worry, thank you. I'm going out to buy something," Chibuzor replied though tempted to accept, he was around when Alex was cooking the rice and the aroma that pervaded the room was hunger stimulating, very enticing and mouth-watering. At that point only good home-training stopped him from asking for a portion, but someone could see in his eyes that he wanted to eat.

He had always debated in his head whether foodstuffs were better than money and vice versa. Having more foodstuffs made him feel anchored like he had a backbone, something he could fall back to but he also felt restrained and confined because he wouldn't be able to buy what he wanted when he wanted— while having more money made him feel like a free bird capable of doing anything he wanted, when he wanted but he felt insecure because there was nothing to fall back to when the money finished.

Chibuzor checked the pocket of the blue trouser that he was wearing earlier that was now on his box— for money then left the room, leaving the hostel to buy bread. On reaching outside he discovered only one shop was opened, he saw girls with boys roaming about and at different corners, some group of boys were drinking and laughing and he wondered why Ifeanyi was not back to the hostel yet.

At the shop, he discovered he could not afford to pay for the bread, and there was nothing reasonable in the shop that was tantamount to the money he was holding. He went back to the hostel and decided to soak garri again. His brother had said that being hungry and being over filled with food are both discomforting.

He agreed that being over filled with food was truly discomforting but he preferred that kind of discomfort now. Reasoning the matter he related it with the statement that money does not bring happiness but it was better to be rich and unhappy than to be poor and still be unhappy.

Chima who was his bunk mate was already in the room snoring out loud. The boy was a loquacious busybody; he was always on the move, exuberant. He reminded Chibuzor of his brother but Chima was a default lout and was obstinately rude at times. He had already had some clashes with Ifeanyi about keeping the room neat and orderly.

His bed was always scattered, his clothes and other properties littered the room at times but anytime he had class or any outing he would iron his clothes so well that the creases on his shirt seemed capable of cutting through cake. He would also polish his shoe painstakingly and thoroughly brushed and cleaned his other foot wares.

Chibuzor soaked his garri, using his last sugar which was insufficient, and the worst part was that the garri swole up soaking up the water, so he had to add more water to avoid it from becoming Eba; though adding water would make it totally tasteless. He had no other option than to ask Alex for sugar but his ego wouldn't let him do that, especially after declining the first offer.

"Oh my God, girls are awesome, see excess food," Ifeanyi said as he opened the door to the room.

"I'm coming for my own oo, now, now, now like this. Let me go and bring my plate sharp sharp, anam abia." Ifeanyi's friend Uchenna said rushing to his room upstairs. Ifeanyi had walked in with a polythene bag containing two food flasks. He put on his phone's torch whilst balancing on Chidi's bed that he had now possessed, his real bed was actually the top bunk, which was stressful to keep climbing and jumping down from every now and then. Ifeanyi brought out the food flasks from the bag and placed them on the floor.

"One cooler is for me and the other one is for whoever is interested. You guys should better start eating before Uchenna gets here, he'll finish everything in seconds."

"I'm here already," Uchenna said gasping for air.

"Wow that was very fast. No, way too fast. Did you fly or something?" Chibuzor asked, amazed. "Or you're high on something?" Chibuzor said in undertones, too low for him to hear, but Alex heard and burst into laughter.

"Ah, you won't understand. I've not eaten better food for over three days and it's not like the last thing I ate was better food," Uchenna said using his spoon to hit his plate.

"Me too I'll eat, I've not eaten since morning." Chima said bringing down his legs and raising up the mosquito net that was hanging in front of his bed. He had woken up when Ifeanyi came in.

"So you're awake, I thought sleep took you to your village, I wish I videoed you snoring as if you haven't slept for days," Chibuzor said, gulping his tasteless garri.

"Abeg, abeg, you won't understand what guys are passing through. Cynthia wants to drain me," Chima said cleaning his eyes and yawning.

"Ah ah, who's Cynthia again? What happened to Nneka and Chioma?" Chibuzor asked looking down.

"Guy *na* long story, my head is paining me, its only food that's on my mind now," Chima said squinting.

"Which food? I hope it is not this one. If it is, better lie back and drop your mosquito net; cause you're not chopping anything, even half a spoon. Nothing!" Ifeanyi said with vigour.

"Ah ah na, boss man, what did I do nau?" Chima asked already suspecting the reason.

"Stay there dey ask me."

"If it is your pot, I go run am this night, I would wash it and I'll arrange my clothes," Chima said in a pleading apologetic tune.

"That's how you use to talk, but in the end you won't do it. Before you eat anything, carry broom and sweep this room."

"Yes sir, Oga Chairman," Chima said looking for the broom to sweep.

"Oboy, my sweat is drying oo, hunger is pressing my neck oo. Let me fetch my own," Uchenna said dragging the bigger food flask.

"Oga leave that thing, that's my own," Ifeanyi said dragging it back.

"You know I was there when you collected it," Uchenna said looking at Ifeanyi wryly.

"And so?" Ifeanyi asked.

"Where did you guys get this food from?" Chibuzor asked inquisitively.

"Must you know? Or you will not eat if I don't tell you? Ifeanyi said looking up at Chibuzor as if he was daring him, knowing very well that he was hungry too, seeing him eating the garri instead of drinking it because it was now in chunks, solidified. The garri still swole because of insufficient sugar. Chibuzor did not reply.

"It was from some girls," Uchenna said now dragging the smaller food flask.

"Nobody asked you Oga broadcaster without pay. Before your minds start going wild in thoughts, it was my sister that gave me, but it was her friend that cooked it," Ifeanyi said with celerity before they enveloped him with questions. "And her friend is the one that insisted on adding an extra cooler for you guys."

"It's like you'll give me that, that your sister's friend's number oo," Uchenna said and laughed mischievously.

"Ah ah no problem, as far as you show me the phone you'll use to collect it," Ifeanyi said and laughed knowing fully well that Uchenna had no phone.

"So who was now that girl you were talking with after that competition? The one I saw you with," Chibuzor asked.

"Was it the one wearing red shirt?" Ifeanyi asked.

"No, the one on black gown," Chibuzor said.

"Oh yeah, that's my sister nau, and the girl that was beckoning on her for them to leave is the friend that I'm talking about," Ifeanyi said as he took one spoon full of beans. Chibuzor adding one and two together knew exactly the girl he was talking about.

"I've finished sweeping, now, can I eat?" Chima asked after rushing to sweep the room.

"You can come and eat, though you did a perfunctory job," Ifeanyi said.

"Jesus is Lord, this beans is sweet oo. She put sugar inside?" Uchenna exclaimed licking his spoon.

"Chibuzor, won't you come down and eat?" Ifeanyi said looking up at Chibuzor, then he turned. *"Oga Alex see beans oo, sweet beans,"* Ifeanyi said.

"Leave them nau, they don't want to eat. Why are you begging them?" Chima said.

"See my pot, just put small of the beans for me, so that I can mix it with that my remaining rice," Alex said closing his hand-out.

"Chibuzor what of you? 'cause I'm not going to wait for you," Chima said as he sat on a stool close to Uchenna who was sitting on Ifeanyi's bed. Chibuzor wanted to refuse, as he had refused to eat Alex's food. But the beans would be perfect to use and finish his garri that he was now having difficulty swallowing.

Besides, Uchenna's comment about the food made him hungrier and he wanted to confirm how sweet the food truly was, knowing fully well who cooked it.

"So what's the name of your sister's friend?" Chibuzor asked as he jumped down from the bunk.

"You, you know how to ask questions oo, if you want to eat come and eat and stop asking questions that cannot fill the stomach," Chima said holding his spoon and waiting to see if Chibuzor was going to eat or not. He had noticed that Chibuzor was always on solos with things concerning food.

"Why do you want to know?" Ifeanyi asked as he dished out beans for Alex knowing that the beans in the other food flask would not be enough for all of them to share.

"Nothing really, just asking," Chibuzor replied abruptly, he did not want to give room for suspicion.

"Hmmm, I would have told you, but since you said nothing, no problem. Nothing spoil."

"Guy, thank you. God bless your sister and her friend," Alex said as he turned to eat. Ifeanyi acknowledged his greeting while masticating his beans.

"Chairman, it's like you would turn the beans you fetched back oo, so that we can turn it inside flat plate where all of us can eat from. Because as it is, you've already cheated us and you're still fetching," Chima said advocating for him and Chibuzor.

"Just leave it like that, I'll add beans for you guys, if you chop together with Uchenna that's when you'll cheat yourself because Uchenna *na* cheetah for food matter," Ifeanyi said dragging their food flask to add more beans.

"Why you dey cast me like this na?" Uchenna said looking at Ifeanyi wryly.
"No vex, but that's the truth," Ifeanyi retorted.

THIRTY EIGHT

CHIGOZIE HAD been trekking inside the school almost every night for tutorials. The idea of getting a first class, not just a first class but a 5.0 had gingered him to be very serious with his books especially with the rumours that the test time table would soon be out. He had been hearing of how a number of students had failed the e-test the last session.

He did not want to fall victim especially for courses he was having difficulty understanding. He had gone for one service in Fellowship of Redeemed Christians (FRC) and they had a guest pastor who preached wonderfully. The preacher was also a lecturer in the school and also in Chigozie's faculty, though he had never seen the man in school before.

The pastor's message sent motivation down his veins. The pastor had dropped so many punch-lines and aphorisms, spicing the message with anecdotes that inspired Chigozie. The man mentioned that it got to a point while still in school that he saw getting B in a course as failure, that why would he get a B when there was A, B was a bad result to present to God who's standard was excellence and B was not an excellent result.

Chigozie that was seeing a C as a good enough result, with an *at-least-I-didn't-fail-mind-set*. He had performed well back in secondary school, his twin being one of the major reasons because they always competed, but his twin wasn't there now, to motivate him. The motivation passed away with the one-year-at-home waiting for admission. But the preaching had triggered that again.

Excellence became his priority and decided to make it his watchword. His reason--- if I wasn't going to have money at least I should have good grades and not feel intimidated by anyone. He remembered almost having aphonia, due to the *cabashing* that faithful morning, the prayer was intense, he had never prayed like that before in his life.

What gingered him to pray was the fact that other students like him were voraciously praying, with vigour, not caring who was looking or staring at them like in his Church back home where most people his age-range were playing big-man. Here in FRC they prayed like the life of their whole family depended on it.

The acrobatics and body movement was more energetic than when somebody was dancing to Afrobeats, the tears, the sweat; the heavy groaning was pervasive, permeating every wall of reservation. The music was the Trojan horse, the tune and melody was fascinating, invigorating, if you didn't pray you must sing; your lips were coaxed to move.

Chigozie had witnessed something similar at CSF during their prayer meeting, they were praying for the success of Missions Twenty Nineteen which was supposed to hold the next week. The gyration and gingered energy in the atmosphere that Monday was overwhelming, the energetic ambience made him watch in awe but he didn't stay till the end because he wanted to meet up with some of his course mates.

But he had made up his mind to attend the programme come what may, also due to the constant talk of the programme by his roommate Akachukwu. He had no idea that there was that level of Pentecostal Christians in the north, where he thought Islam prevailed, though they were everywhere but he couldn't imagine this level of Christianity would be found in the North. He saw a lot of northerners that were Christians, changing his former perception about the North in general.

It was now Thursday, earlier that day someone had invited him to *House on the Rock* Church next Sunday saying that one Apostle was coming to preach. He had not heard of him before but it seemed like he was well known, so he decided to go since he did not have a stable place of worship yet. Every Sunday, since he came to the school, he had been moving from one church to another, checking out to see which one would be conducive enough for him to stay in.

On reaching the school gate, he started feeling hungry. He had not eaten anything since he took doughnut early that afternoon during their break period around 1.00 o'clock. He did not have time to cook because he had lectures from nine in the morning till six that evening, Thursdays had always been bad days for him since he was in secondary school, the day was always boring, long and dry as if it was cursed.

Sabio, who had been free almost all day did not cook for them either. He had cooked Indomie just for himself finishing the gas in the process and did not tell anybody until Wole came back that afternoon inquiring why the gas cylinder did not rapport with the fire he was igniting.

"Sabio! ... How about that N₁₅o you're owing me? I want to buy something, *hunger is sending me voice note,*" Chigozie said calling out to Sabio who was walking behind him operating his phone. "Are you hearing me?"

"Dude, I thought I've given you," Sabio said still operating his phone.

"You've not given me anything guy. Give me now let me buy something to eat," Chigozie said standing and waiting for him. *'When they are asking for the money they'll be doing like their life depended on it; begging like they'll soon die. Time to pay, they'll be behaving like you're begging them for money, your own money fa,'* Chigozie said in his mind.

"Guy, sorry abeg, I thought I've given you and I'm not with money here, it's just twenty Naira with me now. Make I give you?" Sabio said as he reached where Chigozie was standing.

"What can twenty naira do; what can twenty naira buy in today's Nigeria apart from pure water, sweet and chewing gum ..."

"It can buy biscuit too," Sabio cut in.

"Biscuit? Something that wouldn't last in your stomach for a minute," Chigozie blurted.

"But *that's* something twenty naira can buy," Sabio said.

"See Sabio, when are you now going to give me the money?" Chigozie asked, trying to feign not being bothered by Sabio's apathetic attitude towards the matter, knowing fully well that he was hungry.

"I'll give you the money tomorrow morning," Sabio said and continued walking.

"No worry, I dey with you. I can give you this night sef, I'm planning to withdraw when we enter school. Guy I dey with you, it's just one fifty, no fear I go remit," Sabio said placidly.

"Very well then, let me not come and be asking you later oo," Chigozie said as he picked up pace.

"No fear," Sabio replied still staring at his phone. *"Kai iPhone battery no dey last, after paying to charge it, now, now, now* it *don go down* again. *I Hope I carried the charger sef,"* Chigozie heard his lament, but did not deign to

comment, he just kept on walking replacing the hunger with anger by increasing his velocity, to get to class on time.

Some students were going in, others were coming out. It was already dark, a night with no moon, the school streets had no working street-lights.

On reaching his department, classes were already full with students. MAT III tutorials had already kicked off, the tutorials he came to school for. Chigozie had no issue with solving Math, but he had no foreknowledge of the course.

He was surprised to see that some students understood the topics, something he had been finding hard, because the lecturer would just come to the class, preach to himself then ask if they understood; no matter what the response was he would just continue from where he stopped before asking.

The method taught in class was an Israelite journey compared to the method used in the tutorials which was like using hot plate to cook beans instead of the lecturer's kerosene-stove method which would waste a lot of time at the e-centre. He had heard that the number of questions might be equal to the number of minutes, making it one minute to one question. Using the method taught in class would be a great disservice to his CGPA. It was like starting a fire on a charcoal-stove to boil water when you could just use electric kettle.

Chigozie perceived that Sabio had gone back probably because he had forgotten his charger because when he turned back after walking for a while, Sabio was nowhere to be found.

There had been no light off campus for over three days. It had been said by older students that there was usually no light, when it was test or exam period; as if the school had planned it so that students would fail, because light affected reading especially in the night when people needed it the most.

Chigozie marvelled that the tutorials were free; the students in three-hundred and two-hundred would stress themselves taking different classes tutorials almost every day, sharing the time they supposed to use to prepare for their tests to be taking tutorials without payment. He wondered what motivated them to act so. Even with such sacrifice, some students would come to the tutorial to make noise or be asking silly questions.

"There are some questions that by just looking at them you could get the answer without solving anything. It's just common sense, but they could be tricky at times, they could put wrong answers as options that would be the same as what you got as an answer after solving. For example they give 8 + 4 which is 12, among the options you'll see options like 2, 4, 32 so if you divided or subtracted or even multiplied, your answer would be there. So be careful..." The person taking them the tutorials was saying.

"*Blood of Jesus! This people are wicked oo,*" one student exclaimed in a lamenting tone from the middle of the class and most of the students burst into laughter, understanding his angst. Chigozie saw Sabio ahead of him leaving the class after the tutorials, as students were dispersing. He wanted to catch up with him so they could trek back off K together.

On reaching the common room area he saw him buying something. Some vendors came to the common room at night to sell drinks and snack for students who came to read especially now that it was test period, the population of students reading overnight had boosted exponentially.

Sabio had bought a drink and was offering it to a girl that was standing by his side who probably also wanted to buy something, they were both backing him facing the people selling.

Chigozie just stood a distance away to watch what was going on, this was the perfect opportunity to collect his money and buy something because hunger had messed up his disposition. The girl refused the offer. As Chigozie started moving closer to meet Sabio, the girl by his side started looking familiar, he wondered where he had seen her.

When the girl turned sideways to talk to another girl beside her, Chigozie immediately swerved changing direction. The girl looked exactly like Funke but he doubted the possibility.

"*How?... When?... What is she doing here?*" He questioned in his mind walking fast. If truly she was the one he couldn't meet her the way he was looking, he hadn't cared about his dressing or how he had been looking. His feet and the lower part of his legs were clad with dust like socks, his slipshod was almost spoilt; it was bruised underneath, to the extent that part of the heel of his leg touched the ground.

He was wearing a worn-out jersey-short and a faded black shirt, the faded colour was obvious at the collar and the zip of his bag was spoilt. His hair was rough; he had not even combed it after bathing in the morning. He just realized that he was in total disarray.

THIRTY NINE

"I HAVE seen small people do great things and big people being timid, and I know it's not about size but mind-set. Even some rich kids end up poor and some poor kids end up rich, mind-set is the reason." Mr Okafor said, talking to Osinachi in their dining room.

"This thing I'm telling you, I've told your elder sister Amaka and your two elder brothers Chibuzor and Chigozie. Though you seem to be the most ambitious of them all, I'm still telling you so that you know that anything you set your mind to do you can achieve.

No matter how bad your background is, there are several people that have excelled and succeeded in life with terrible backgrounds and many of them don't serve God as we do. With God on your side you have a greater advantage, just like having expo in an exam, sorry; it's just like knowing all the questions and the answers to an exam you're about to write; it gives you so much advantage, you can only fail if you're desperately determined to. You don't have to cheat; God would always be there for you.

I'm not saying life would be bread and butter or Ice-cream... (Mrs Okafor who was busy watching TV in their sitting room turned looking at her husband with an inquiring expression); not you Ice-cream." He answered her and winked. "I hope you understand what I'm saying Osibaby?" Mr Okafor asked turning back to his daughter.

"Yes sir!" she replied.

"Read your books, concentrate on them so you would do exceedingly well, I know you would do so well being an Einstein, but don't depend solely on your books, your brother Chigozie on the other hand is bent solely on doing business. Think of other businesses you can put your hands into, a good business would pay more than most professional jobs you can think of, as you can see we were doing much better when we still had business outside work.

And see, making money is not the only factor of making wealth, but also managing the money that you have made. If you are making up to one million every month but you don't manage it well, it would still be insufficient for you.

Learn to live within your means, buy what you can afford, spend your time on what would add value to your life, and always put God first."

"Daddy what is insufficient?" Osinachi asked finally, she had been trying to reason the meaning, the word sounded familiar.

"Insufficient simply means not enough, in short supply. Do you understand?"

"Yes sir," Osinachi replied.

"Alright then, you are free to go."

"Who left this pot of soup wide open?" Amaka shouted when she entered the kitchen, thinking it was Osinachi.

"It's mummy!" Osinachi replied from the sitting room.

"Oya go and put hot water on fire, so that your sister would make Eba for night food," Mrs Okafor said.

Osinachi, not wanting to go was dragging her leg, on reaching the dining room leading to the kitchen she ran back.

"Mummy there's no hot water to put on fire?" Osinachi said cheekily.

"What do you mean? Are you trying to tell me that the water we bought just this afternoon has finished? That there is no water at all to put on fire?"

"There is water to put on fire but it's not hot." Osinachi said brazen-faced. Amaka burst into laughter in the kitchen.

"Osinachi if you make me stand up from here eh," Mrs Okafor said, getting her point but feigning to stand up with her hands up. Osinachi dashed to the kitchen, breathing hard. Amaka had left the sitting room earlier due to her mother's constant comments on the soap opera they were watching.

Mrs Okafor had been working almost throughout the day, amending and sewing, from one cloth to another, she had been getting work from some church members. She saw it as a blessing from God, because anybody she sewed for really appreciated and more jobs kept coming.

She had come to the sitting room to relax and watch TV to get her mind off work.

FORTY

MR OKAFOR jerked up from his sleep sweating, the way he had woken up made his wife to wake up too, but as she saw him walk into the bathroom she slept back. Mr Okafor went to the bathroom and washed his face and came back to the room. He sat on the bed for a while then turned to wake his wife.

After talking to Osinachi earlier that night he went to their room to pray and after that he slept off out of tiredness; about an hour later his wife woke him up to eat. After eating he dozed off again. Now it was around three in the morning, it was night silent.

"Ice-cream, please wake up," he called his wife in a hushed tone. She rose her head up and looked at him with squinted eyes for about three seconds then turned to lie down. Adjusting her body and using the blanket to cover herself very well.

"Ice-cream, Nwaozioma please wake up," Mr Okafor called, tapping her gently.

"Sugarcane what is it nau? Nnamdi what did I do to you that you don't want me to sleep this night, I'm tired please allow me to sleep in peace," Mrs Okafor said shrugging, waving off his hand like she would do to wave off a hungry singing mosquito which kept coming now and then. Since lights went off earlier that night, the fan couldn't work to drive mosquitos away.

"Ice-cream sit up please, I had a bad dream," Mr Okafor said placidly and Mrs Nwaozioma turned abruptly.

"A bad dream? It's not the first time nau, please sleep tomorrow we would pray about it," Mrs Okafor said and turned back, with sleep in her eyes and insufficient rest in her bones.

"I need a hug," Mr Okafor said cheekily.

"Like seriously?" Mrs Nwaozioma said sitting up. She could not really figure out his face to see his expression in the dark.

"Yes I'm serious," he replied flatly.

"Sugarcane... I'm not ready for this oo. I'm really, really tired; I wish you could see my eyes. I don't know what you want from me this night. Hmmm, if I hug you, are you going to sleep and let me sleep?" Mrs Nwaozioma asked with heavy eyelids. She had been tailoring until about an hour ago when power the distribution company did their thing.

"Yes, I will. I just need to hold you," Mr Okafor said. Mrs Okafor then drew closer to him, and hugged him resting her head on his chest. Mr Okafor then wrapped his hands round her laying his back on the bed.

"Ice-cream, the pressure at my work place is becoming too much, I don't know if I can take it anymore, I don't know how long I can hang on. We're languishing in indigence; penury wants to be our middle name almost like that of *ukpa mkpume* aki. This life we're living is not what I planned for you my love, and our children.

These guys at my work place are offering me real money, just to add some Zeros and they've been threats, warnings that if I don't give in to their demands there would be consequences.

Ice-cream, if I give in, it's only our, my belief that would be tarnished but at least we would be living well, way better than we are right now. But how can I teach our children the ways of God, what mind would I have to tell them to do the right thing and stand for righteousness?

My love I'm in a death sentencing dilemma," Mr Okafor narrated with a shaky voice. He knew his wife was really tired, he contemplated whether to tell her the bad dream he had or not. He knew his wife well, the tables could turn, and he would be the one begging for sleep while she would be motivated to pray even to the extent of waking their children to join them in prayer.

"My husband, please just hang on, hold on to God. The Lord will see us through. Just know I love you, no matter what," Mrs Nwaozioma said with a sleepy voice. Mr Okafor knew his wife did not understand the gravity of the dream he had, so he decided to narrate it though he could not remember everything.

"Ice-cream what happened in the dream was that we were on our way from church; all of us were in that our car including Chibuzor and Chigozie, on the highway and all the cars I was seeing began to disappear, then suddenly men with big guns appeared in front of the car, they were on masks but I could recognize them. They were my colleagues, they began to laugh saying last warning, and started shooting in the air incessantly, and then I woke up, it looked so real." Mr Okafor narrated. He got no reply but a hushed snore. He then looked at his wife. "Ice-cream, Ice-cream," he whispered her name with oomph and still got no reply, she had already dozed off, probably since she finished talking.

FORTY ONE

"MY HUSBAND has not been giving me any issue lately; he had been lenient ever since the last incident, surprisingly. I feel God has started to answer my prayers. There was even a time; I don't know whether by omission that he called Joseph by his name, not Yusuf," Mrs Hannatu said to Mrs Adaeze after service.

The Sunday sun was sheen and radiant, candidly hot, making everyone sweat. It was the last Sunday of the month which was dedicated to thanksgiving in their church. Most of the people that came out for their thanksgiving were affluent families. Mrs Adaeze had also come out for thanksgiving— someone had blessed her with a brand new car, which was the Camry that they were standing by.

"This proves the Bible passage which says; "To him who had much, more would be given to him but he that had not, even that which he had would be taken away from him," Mrs Hannatu thought knowing Mrs Adaeze had more than two cars already. She had come to congratulate her when Mrs Adaeze started asking her about her family--- her husband and Joseph.

"Yes, it's truly the Lord's doing. I'm really happy for you, just keep on praying, because the devil is never happy that you're happy. The Lord would see you through my sister," Mrs Adaeze said shading her eyes from the sun.

"Yes ma, thank you ma," Mrs Hannatu replied.

FORTY TWO

"WE DEDICATE these children Shola, Shade and Segun in the name of the Father, 'Amen' and of the Son, 'Amen' and of the Holy Spirit!" The congregation chorused "Amen!" to the prayer of the pastor.

Then everyone started clapping and cheering including Mrs Hannatu. She had gone for a church member's child dedication at a different branch, the branch that was closer to her house which she was going to— before she started going to the Headquarters.

Mrs Hannatu had gone home with Joseph after service, surprised not to see her husband home, she wanted to leave Joseph home then go for the child dedication. Seeing that her husband wasn't home, she left him at their neighbour's house, the same neighbour whose children went to the same school with her son, fortunately they were already back from Church.

She wondered where her husband was, knowing he was always at home on Sunday. He usually had no engagements during the weekends especially on Sunday.

The person whose children were being dedicated was her close friend who had had no child for the five years of her marriage. Her previous conception ended in a miscarriage and she had not conceived before though she had been praying and believing God for a child for the past four years.

Now God blessed her with triplets, shutting the mouths of her enemies and so-called friends and acquaintances that badmouthed her, calling her malicious names even those who weren't married yet especially relatives from her paternal side and in-laws who did not like her. Some of them had come for the dedication like they were her closest of companions throughout the years.

Mrs Hannatu had known her since they were in the University, they weren't that close then until they met again after school. She had prayed for her concerning her childlessness, and was glad her prayers were heard. She couldn't miss the dedication of the children by any means.

She was part of the people serving food for the gazillion number of people who came picking up their plates and lining up to select the food they wanted from a range of delicacies available. For "swallow", there was Semo, Eba, Amala and Akpu with different soups like Egusi, Vegetable, Ewedu, Okra, Obgono, Afang and so on.

There was also varieties of rice such as white rice eaten with stew and Ofada rice which was also eaten with stew though a different kind, there was also Jollof rice and fried rice which were usually served together with salad or Moi-moi with eggs in it.

There were small chops consisting of buns, samosa and mini sausage rolls which were already served on the tables. Drinks were also available; mostly in cans and plastics. It was a Yoruba occasion therefore food was prodigiously abundant, the music had the western ambience with the life band making great use of the talking drum.

Mrs Hannatu was stunned by the good amount of people that came to carry swallow to eat, she had even doubted that people would see the swallow as an option to eat outside their homes in broad day light.

She didn't really enjoy eating outside even though it was rice she was eating, she couldn't imagine herself having *swallow* as a choice because whether she used her hands or a fork it would be a disaster. She felt petrified by the idea; she couldn't stand that blushing sensation. She had just seen a young man licking soup off his fingers. *In public!* she exclaimed in her mind, and shuddered at the sight.

There were all manner of people at the occasion. The poor and classless walked and talked anyhow with boisterous laughter, they argued loudly, ate voraciously, and licked their fingers saying *'this food sweet oo'* defending their lack of etiquettes. They were usually the first to line up for food, some even lining up for the second time for more food when people who hadn't eaten were still on the line. They were also not bashful to display the latest dance move they had learnt.

From the poor and classy— some overtly attempted to act chic, speaking in accents obviously worn for the occasion, they ate with fork they couldn't use, used over constructed English, and wore *'see me!'* type of clothes while the others just played along, tried their best to act normal following all the rules, 'stand up' they stand, 'line up for food" they line up— they wait till the final end of the ceremony, they struggle to leave some food in the plate, and make it a bit obvious they didn't finish their food.

The rich and classless acted like they were in charge; they knew everything, wanted to contribute in everything, dictated what food should be given to them, ate and talked, giving their views to any topic of discussion, boasted at times. They finish their food and demand for a certain type of drink; sprayed money for show-off, and occasionally had confrontations with the MC, and they would hoist their phones ostensibly high to see the time or see who was calling them.

The rich and classy— hardly stay till the end of the occasion, they make their presence known to the celebrants and themselves, if they ate they were picky taking food like meat or fish, Moi-moi, salad, fruit-salad and stuffs like that and they never finish their food, probably as a sign of opulence, they were usually quiet, talking in hushed tones to their counterparts, laughing like they lost their voice.

Mrs Hannatu observed this as she served people food. Her friend's husband was affluent and well known in their church so the reception was glutted with church members and other well-wishers including the apathetic ones.

The MC was doing what MC's knew how to do best, creating scenarios that would make people bring out money. He had put the chairman of the ceremony in a tight corner, bathing him with names of opulence, inundating him with copious parlance of affluence. The chairman had no option but to spend to save face.

So many people had fallen prey, to the malicious scheme of some Nigerian Emcees. After the offering for the child had been taken, women were called out to dance with the mother in celebration. Mrs Hannatu was done serving food, so she tagged along. At this point people had started dispersing because they had passed the climax of the occasion which was eating.

After eating, people saw no reason to keep waiting; they had fulfilled their purpose for coming, after showing love and support to the celebrants.

After the dance and spraying of money and some other activities Mrs Hannatu wanting to leave, greeted her friend goodbye and carried each of the triplets, dropping money for each of them.

Rushing home thinking about Joseph, she had bought some snacks for him before leaving but she knew that by now he would be famished. On the way, her car started jerking to the extent that she had to pack, she wondered what was the reason, she then discovered that her fuel was low but her car hadn't done like that before and there was no filling station around.

She knew calling her husband would be a waste of time but she reasoned that since he had been acting differently, more positive, he may be of help. She tried calling him, for three good times and it rang to the end which sounded bad, she tried again and the configured lady that served as customer care said; "the number you've dialled is unreachable at the moment, please try again later."

Without any courtesy sef, she didn't even say thank you," Mrs Hannatu lamented in her mind. She then tried using her other Sim, probably the previous one had no service. Dialling with the second Sim, the configured lady had the guts to say *"dear customer, your account balance is too low to complete this call, recharge as soon as possible and try again, or dial *233* to borrow credit and complete your call."*

The configured lady with the sweet placid voice was about to repeat the heinous message when she cut the call out of frustration. She locked the car, abandoning it; she boarded a bike home which was not too far from where she was; still wondering why her husband had not picked the call the time it went *through.*

"I hope he is okay?" she thought. On reaching home she tried using the key to unlock the door but discovered that it was already open. "Ha thank God my Husband is back," she said in her mind with relief, also hoping he had carried Joseph. She closed the door behind her, walking to their bedroom; she saw his shirt on the floor.

"Oh Habib when will you stop doing this?" She said in her mind then started smiling; her husband childish attitude sometimes amazed her, she liked his erratic carefree disposition towards some things at times. She

carried his shirt sniffing his fragrance, now she wanted him, she wanted him to have her.

"Habib, honey," she hollered amorously, opening the door to their bedroom. As the door opened she was awestruck, she couldn't comprehend what her eyes were seeing; her husband was on their bed wearing only his boxers and was busy lustfully kissing a nubile lady who was wearing nothing except a shabbily worn lingerie on their matrimonial bed.

"Habib!" She ineptly screamed his name. Speechless she dropped all she was holding, his shirt, her phone, her bag and mouth which was left agape, placing her hand on the wall to balance herself. *"could this be a nightmare?"* she banged the door and opened it again to confirm, the lady was busy trying to cover herself up with Hannatu's wrapper, shamelessly, while her husband was just staring at her without moving.

Her hands started shaking, vibrating uncontrollably, she was in utmost shock. She never imagined it would get to this point, she quickly picked up her phone and bag and scurried towards the sitting room, she expected that her husband would run after her, she anticipated that he would call out her name to stop her, she thought he loved her but all she could hear was hushed laughter from her husband, she then noticed a black hijab lying on the floor close to their black couch by the wall.

Hot tears poured down her shaking cheeks. She felt like dying, though death didn't seem to be enough but it seemed like the perfect panacea; her heart was broken, shattered like a ceramic vase dashed against a concrete wall.

She ran to the kitchen grabbed a knife and ran back to the room, she darted it at her husband's head, unplugged it from his head and stabbed the lady deep in her bare stomach and left her to bleed to death.

She imagined, but she couldn't do that, she just shook her head with tears still profusely running down her cheeks. She scampered out of the sitting room after seeing the Hijab, hoping her son was still where she left him.

PREJUDICE is a storyline that tells the tale of conflicts resulting from misgivings between faiths, cultures, generations and social classes. This novel brings before us the struggles everyone can honestly identify with as it tells of people who strive earnestly to break loose from such shackles; sometimes successfully, other times getting into deeper struggles as a result.

This novel is a pleasant narrative anyone would like to read from start to finish. The plots are very tight and full of suspense—it is a skillful piece of art indeed. PREJUDICE is proof to the fact that talents and skills are always there looking for a window to be showcased.

Emmanuel Ikechukwu Azubuike, although an undergraduate student of environmental sciences proves to be versatile on the drawing board of societal happenings even as he is in sketching towns and cities. Above all, he has shown here very clearly that he knows what is happening around the world he has come to regard as home.